"Celia, where's the stuff my mom gave you for Help India? My favorite T-shirt was in there."

"Oh, Carrie, I'm sorry," Celia said, finally focusing on Carrie's face again. "The Airway Express people picked those boxes up a couple of hours ago."

Carrie suddenly felt nauseated for the second time that day. She sat down on the closest footrest and put her head between her legs. Vivid flashes of triumphant moments with the T flashed through her mind. . . .

"Oh, wait. I've got the receipt right here," Celia said suddenly. "We can call them. Maybe we can still get it back."

Carrie's head jerked up so fast she gave herself whiplash. The pink slip of paper looked like gold to her. Celia rushed out and came back a moment later with a cordless phone. She dialed the number and held the phone to her ear, smiling encouragingly at Carrie.

"Hello? Yes, I'm calling to inquire about packages I sent out this afternoon. I'd like to stop them if I can," Celia said into the phone, glancing hopefully at Carrie, who crossed her fingers on both hands.

"Yes, the receipt number is 2789457," Celia said.

Time froze. Carrie couldn't breathe.

"Yes, I see. Well, thank you for checking," Celia said. She looked down and hit the off button on the phone. "I'm sorry dear. The plane has already left for India."

Also by Kate Brian

Sweet 16

Megan Meade's Guide to the McGowan Boys

The Virginity Club

The Princess and the Pauper

The Private series:

Private

Invitation Only

Untouchable

Lucky T

by

KATE BRIAN

SIMON PULSE
New York London Toronto Sydney

Produced by Alloy Entertainment
141 West 26th Street, New York, NY 10001

SIMON PULSE
An imprint of Simon & Schuster Children's Publishing Division
1230 Avenue of the Americas, New York, NY 10020
Copyright © 2005 by Alloy Entertainment
All rights reserved, including the right of reproduction in whole or in part in any form.
SIMON PULSE and colophon are registered trademarks of Simon & Schuster, Inc.
Also available in a Simon & Schuster Books for Young Readers hardcover edition.
Designed by Christopher Grassi
The text of this book was set in New Baskerville.
Manufactured in the United States of America
First Simon Pulse edition March 2007
10 9 8 7 6 5 4 3 2 1
The Library of Congress has cataloged the hardcover edition as follows:
Brian, Kate.
Lucky T / by Kate Brian.—1st ed.
291 p. 24 cm.
Summary: Carrie gets upset when her mother gives her lucky T-shirt to Help India; now she's only having bad luck, so she decides to travel halfway around the world to get her lucky shirt back.
ISBN-13: 978-0-689-87351-5 (hc.)
ISBN-10: 0-689-87351-4 (hc.)
[1. Superstition—Fiction. 2. Luck—Fiction. 3. Teenagers—Fiction.
4. T-shirts—Fiction. 5. Lost and found possessions—India—Fiction.
5. Charms—Fiction.]
[Fic]—dc22
2005299064
ISBN-13: 978-1-4169-3545-2 (pbk.)
ISBN-10: 1-4169-3545-2 (pbk.)

For Manisha and Aimee

Acknowledgments

Special thanks to Claudia Gabel and Emily Thomas for all their help on this book. And to Lisa and Matt, who cheered me on over the hurdles.

Lucky T

Chapter One

On a warm and sunny Saturday morning, Carrie Fitzgerald stepped out of her walk-in closet wearing a lime green miniskirt. It was so short, she was positive she could never, under any circumstances, bend over in it. Her blond hair was held up in an impromptu bun with a No. 2 pencil. She had just run up to her room with her best friend, Piper Breslin, and begun trying on a multitude of eye-popping outfits that they bought during their crack-of-dawn shopping spree. The Westfield San Francisco shopping center had never been hit that hard that early in the morning before.

"Does this make me look sexy or skanky?" Carrie asked.

Piper checked herself out in Carrie's floor-length mirror and stuck her tongue out at her reflection. The electric blue tank top that she'd grabbed off Carrie's reject pile was clinging in all the wrong places. While Carrie had a very sleek figure that would make a supermodel envious, Piper was on the shorter, slightly rounder side.

"How do I put this without hurting your feelings?" Piper said with a smirk. "There's a hooker in LA that wants her skirt back."

"Hey, I can't help that I'm all legs." Carrie tugged at the hem of the skirt, hoping a few more inches of material would magically grow.

"I don't know how you do it," Piper said as she watched Carrie gawk at herself in front of her mirror. She could totally tell that Carrie was admiring the lift of the push-up bra she had bought at Victoria's Secret.

"Do what? Look like a streetwalker no matter what I put on?" Carrie joked, her brown eyes teasing. "Why do I have to be so tall and skinny?"

"Yep, tall and skinny. With big boobs. Must be a nightmare," Piper said with a deep sigh of frustration. "How do you manage to look so good even when you look bad?"

Carrie smiled. This is one of the many reasons she and Piper had been soldered together at the hip since kindergarten. They had this unbelievable relationship that bordered on sisterhood. No one else could tell Carrie that she looked cheap and then seconds later compliment her. No one else would put up with Carrie's complaining about sprouting up to five foot ten earlier in the year (despite the fact that it helped her make the varsity basketball team, even though she was only a sophomore). No one else could ever replace Piper as Carrie's best friend.

"C'mon, Piper. Let's stay focused. I have to find the perfect outfit for tonight," Carrie said as she threw a few more clothes-draped hangers on her bed.

"So what are you and Jason doing for your anniversary?" Piper asked while yanking off the blue tank top. The static electricity made her long, curly brown locks frizz out.

"I don't know. I'm just glad that we're doing whatever it is alone. We've been hanging out in these big groups lately." Carrie put her hands on her hips and peered at the three remaining items that lay in front of her—a pair of cropped green cargo pants, a long denim skirt with a slit up the side, and a short white ruffly skirt—wondering which one Jason would like. She really wanted to look good for him on their one-year anniversary, especially because he took such good care of himself. Jason Miller was the only guy in their school who actually took some pride in his appearance. An all-star player on the football team, Jason had a rock-hard body and a gorgeous-looking face that Carrie got to cover in kisses every day.

"Well, you two will have lots of fun," Piper said seductively. "If you know what I mean."

"Ick, stop. That dirty voice really creeps me out." Carrie took off her skirt and the red honeycomb-stitch sweater she was wearing and then grabbed a pair of Miss Sixty low riders. Piper was right, though. Being with Jason was a lot of fun. Every Sunday they drank lattes and ate chocolate chip scones in a different Starbucks within the borders of downtown San Francisco. They had a regular movie night at the Castro Theater on Market Street. On the weekends they usually ran around to concerts and sporting events and house parties.

Yet the only thing they didn't do was talk about anything substantial, which Carrie always thought was a bit weird. Not that Jason would just sit next to her and space out. But still, it wasn't as if he and Carrie ever got into a heated discussion about the death penalty or even traded their most-embarrassing-moment stories. Tonight, however, things were going to change. Carrie was all about learning what was going on in Jason's brain (in addition to the kissing, of course).

"Did you get him a present?" Piper asked. She flopped backward onto Carrie's bed and spread her arms out so that they draped off the edges.

"We agreed not to buy each other anything," Carrie replied. "Wait a minute—he doesn't have a surprise for me or something, does he?"

Piper stretched her arms above her head. "Not that I know of."

"Come on," Carrie persisted as she poked Piper in the stomach. "What did he get me?"

"Ow! Carrie, I swear," Piper said, trying to fend her

off. "He saves all his deepest, darkest secrets for my brother. Now stop jabbing me with your bony fingers."

"But if you knew something, you would tell me, right?" Carrie said.

"Yes, of course," Piper huffed. "If I find out anything between now and tonight, I promise I will call you."

"Good," Carrie said with a satisfied grin.

"Why don't you wear that cute floral dress you wore to the freshman dance last year?"

"Because I totally spill out of that now," Carrie replied.

"Uh, that's the point."

"Very funny," Carrie said while returning to the closet. "I have a shirt in mind anyway. I just need to find something else to go with it."

Piper sat up and began to rearrange Carrie's pillows so that she could prop herself up and watch her friend try on the next outfit, which was her tenth of the afternoon. Underneath the avalanche of fluffy shams and a few stray stuffed animals, Piper noticed that something was wedged between the headboard and the mattress.

"Hey, something's stuck in your bed," Piper said, yanking on the object forcefully.

Carrie ran out from the confines of her closet and yelped as if Piper had stepped on a small puppy. "Wait, no! You'll rip it!"

But in a few seconds Piper finally pulled whatever it

was loose, and her mouth went completely agape. In her hands was an old T-shirt that Piper thought Carrie would have thrown out years ago. After all, she got it when she was in fifth grade.

"I can't believe you still have this," Piper said with astonishment.

Carrie was completely embarrassed. "I know it's weird. Please don't tell anyone, okay?"

There could only be one explanation for why Carrie wanted to keep this under wraps.

"You don't still—you can't possibly—" Piper stammered.

"I know you don't believe me, Piper," Carrie said as she put the T-shirt on very carefully. "But it's true. This shirt is lucky."

"I can't do it," Carrie said to Piper, who was now standing in the middle of Carrie's closet, rummaging through the crowded racks.

"Yes, you can," Piper replied confidently.

Carrie was now lying faceup on her neatly made queen-size bed. She looked around her room, which was much more airy and sunny now that summer was approaching. Her cream-colored walls were decorated with posters of foreign landscapes her father had sent her from his many trips, hung only at right angles. Her notebooks were neatly stacked on her antique desk and all her books shelved by height on the built-in bookcases. In general, Carrie reserved her mess for the closet, where she could always close the door on it.

But now Piper was attacking it like Mary Poppins on Red Bull.

"This is a waste of time," Carrie said. "I'm not going to take it off."

Piper wasn't deterred at all. "This superstition thing has gone too far, Carrie. Ever since you got this T-shirt, you've been obsessed with luck."

"That's not true."

"Really? You don't convulse at the sound of a plate breaking or hyperventilate when I step on a crack? Do you *really* think my mother's back is going to break?"

"No!" Carrie said, picking up a stuffed porpoise and throwing it at Piper.

"So you'll stop this nonsense and take off that T-shirt?"

Carrie sat up and looked Piper in the eye. "No!"

Piper buried her head in her hands and walked slowly over to Carrie. "Okay, explain yourself, because I have no idea what's going on in that fat head of yours."

"My head isn't fat," Carrie said. "It just seems bigger because—"

"Yeah, you're tall and skinny. Whatever."

Carrie smiled down at the familiar green star on the chest of her red baby T. This shirt had brought her luck in every area of her life, and wearing it made her feel as if she could do anything. She had the proof to back it up.

"I'm telling you, every good thing that has happened to me is because of this lucky T."

Carrie had an extensive list going of all the positive moments that occurred after she got the T-shirt. She wore the lucky T to varsity basketball tryouts and was the only sophomore who made the cut. She had the shirt on during auditions for every school play since the fifth grade and won the lead role every time. Her grades had soared and she hadn't gotten anything less than an A on any test, which made sense because Carrie always wore her lucky T on exam days.

Piper didn't seem the least bit convinced. "So you're saying it's more believable that the shirt has magical powers than you're just an awesome person who achieves great things?"

"Girls!" Carrie's mother called up from the kitchen. "Lunch will be ready in fifteen minutes. What're you doing up there?"

Carrie was about to answer when she heard the sound of her mother coming up the stairs. Knowing Carrie and Piper were modeling their new clothes as they usually did after squandering their allowances, her mother would want in on the fashion show.

"I hope you both didn't spend your life savings," her mother said when she entered the room. She wore a wry smile on her smooth, cream-complexioned face (the woman never left the house without her SPF 45 slathered on). Her light brown hair was pulled into a high ponytail, only the gray streaks here and there indicating that she was not, in fact, Carrie's sister.

"Nope, we just spent yours," Carrie said playfully.

Her mother didn't really invest much money in her own wardrobe. Thus she had worn her current outfit of batik-print skirt, huge purple sweater, and beaded necklace every day since she had welcomed Carrie into existence. She did, however, spoil Carrie when it came to clothes, and Carrie knew it was mostly because her mother was still feeling pretty bad about the divorce, even though it had been years and years ago.

"Well, Carrie, since you and Piper are already fooling around in the closet, why don't you make a pile of any stuff you might want to toss and I'll give it to Celia?" her mother said, turning from the door.

Carrie's mother's best friend, Celia DeMarco, was always collecting clothes and canned goods for some charity or another.

"What's the cause of the week?" Carrie asked.

"India, I think," her mother said, brow furrowing. "Or is it Tibet? I don't know. I'll ask her. I'd help, but I have to keep an eye on the cucumber soup."

"Cucumber soup?" Piper looked as if she might puke.

"I was kind of hoping for burgers," Carrie said.

"Sweetie, we had meat loaf on Thursday. That's enough red meat for one week," her mother said.

"But I need my protein!" Carrie protested.

"I'll throw in some tofu," her mother replied, and then headed back to the kitchen.

"Having a nutritionist for a mother sucks on so many levels," Carrie pouted.

"So, are you going to answer my question?" Piper said, returning to the depths of the closet.

Carrie begrudgingly got off her bed and met Piper in a mound of clothes. She was really hoping that her mom's interruption would have somehow confused Piper enough so that she'd forget what they were talking about.

Maybe the T-shirt wasn't that lucky after all.

But just when Carrie had begun to question the whole theory, she got down on all fours, yanked a tangled button-down from the floor, and paused. There, sitting at the very back corner of the closet, was the Skechers box she had used as a time capsule back in middle school. It was tattered around the edges and covered in smiley face stickers with the warning *Open and Die!!!* scrawled across the top in red marker. Carrie smirked, sat down cross-legged, and pulled the box reverently onto her lap.

"What's that?" Piper asked, plopping down next to her.

Grinning in anticipation, Carrie carefully removed the rubber bands that held the box together, snapping a couple in the process. She lifted the box top and was greeted by a glossy photo of her and Piper, age ten, dressed up as flappers for Halloween. Wearing far too much makeup and glitter, she and Piper were striking modeling poses—one hand to the hip, the other to the head—and grinning at the camera.

"Oh God. I remember that Halloween. You forced me into dressing up like that when I wanted to be a witch," Piper said with a laugh.

"Ugh, you and your witch phase," Carrie said. "I'm so glad you outgrew that."

Next up was the program for the fifth-grade play, *Anne of Green Gables.* Carrie opened to the cast list, a whoosh of giddiness rushing over her. How was it that after all this time, it was still so cool to see her name right there at the top? She ran her fingertips over the type, then down the list to Piper's name.

"Hey, Orphan Girl #2," Carrie said. "You still remember your one and only line?"

"Eh, it was something about you having fiery red hair," Piper replied.

"Wish we hadn't used my wig to mop up the Great Diet Coke Spill of 1999." Carrie giggled.

Under the program was a heavy sheet of white paper, folded in thirds like a letter. Carrie opened it and her heart nearly stopped.

"This is it," Carrie said, handing the letter to Piper.

Piper leaned back against a bunch of ordinary shirts that hung from the closet wall and read about Carrie's lucky T.

International Airways ▬

Dear Carrie Ann,

The air in Morocco is heavy and thick and full of spices. Walking through a crowded market district yesterday I almost got dizzy from all the colors and scents and sounds. I stumbled into a souvenir shop to take a breather from it all and met this crazy woman. You would have loved her. She had braids all over her head and her eyes were drawn out with makeup so she looked like a cat. We started talking and when she heard I had a daughter, she insisted I buy the enclosed for you. She swears it will bring you good luck. I don't know if that's true, but I hope it is. No one deserves good luck more than my best girl. And besides, I figured it might be BAD luck to pass it up. (I know it looks like something a tourist would wear—the shirt is pretty much the flag of Morocco, after all—but I swear the lady said the green bejeweled star is all hand-stitched!)

I think of you every second when I'm on these adventures, wishing you were with me so you could see all the beauty there is in this world. One day we'll take a trip—just you and me—anywhere you want to go.

I'll see you soon, kiddo. In the meantime, wear this lucky T and remember that I'm thinking about you all the time.

Love and kisses,

Dad

As she finished reading, Piper gazed at Carrie, who suddenly seemed very sad.

"I remember when I first read this letter," Carrie said, taking the paper out of Piper's hands. "It was on the day it all changed. . . ."

THE DAY IT ALL CHANGED:
THE INCITING UNLUCKY MOMENT

Sloppy joe. Of all the things in the world Carrie could have spilled on her brand-new, pink Abercrombie hoodie, it had to be sloppy joe. Not only was it gloppy and mealy and a bizarre orangey brown that screamed, "I will never come out no matter how many times your mom washes me!" it also advertised to the world that she had dared to try to eat the sloppy joe at all. Something no sane person who had a life at this school would ever do.

Carrie rushed to her locker, holding her arm at an unnatural angle over her chest in an attempt to hide the stain. This had to be the worst day ever in the history of fifth graders. Not only had she missed the bus by five seconds, thereby giving Chris Beren and Greg McCaffrey ample time to laugh at her through the back window as it pulled away and left her in the dust, halfway on her run to school she had realized she'd forgotten the index cards for her oral book report this afternoon. She had been nervously awaiting the humiliation of English class and the inevitable detention all day, and now this. It was going to be bad enough telling Ms. Russo she wasn't prepared for her report while everyone stared at her. But there was no way she could do it with this stain spread across on her chest. She'd die first.

Carrie yanked open her locker and dropped to her knees to pull out the duffel bag that was wedged in the back. Inside was a big red T-shirt with a glittery green star on the front. A T-shirt that she had, in the weeks since it arrived, refused to wear. Just looking at it made her face flush with anger and hurt. Her father had left. Her father had left and all she got was this lousy T-shirt.

She hated the thing. He'd bestowed it upon her as if it was some kind of consolation prize. As if it would make everything okay. "You can't have a dad around, but hey! You've got this T-shirt!" How lame could he be? And it was supposed to be lucky? Please. As if anything her dad gave her could be lucky. But at the same time she couldn't bring herself to throw it away. The thought of her dad in that shop in Morocco, of him telling some strange lady about her, of how he was psyched to send her something that might bring her luck—it made her heart swell. It was crazy, the number of emotions one stupid T-shirt could bring out of her. She was going schizo and she was only ten years old.

The warning bell rang and Carrie's heart hit her throat. There was no choice. This was all she had to change into. She ran to the bathroom with the T-shirt clutched in her fist. All she had to do was make it through the rest of the day. Then she could go home and have her nervous breakdown.

THE DAY IT ALL CHANGED:
LUCKY MOMENT #1

Okay, just tell her the truth. Tell her the truth and maybe she won't embarrass you to death, Carrie thought as Ms. Russo stepped to the front of the room. The woman was at least six feet tall, with short brown hair and broader shoulders than Mr. Latke, the former-U.S.-wrestler-gym teacher. There wasn't a more intimidating person on earth. You did not forget homework for Ms. Russo. It just didn't happen.

"Well, class, I hope you're all prepared for your oral book reports," she said, raising one eyebrow behind her glasses as she scanned the room. Twenty fifth graders froze in place, afraid even to breathe in front of her.

Since the beginning of the year, no matter what, Carrie was always in the first group of kids picked to do oral reports or read aloud from books. Not only that, Ms. Russo only called on Carrie to answer the questions she didn't know the answers to, never the ones she did know. When it came to Ms. Russo's class, Carrie never seemed to luck out.

15

I'm dead. I am so, so, so, so dead, Carrie thought.

And then the woman did the oddest thing. She smiled. "But only three of you will have time to present today because today is Lauren Dillon's birthday and her mother has sent us all cupcakes!"

Nineteen fifth graders all turned to look, slack-jawed, at Lauren Dillon, whose face went from its natural milky white to fire-engine red in less than ten seconds.

"And those three lucky students are . . ." Ms. Russo dipped her hand into the plastic top hat she always placed their names in for such butterfly-in-the-stomach occasions. It read *Congratulations!* across the brim in silver letters. Carrie and her friends thought this was kind of a sick joke considering what it was used for.

Please don't say my name . . . please don't say my name . . .

Carrie didn't really think the silent begging was going to work since it never did, but there wasn't much else she could do.

Ms. Russo pulled out the first piece of paper and unfolded it. "Carlos Almeda."

Carlos groaned. Carrie's heart soared.

Please don't say my name . . . please don't say my name . . .

"Ashley Walters."

Ashley, A student that she was, sat up slightly taller and smiled.

"And . . ."

Please don't say my name . . . please don't—

"Micah Taylor!"

Carrie's eyes popped open. She hadn't even realized she'd scrunched them shut. This had to be some kind of miracle. No one was ever going to know she forgot her book report. There would be no public humiliation. No detention. She couldn't believe her luck.

THE DAY IT ALL CHANGED:
LUCKY MOMENT #2

Half an hour and three boring book reports later, the class gathered around Ms. Russo's desk to check out the cupcakes. They were chocolate with white icing and pretty yellow and pink flowers all over them.

"Ooh . . . I want that one," Ashley Walters said, pointing out the cupcake in the back corner. The one with the huge pink flower on top.

"Definitely the best flower," Abby Simpson agreed with a little nod. Abby was an authority on all things in the world that were the best of their kind.

"Back to your seats, class," Ms. Russo said, clapping. "I'll hand out the cupcakes."

There was no question of who would get the cupcake

17

with the big pink flower. Abby Simpson would get it. Abby Simpson got everything. All the teachers loved her. All the students loved her. Abby Simpson's life was perfect and everyone in the world seemed to silently agree that this was the way it should be and that they would help perpetuate this reality in any way possible.

Carrie didn't even bother to covet the big pink flower. It was Abby's, plain and simple.

She watched as Ms. Russo handed out the cupcakes, one by one, going up and down the aisles. She sat back slightly when Ms. Russo came to her. When the cupcake was placed in front of her, her brown eyes widened.

It was the cupcake with the huge pink flower.

Carrie turned to look at Ashley. Ashley gaped at the cupcake, as did Carlos and Greg and Delores Mancini. The cupcake had not been given to Abby. Their entire universe was askew.

THE DAY IT ALL CHANGED:
LUCKY MOMENT #3

That afternoon Carrie walked out of math class after receiving a 100 percent grade on a pop quiz and was instantly grabbed by Piper. Piper's brown hair had been twisted up into five mini-buns that morning and they were all popping out and unraveling at random angles all over her head. The hair, along with the fact that she was wide-eyed and frantically jumping up and down, made her look like a mad scientist.

"Carrie! You got it! You got Anne!" Piper screeched, her braces flashing.

"I did!?" Carrie shouted, all her blood rushing to her head.

Each year in primary school one class in each grade got to put on a play for the rest of the school, and each year Carrie had hoped it would be her class. But year after year some other teacher's students had been chosen and Carrie had never gotten the chance even to step foot onstage. Whenever she had been ushered into the auditorium to watch another production, she had imagined herself up there, smiling under the lights, wearing some amazing costume, delivering her memorized lines perfectly. She had envied the kids who walked around with their dog-eared scripts and got to spend an hour after lunch each day rehearsing in the auditorium. It all seemed like so much fun. And Carrie always knew she could be a great actress if given the chance. Wasn't her mother always telling her how dramatic she was?

Now she was in middle school. And in middle school they put on only one play a year and everyone got to try out. The auditions last week had been intensely nerve-racking, but Carrie had done her best and had been dreaming about winning a role ever since. Something with a couple of lines, maybe. Maybe even something with a lot of lines.

But the lead? She never thought she would get the lead.

"You have to see!" Piper said, grabbing Carrie's hand and pulling her down the hall.

"The cast list isn't supposed to be posted till tomorrow," Carrie said as she dodged other students, her heart pounding a mile a minute.

"I know. But I was just coming back from gym and I saw it and your name is right on top," Piper replied. "Come on!"

Piper and Carrie ran together back down the crowded hallway to the auditorium where a klatch of people had already formed around the list on the door.

"Excuse me! Big star coming through!" Piper shouted, shoving people this way and that.

"Congratulations, Carrie," Melissa Staller said as they passed by.

"You're Anne!" Danielle Yung screeched, grabbing her up in a hug.

But Carrie didn't believe it until she saw it, right there in front of her eyes.

Anne Shirley . . . . Carrie Fitzgerald.

Piper was right. Carrie was a big star!

THE DAY IT ALL CHANGED:
LUCKY MOMENT #4

Carrie was still grinning when her bus pulled up to her stop that afternoon. It was a beautiful, blue-sky day in San Francisco, and from the top of her hill she could see the sun reflecting off the bay water and glinting against the Golden Gate Bridge. Why had she never noticed the perfect view before? Why had she never noticed how perfect everything was?

The door popped open and Carrie got out of her seat.

"Carrie! Wait!"

It was Abby Simpson. She walked up from the back of the bus, where she sat with her friends every single day. Her blond curls framed her angelic face as she blithely blew a big Hubba Bubba bubble that popped and went right back into her mouth instead of sticking all over her face. She was wearing those cool new strappy sandals that no one else's parents let them wear. And her toenails were painted hot pink with a Hello Kitty sticker on each of the big toes.

"Here," she said to Carrie, holding out a small pink envelope. "Hope you can come," she added with a smile.

Stunned, Carrie took the envelope and stared at it.

"Thanks," she muttered.

"Oh," Abby said. "Nice shirt."

Somehow Carrie turned and managed to step down from the bus without letting her quaking knees go out

21

from under her. She couldn't believe what she was holding in her hand. As soon as the bus disappeared around the corner, Carrie tore into the pink envelope.

It read in swirly gold script: *Abby's Having a Birthday Slumber Party and You're Invited!* Carrie grinned. An invitation to one of Abby's parties! She had been waiting for this her entire life. Her moment had finally arrived.

"This is the best day ever!" Carrie said aloud, turning to run down the block. She couldn't wait to tell her mother about everything that had happened. About the book report and the cupcake and the quiz and the play and the party. It was the luckiest day of her life.

Carrie paused at the foot of the steps that led up to her house, suddenly recalling the panicked rush she had left in that morning. Hadn't this started out as the unluckiest day ever? With the book report and the sloppy joe incident?

She looked down at the invite again and saw the green star on her chest glittering up at her. Her heart did a cartwheel. The T-shirt. All the good stuff had started happening after she put on the T-shirt. Was it possible? Could it be that this T-shirt really was good luck?

Suddenly Carrie was overcome with a warm and fuzzy feeling that started in her chest and radiated out through her entire body. This T-shirt was magical. This T-shirt had changed her life. And she was never taking it off again.

✻   ✻   ✻

"So why didn't you ever tell me this story before? Anytime I ever asked you why the shirt was lucky, you just said, 'Because,'" Piper said.

"I don't know. I was afraid you might think I was an idiot," Carrie explained.

"Ugh, I would never think that," Piper replied. "But I still don't understand why you believe the shirt is lucky. So you had *one* good day."

"No, there's more to it than that," Carrie said assuredly, dropping the letter back in the box and replacing the rubber bands. "Amazing things happen to me when I wear it. Like the day last spring when you told me that your brother's best friend from camp, Jason Miller—the guy you'd been saying was perfect for me since the sixth grade—was transferring to our school."

"Pure coincidence," Piper remarked.

"I wore it the day Jason asked me out," Carrie retorted.

"Every girl in school was jealous," Piper remembered.

"I had it on during my PSATs and got a 1450 combined."

"Yeah, that's kind of odd. You're not *that* smart," Piper said sarcastically.

"Oh, that's nice," Carrie joked.

Suddenly Piper's face got serious. "Carrie, I'm just concerned that you might be holding on to this idea for the wrong reason."

"What reason is that?" Carrie asked as she discarded unwanted clothes into a pile on the closet floor.

"It's not going to make your dad come home."

Carrie stopped dead in her tracks. "Excuse me?"

Piper sensed the tension in Carrie's voice, so she tried to be a little gentler. "I know that you miss him and that you only get to see him two or three times a year. But he's been working out of New York for years now. I don't think wearing the shirt is going to make him move back to San Fran."

Carrie stood in silence for a moment as she picked up a chunky gray sweater of her dad's that would never come back in style. True, she was mad at him when he first moved out. In fact, for years after that, she was really angry that he never seemed to make much of an effort to spend time with her at all. While Carrie tried to let go of the bitter feelings little by little, in Carrie's mind the luck of the T knew no boundaries. It had the power to do anything, and since all those good things started to happen the instant she put it on, maybe a part of her *had* hoped that one day, it would make her lucky enough to bring her family back together. Carrie wasn't ready to give up that hope. Not now. Not ever.

"Piper, I don't know why you're so worried about this. So I think this T-shirt is lucky. Big deal! What's it to you?" Carrie's tone of voice had an edge to it that Piper wasn't used to at all.

"Lunch is on the table!" Carrie's mom shouted from downstairs.

"Coming!" Carrie yelled. She stomped out of the closet, put a pile of clothes near her door, and then turned to look at Piper.

"You're right, Carrie. It shouldn't bother me at all," Piper said sullenly. "I'm sorry I even said anything about it."

Carrie sighed. She realized that snapping at Piper wasn't going to help anything. Besides, Piper was just looking out for her. Carrie walked over to Piper and put her arm around her friend's shoulders. "Listen, it doesn't matter. Everything is fine. Better than fine, actually. I'm going to have a wonderful date with Jason tonight. You're going to have a fun time at your brother's party."

"We'll see. I don't have the advantage of owning a lucky T-shirt, though," Piper teased.

"Wish I could spare mine," Carrie said with a wink. "Nah, even if I could, I wouldn't give it to you."

"Care, that's so mean!" Piper pinched Carrie's upper arm.

"I'm only teasing."

"Girls, let's go!" Carrie's mom shouted again. The distinct smell of cooked cucumbers wafted throughout the house.

"If we're summoned again, she'll make us eat sprouts and flaxseed oil," Carrie said woefully.

25

Then she took Piper by the hand and they scampered down the stairs. When they got to the kitchen, they saw Carrie's mother pouring a vat of cucumber soup down the trash compactor.

"What happened?" Carrie asked.

"I think the tofu was bad. It started smelling very odd," her mother replied. "And Celia called. She's having some crisis with her meditation class and wants me to come over and help her recenter. You're going to have to grab lunch with Piper."

Carrie pressed her lips together to avoid breaking into a grin. Piper was doing everything she could to stop herself from unleashing a full-blown hyena laugh.

"Try not to be too smug, ladies," her mother joked. Then she kissed them on the forehead, grabbed her purse, and headed for the door. "I'll see you both later, and have fun tonight!"

"Good luck finding Celia's center," Piper called out.

They both looked down at the sparkling green star on Carrie's chest and grinned. Another checkmark was added to the lucky T's win column.

"Mickey-D's, here we come!" Carrie said, knowing that as long as she had the shirt, life was pretty much near perfect.

Chapter Two

Late that afternoon Carrie walked out of her bathroom after well over an hour of primping. She was wearing her favorite, snug, hip-slung jeans and a lacy white bra. Her hair was perfectly fluffed and her skin was glowing beneath a thin layer of tinted moisturizer. She smiled at her reflection in the mirror above her huge oak dresser as she opened the second drawer. Her big brown eyes were full of anticipation, her flawless skin (save for a few nose freckles) flushed from the heat of the hair dryer. She looked out her window and saw that a few ominous-looking clouds were rolling in off the bay, but no matter. A little rain couldn't bring her down. Tonight was going to be romantic and wonderful—she could feel it.

She was just about to put on a bit of the perfume that Jason liked when out of her peripheral vision she saw that her lucky T was not hanging off the doorknob where she had last left it. She spun around and looked again. That was weird. She could have sworn she put it there when she went to take a shower.

Carrie quickly scanned her room to make sure that she hadn't set it on the bed or accidentally thrown it in the hamper. She dug through the two piles of dirty shirts and found nothing. Confused, she rifled through all the drawers in her dresser, knowing that she never put it away, but she had to check just to make sure. As she suspected, the lucky T wasn't there.

Frantically Carrie opened her closet door, glancing at the uncluttered floor. No sign of a glittery green star anywhere. Pulse pounding now, Carrie returned to the dresser and pulled everything out of every drawer, dumping it all in mounds on the carpet. She hit her knees and sorted through sweaters, sweatshirts, polos, and pj's, but it wasn't there.

Okay, don't panic. It's not like you lost it, she told herself. There was no way she would ever do a thing like that. Not with her lucky T. She had just done a load of laundry earlier. Perhaps she tossed it in with the other clothes and spaced about it. Yeah. That was it.

Carrie raced out of her room down the stairs to the second floor, where her mom's room was, and down the second set of stairs to the first floor. She blew by her mom, who was, as ever, hunched over a cookbook in the kitchen, and slid in socked feet into the laundry room.

"Carrie?" her mom said, sounding concerned.

"Yeah?" Carrie said.

There were three tall laundry bins in the small room: one for whites, one for delicates, and one for darks. Carrie picked up the delicates bin and dumped it over on the floor, then closed her eyes and said a little prayer before digging through it. The T-shirt wasn't there.

"Everything okay?" her mother called.

Carrie's heart was somewhere in the vicinity of her kidneys. She turned and dumped out the contents of the second and third hampers, knowing she wasn't going to find it. Knowing she hadn't put it in the laundry but hoping for some kind of miracle, some kind of rift in the space-time continuum. Anything that could alter reality.

"Yeah!" Carrie replied, her voice strained. She picked through the clothes on the floor. Nothing. Nada. Zip.

Biting her lip, Carrie slowly stood. She took a deep breath, trying hard not to panic, and turned toward the kitchen. Her mother wore a flowered skirt, a purple T-shirt, her ever-present beads, and an overly stained apron that read *Quiche the Cook* across the front. Her hair was pulled back in a loose bun and her eyebrows knit together over her nose as she looked at Carrie.

"Mom?" Carrie said flatly, crossing her fingers at her side. "Have you seen my T-shirt?"

Her mother blinked. "Sorry, sweetie," she said. "You're going to have to be more specific."

Carrie stepped into the kitchen and up to the opposite

side of the counter from her mother. She placed her hands flat on the surface to ground herself. There was a good chance she might freak out and bounce from wall to wall to ceiling to wall as if she were a cartoon character gone mad.

"You know, the red one with the star?" she said. "The one I've had forever? Have you seen it?"

"Oh, yeah," her mother said, tapping a wooden spoon against the counter as she returned her attention to the cookbook. "Wasn't that in the pile of clothes you left me for Celia? She rode back with me to pick up our items. You were in the shower so I went into your room, saw the stuff on the floor, and gave it to her."

Carrie had lived through a few earthquakes in her life, but nothing compared to this one. The floor tilted beneath her. The entire house came crashing down around her. She clutched the countertop for dear life as a sinkhole the size of Texas opened up beneath her feet, threatening to swallow the entire city.

Her T-shirt. Her lucky T-shirt. It was . . . *gone?*

"You . . . did . . . what?" she croaked.

Her mother, astutely sensing something was awry, looked up again. Her whole face creased when she saw the pained expression on her daughter's face.

"What's wrong?" she asked.

"Mom, that shirt was not in my giveaway pile. It couldn't have been. I would never, ever, ever give that shirt away."

"I'm sorry, Carrie," her mother said. "But I remember it being right on top."

Carrie's throat closed up, making it impossible to swallow or breathe. Suddenly it all seemed to make sense. The lucky T must have slid off the doorknob and fallen right onto that huge pile of clothes she had left for Celia.

Oh God, she thought. *I'm going to vomit.*

Carrie experienced tunnel vision for the first time ever. She could see one thing and one thing only—the telephone. She walked across the room and grabbed it off the wall. Maybe Celia hadn't given the T-shirt away yet. Maybe there was still time.

As she frantically dialed Celia's number, her mother accidentally bumped into the kitchen table and knocked over the saltshaker with her elbow, spilling its contents everywhere. Carrie almost fainted. Just what she needed right now—bad luck.

"Mom! Salt!" she cried.

Her mother, who was quite used to Carrie's superstition obsession, automatically grabbed a pinch and tossed it over her shoulder. Her motherly instinct clearly kicked in and told her that this was the only way to prevent some kind of psychotic break in her daughter.

Carrie listened carefully to the phone. Busy signal!

"Who doesn't have call waiting!?" Carrie cried, pressing the off button. She hit talk again and looked steadily at her mother. "What's her cell?"

31

"She doesn't have a cell," her mom replied.

"Ah! She's living in the Dark Ages," Carrie said. "Why are you even friends with this freak? I mean, does she even *want* friends? Because it's not like they can get in touch with her."

"Okay, since you're upset, I'm going to forgive the fact that you just called my oldest and dearest friend a freak," her mother said. "Now, let's just calm down."

"I can't calm down, Mom! You gave away my favorite shirt without even asking me!" Carrie shouted.

Something inside her snapped. As she slammed the phone on its cradle, hot tears sprang to her eyes. This was not happening. It couldn't be gone. It just couldn't be. All of the good things she had hoped and dreamed about, especially one in particular, might never come true now.

"Carrie, let's just take a step back here and look at this from another perspective," her mother said in her best soothing tone. "Come on, now. It's just a shirt."

"It's not," Carrie said, turning to face her. "It's really important to me, Mom. You have to take me over there."

Deep down, Carrie wanted to go into the whole story about how the shirt was lucky and her life would fall apart if she didn't have it in her possession within the next sixty seconds. She also wanted to say why she was so sentimental about it, that her dad had sent it to her and wearing it made her feel closer to him in a way that no one would really ever be able to understand. But Carrie knew that talking about her father always put her mother in a foul mood. While she seemed to be better these days, Carrie's mom was still dealing with her emotions surrounding the divorce. Carrie hated having to always walk on eggshells around her mom, though, especially now, when she needed her to comprehend how desperate the situation was. Yet Carrie couldn't find it in her heart to offer any more of an explanation.

"But Carrie, I don't understand why—"

"Please, Mom," Carrie said, holding her breath. "I can't lose that T-shirt."

Carrie slammed the door to her mom's Escape Hybrid and sprinted up the walk to Celia's house. The door frame was surrounded by wind chimes of all shapes, sizes, and materials that tinkled and bonged as Carrie blew by. She rang the bell, then bounced up and down on the balls of her feet as she waited. She was one huge ball of nervous energy. Anyone coming in between her and her lucky T, beware!

Please. Please . . . please . . . please, Carrie thought, clenching her hands into fists. Fingers on both hands were crossed now. *Please just don't let it be too late.*

The door swung open and there Celia stood, her short gray hair sticking out straight from both sides of her head. Her floor-length dress looked as if it was made out of a hundred different scarves of all patterns and colors. A pair of beaded earrings hung so low they grazed her shoulders and strained her earlobes. Celia smiled broadly to find Carrie on her front step and her mother bringing up the rear.

"What's all this?" she asked.

"I need my T-shirt back," Carrie said, every muscle in her body coiled.

"Sorry to barge in, Ceil," her mother added.

Celia looked from Carrie to her mother and back again. "I'm sorry. What T-shirt?" She turned and walked back into the house, leaving the door agape. Carrie followed, trying hard not to let her panic and impatience get the best of her. She had known Celia her entire life and the snail's pace at which the woman did everything other than talk sometimes drove her up a wall. But even if she did have some freakish tendencies, like her Wicca cooking group, her multicultural anti-Thanksgiving feast, and her ability to fluently speak Tolkien's Elven language, Celia was to her mother as Piper was to Carrie. She was kind and had always been there for them, so it would have been incredibly uncouth to tear her head off.

They followed Celia into her sunroom, where her daughter, Doreen, sat on the divan repeating foreign language words back to the CD player. Doreen's nose was buried in a travel guide for India. She was wearing a *Beauty and the Beast* on Broadway sweatshirt and black jeans. Her waist-length black hair hung in two heavy braids down her back. Carrie always thought that with a trendy haircut and some non-fleece wardrobe items,

Doreen might actually be pretty, but no matter how hard Carrie had tried to convince her over the years, Doreen had zero interest in changing. In fact, the only thing that had changed was Doreen's attitude, which went from sweet to smart-ass as soon as Carrie and Piper became best buddies.

At one time, many, many moons ago, Carrie, Piper, and Doreen had all been close friends, although Doreen was a year behind them in school. Carrie and Piper used to like putting on musicals in Doreen's basement, watching Nickelodeon, and reading princess books. But when Carrie and Piper had hit fifth grade, suddenly they didn't care about those things anymore. Carrie was acting in actual plays, participating in sports, and going to parties. Piper never left Carrie's side. Even though it wasn't intentional, Doreen was left behind, and the wedge between them got bigger once she began attending a private alternative Pass/Fail day school, which Carrie thought made Doreen feel entitled to act all superior. Now when Carrie was in Doreen's presence, all she got was lip, which Carrie had to ignore if both their parents were in the room. Otherwise Carrie went toe-to-toe with Doreen every chance she got.

"*Mangsho!* Meat!" Doreen repeated the monotone voice on the CD.

"Look who's here!" Celia announced, as if there wasn't a thick panic in the air that demanded immediate attention.

Doreen barely glanced up from her book. "Hey, *boka,*" she said flatly.

"Hey," Carrie replied. She was pretty sure that Doreen just insulted her there, but she couldn't prove it.

"We're studying up on our Bengali for our trip to India this summer," Celia said excitedly, her green eyes sparkling. "You know, most people in India speak Hindu, but it Calcutta, where we're going, Bengali is the most widely spoken language."

"Really? That's interesting," Carrie said quickly. Normally she might actually have asked follow-up questions about trivia like this, but at the moment she couldn't have cared less. "Celia, I—"

"We'll be leaving two weeks after the school year ends and we'll be staying at a hostel with these friends of mine from the Peace Corps," Celia continued. "Oh, they can't wait to have us. You should see the amount of work that needs to be done over there, Melena," she added, addressing Carrie's mother. "It's just so tragic—"

"Um, Celia?" Carrie attempted to interrupt.

"*Bhat!* Rice!" Doreen announced, and then tugged at the sleeve of her oversized sweatshirt.

"Their people have no place to sleep, almost nothing to eat," Celia continued. "We'll be helping build housing for a number of underprivileged families. You wouldn't believe . . ."

Carrie shot her mom a "help me" look. Her mother returned a "what can I do?" expression. No one ever got a word in edgewise once Celia got off on one of her ramblings.

"It will be hard work, but we're ready for it, aren't we, Doreen?"

"*Svikara!*" Doreen shouted before pulling one of her braids over her shoulder so she could stick the end of it in her mouth.

"That means 'affirmative,'" Celia said, temporarily distracted from her story. "Doreen, please don't chew on your hair." Doreen dropped her braid and Carrie grabbed her opportunity.

"Celia, where's the stuff my mom gave you for Help India?" she blurted, the words coming out in a rush. "My favorite T-shirt was in there."

Celia stared at her, stunned, as if she had forgotten Carrie and her mother were there for a reason. She blinked and looked around her and for a split second Carrie had hope. If Celia was looking around, that meant the shirt was still here somewhere. Maybe in this very room. She was so close she could practically feel the soft cotton beneath her fingertips.

"Oh, Carrie, I'm sorry," Celia said, finally focusing on Carrie's face again. "The Airway Express people picked those boxes up a couple of hours ago."

Carrie suddenly felt nauseated for the second time that day. She sat down on the closest footrest and put her head between her legs. Vivid flashes of triumphant moments with the T flashed through her mind—winning the eighth-grade poetry contest, scoring a first-floor locker right near both the exit and the bathroom, getting the last size six of that to-die-for dress for the freshman dance. Was this what it was like to have your life flash before your eyes?

"I'm sorry, Carrie," her mother said, rubbing her back.

"Oh, wait. I've got the receipt right here," Celia said suddenly. "We can call them. Maybe we can still get it back."

Carrie's head jerked up so fast she gave herself whiplash. The pink slip of paper looked like gold to her. Celia rushed out and came back a moment later with a cordless phone. She dialed the number and held the phone to her ear, smiling encouragingly at Carrie.

"Hello? Yes, I'm calling to inquire about packages I sent out this afternoon. I'd like to stop them if I can," Celia said into the phone, glancing hopefully at Carrie, who crossed her fingers on both hands.

"Yes, the receipt number is 2789457," Celia said.

Time froze. Carrie couldn't breathe. Her mother's hand stopped moving on her back. "*Jawl!* Water!" Doreen could be heard shouting in the background.

"Yes, I see. Well, thank you for checking," Celia said. She looked down and hit the off button on the phone. "I'm sorry, dear. The plane has already left for India."

"No!" That was it. Carrie crumbled right there in front of everyone. The tears finally let fly and she pressed the cuffs of her sweater sleeves into her eyes, bending at the waist. This wasn't happening. It couldn't be. "Nonononono!"

She saw the whole gut-wrenching scene in her mind's eye. It was really gone. Gone forever. It was too horrifying to contemplate.

"It's just a T-shirt, Carrie," Doreen said. "God, could you *be* any more dramatic?"

Carrie had never wanted to strangle anyone so much in her life. She got up and ran out of the room, through the house, and back out the front door. A light drizzle was just starting to fall as she raced across the road and dove into her mother's environmentally conscious car. This couldn't be. She could not imagine what her life would be without her lucky T. Her good luck was over. Gone. Kaput. What would her future look like now?

Carrie began to miss her father with a longing, twisting ache. She imagined the last time they were together, which was almost a year ago. He was on a layover in San Francisco, en route on a long international flight. She begged her mom to take her to the airport so that she could see him. Carrie's mom waited outside in the car, not willing to escort her daughter inside and risk running into him. Carrie and her dad spent fifteen minutes eating at a Pizza Hut Express, talking about boys and sports. Right before he had to board the plane, her father picked her up in this enormously tight hug and told her that he loved her. Then she watched him walk away.

And now it was as if he was gone all over again.

The driver's side door opened and Carrie's mother got in. "Oh, sweetie," she said. "I'm so sorry. I had no idea that shirt meant so much to you."

"It's okay. It's . . . it's not your fault," Carrie said flatly, realizing now that she should have confided in her mother about the lucky T a long time ago, because if she had, there was no way her mom would have given it away, even if the charity pile had been completely wrapped in it.

"Do you want to go get something to eat?" her mother asked. "I'll even take you to McDonald's."

Carrie shook her head. She appreciated the gesture, but the last thing she wanted to do just then was eat.

"Thanks anyway, Mom," she said. "I just wanna go home."

As soon as Carrie went up to her bedroom, she picked up the phone and called Piper. Thankfully, she picked up on the first ring.

"Hey, Carrie, what's—"

"Piper, the worst thing in the world just happened," Carrie sobbed.

"Oh my God, you sound frantic. Are your parents okay?" Piper asked with concern.

"Yes, they're fine," Carrie said, trying to get ahold of herself. "It's just that . . . my . . . my lucky T . . . is . . . GONE!"

There was silence on the line for a minute.

"Piper, you still there?"

"Did you just say your lucky T-shirt is gone? Because I swear it sounded like someone had just bludgeoned your entire family to death."

Carrie let out a little bit of a laugh as she flopped facedown on her bed. "Be serious, okay? I'm really upset about this."

"I know, I know," Piper said. "Why don't you retrace your steps and try to remember where you left it?"

"No, it's not lost. It's gone. As in accidentally given to Celia's clothing drive and then shipped off to India," Carrie said in a wobbly voice.

"Whoa, that's not good," Piper replied.

"No, it's worse than 'not good.' It's abysmally tragic!"

"Carrie, you know I love you, but I think you're freaking out way too much about this."

"Of course I'm freaking out! Did we not talk about this today? Did I not tell you what the shirt means to me?" Carrie was becoming extremely agitated by Piper's nonchalant attitude.

"Yes, you're right. I'm sorry," Piper said. "I just wish there was some way I could get you to see that everything will be okay."

"Me too," Carrie said, sniffling.

"Want me to come over?"

"No, Jason's going to pick me up soon," Carrie said while burying her head in a pillow.

"Well, when I was sad, my grandfather always used

to say this," Piper said. "A penny saved is just another damn thing for the cat to knock off the dresser."

Carrie rolled over on her back and looked up at the ceiling, feeling hopeless. "How is that helpful in any way?"

"I have no idea," Piper said. "My grandfather was crazy. It's the only thing he ever said to me that made even the slightest amount of sense."

Leave it to Piper to make Carrie laugh at a time like this.

Chapter Three

When Carrie saw Jason standing on her doorstep that evening, she understood firsthand the meaning of the phrase "a sight for sore eyes." Hers were definitely sore from crying away half the afternoon, and just looking at him in his American Eagle rugby shirt and rugged FCUK denim jacket, his light brown hair perfectly tousled and his blue eyes all soulful, made her feel instantly, if not totally, better.

"I'm so glad to see you," she said, stepping out and closing the door behind her. It was pouring now, which meant that Carrie had to cuddle close to him under the awning in order to stay dry. Not that she minded. Being next to Jason's warm athlete's body always made her feel tingly all over.

Jason squirmed a bit. "Actually, I was thinking maybe I'd come in for a while."

"Would you mind if we went somewhere else? I've had such a bad day and I'd really like to shake it off," Carrie said. She didn't even bother waiting for a response. Instead Carrie pulled the hood on her rain jacket up over her face and ran down the stairs. The rain pounded against the vinyl around her ears and she ducked quickly into his Jeep, which was double-parked in front of the gate.

Jason climbed in a second later, shook his head, and groaned. "I hate rain."

"You hate it? My hair's been a frizz ball ever since it started," Carrie grumbled. If she had her T-shirt, it might not be sunny and dry, but she'd definitely look perfect right about now. "I must look awful, huh?"

She waited for him to tell her that she was crazy and that she looked amazing, but he didn't even glance in her direction. Unbelievable. Wasn't that standard boyfriend protocol? She started to feel a rumbling in her stomach—a telltale sign that she was getting real anxious. Carrie tried to push her concern aside and forced a smile.

"So, where're we going?" she asked, hoping he'd planned a fun evening for them. Thankfully, it was their anniversary. She needed a major distraction. She needed romantic candlelight. She needed some big-time lovin'.

"Carrie, I'm sorry you've had a bad day . . . but I was hoping we could talk," Jason said, running his hand along the steering wheel, down, up, down, up. He was obviously nervous. Carrie could see a little bit of sweat gleaming on his forehead.

"Okay . . ." Carrie said apprehensively. "Talk about what?"

"About . . . us," Jason said, hazarding a weak glance in her direction.

Okay, bad sign. Jason wasn't a talker to begin with and tonight Carrie was planning on cracking him open and seeing what was inside. But from the look on his face, which was pretty panic-stricken, she had a strong feeling that whatever was happening in his mind was not good at all. Her emotions already raw, she felt her breath start to quicken and began wringing her hands.

"What about us?" she asked.

"I just . . . I don't know if it's . . . working out," Jason mumbled while staring out at the droplets popping against the windshield.

Oh my God, this is not happening, Carrie thought.

"What's not working out?" she asked, accessing her emergency calm reserve as quickly as possible. "I don't understand."

He opened his hands and then curled them into fists and pressed them together. "It's just . . . we've been together a year, you know?"

"It's our anniversary," Carrie replied.

"Well, that's the thing," he said. "There's this party over at Doug's—all the guys are there watching basketball right now. I mean, it's the *finals*. And I have to do this anniversary thing—"

"Have to?" Carrie blurted, her heart palpitating out

of control. "I thought you wanted to be with me, not that you *had* to."

"I do . . . I mean . . . I just . . . This is all coming out wrong," Jason said, looking at her with a pleading expression.

Carrie stared back at him. What did he want her to do, make it easier for him to break up with her? Well, that wasn't going to happen. For a few moments the only sounds were the splatters of raindrops as they battered the car.

"Look," Jason said, searching for the right words. "I just want to be able to hang out with my friends. It's not that I don't like you, it's just—"

"You don't like me enough," Carrie said as she felt tears well up in her eyes again. She blinked them back angrily. She'd thought she was all cried out, but that was back when she had believed she was going out with her cute-as-hell boyfriend to have an incredible time and get her mind off The Day It All Changed to Crap, Part I. But the reality was clear. She was experiencing her first breakup and her first horrible moment after the loss of her lucky T. If only Piper were here. She'd finally be able to convince her best friend of the simple truth: life with lucky T = good; life without lucky T = bad.

"Carrie, I feel terrible about this," Jason said when he noticed the tears.

The tender tone of his voice was pushing Carrie over the edge into an alternate universe her mom liked to call The Temper Zone. Ever since she was little, she had the tendency to fly off the handle when things weren't going her way, and Carrie had a feeling that was going to be happening a lot more often now. Even so, she tried really hard to be graceful under pressure.

"Well, Jason, you certainly know how to show a girl a good time," Carrie said snidely. "Woo-hoo! Happy anniversary!"

She fumbled her way out of the car and slammed the door behind her. She raced back up to the house, taking the many rain-slicked steps two at a time. She couldn't believe this was happening. Everyone always said they were the perfect couple. That's exactly how Carrie saw her and Jason too. She was secretly hoping that they had something that would last forever or at least until their first year of college. How could he dump her on their anniversary? Did Jason have an iceberg for a heart or what?

"Carrie!" Jason shouted behind her, causing her heart to leap. Maybe he'd realized he made a mistake. Maybe he was coming after her. Carrie turned around under the awning and saw him leaning over the passenger side seat, peering out the opened window so he could face her.

"Yeah?" she said loudly.

"So, we're broken up, right?" he asked.

"*What?!*" she yelled, not quite able to believe what she'd just heard.

"I mean, I just want to be clear," he said. "We're not together anymore."

She wanted to hurl something at him. Something big and very, very heavy. She was now entering . . . The Temper Zone.

Carrie took long strides back toward Jason and his precious Jeep that always smelled of Barbecue Lays, which at one point she really liked, but now the thought of it made her sick. The rain was pummeling her, yet Carrie didn't care how soaked she got. She and Jason were going to have words, all right. She was about to tell him everything that was on her mind and it wasn't going to be pretty. She was going to tell him that after he worked out and he took off his sneakers, the odor was so nasty it had killed every plant in her room. She was going to recommend that he invest in Proactiv because chronic back acne is not exactly a bonus. She was seconds away from revealing that she would have waved him on to third base if he didn't royally suck in the making-out department, which wasn't really true, but who cared? Carrie wanted to hit below the belt and make Jason feel as horrible as she did.

But when she approached his side of the window, all riled up and ready to rip, Jason's car pulled away and drove through a large collection of puddles down the street, then around the corner until he was out of sight.

There was nothing else Carrie could do but walk inside.

Carrie sneaked upstairs, avoiding her mom, who was watching TV in the living room. She only felt like talking with one person right now, and that was Piper. Carrie went into her bedroom, and the first thing she did before grabbing a big towel was dig out her cell from her purse and dial Piper's number.

As she listened to the phone ring, Carrie's thoughts kept going back to Jason. God, what was *wrong* with him? True, he wasn't a genius, and he never really had anything important to say except for, "Man, *The Matrix* rules." But they had lots of fun together, and Carrie thought she was safe with Jason. She had hoped that he was going to stick around for a long time, unlike the other major male figure in her life. She thought she was about to learn all these interesting things about him, but when he finally opened up, it was to push her away. Carrie's world was crumbling before her very eyes, and just then she wanted to speak with Piper even more than she wanted her lucky T back.

The line rang four times and the voice mail picked up. She could feel a steady stream of tears flowing down her flushed cheeks. Carrie sniffled hard and left a message.

"P, it's me. I really need to talk. You're never going to believe what Jason did. Call me back as soon as you get this."

Then she hung up the phone, lay facedown on her bed, pulled the comforter over her cold, shivering body, and sobbed as much as she did the morning her parents sat her down and said, "Mommy and Daddy aren't going to live together anymore."

When her cell phone rang an hour later, Carrie snapped out of her emotional-exhaustion-induced slumber and lunged for it.

"Hello?"

"Carrie, I just heard. Are you okay?" Piper asked.

"I am so not okay," Carrie replied, relieved beyond belief to be talking with Piper. She sat up straight on her bed for the first time since she'd walked back into the house. "Let's just say Jason Miller is total scum."

There was a sudden loud and raucous cheer on the other end of the line and Carrie held the phone away from her ear.

"Where the heck are you?" she asked Piper.

Fumbling noises were followed by the sound of a door closing. A couple of muffled whispers and for a moment everything was silent.

"I told you earlier, remember? My brother is throwing this NBA party. Everyone is over here watching the Blazers game," Piper said.

There was a thud inside Carrie's chest like she'd never felt before. "Wait a minute, is *Jason* there?"

Piper sighed. "Yeah, he is. And he told me what happened. He—"

"So you didn't even listen to my message?" Carrie asked, swallowing hard.

"Well, I didn't hear the phone, Carrie. It's kind of noisy in here. Fifteen guys. Lots of testosterone. You know how it is."

Carrie was on her feet now, pacing back and forth next to her bed. She clutched the phone for dear life. "Wait a minute, wait a minute. How long has he been there?"

"I don't know . . . half an hour, maybe?" Piper said.

He broke up with me and went straight to the party, Carrie thought, half seething, half drowning in humiliation. *He's hanging out with my best friend while I sit here alone crying my eyes dry.*

"So when did you decide it was right to call me? During the halftime show or when Doug and his friends went out to recruit bums to buy beer for them at the Shop-N-Go?" Carrie asked mockingly.

The betrayal was almost too much to handle. Piper was supposed to be there for her in times like this. But instead she had missed her call for help because she was watching basketball with the very guy who had broken her heart.

"Listen, I know you're really pissed off," Piper said, trying to console her. "Why don't you tell me what happened?"

"It sounds like you already know what happened," Carrie said flatly.

"Carrie, obviously I didn't know he was coming," Piper said. "I thought you guys were going to be out all night."

Carrie's heart ached even more, thinking about the romantic night she should have had. "Yeah, so did I."

"Look, Carrie, I know it's hard right now, but it's gonna be okay," Piper said. "Sometimes people just grow apart."

Carrie wrapped her free arm around herself and held on tight. "Is that what he told you?"

"Yeah. And he feels really bad about the whole thing. He actually said he hoped you guys could still be friends."

This was unbelievable. Piper was pleading Jason's case! She was supposed to listen to Carrie's story and be appalled and righteously indignant and was supposed to vow never to talk to Jason again for the rest of her life. But instead Jason had gotten to her first and told her some watered-down version of the story, which for some reason Piper believed without hearing Carrie's point of view. This was so out of whack and hurtful to Carrie that she couldn't help but visit The Zone again.

"This is complete BS," Carrie snapped. "I can't believe you're taking his side."

"I'm not taking anyone's side," Piper said.

"Yes, you are!" Carrie shouted. "I thought we were best friends, Piper. I thought I could count on you. But on the night my boyfriend callously dumps me, you're telling me I should still be his friend? He's probably sitting there watching you talk to me."

The silence on the other end of the line said it all.

"Oh my God! He is! He's sitting right there!" Carrie

cried. The very thought of Jason listening in their conversation, watching Piper for signs of how things were going, made Carrie want to hurl. She had never felt so wronged.

"Carrie, you guys are both my friends," Piper said. "I didn't know what to do. I'm sorry, but—"

"I'm sorry too, Piper," Carrie interrupted. "Sorry that I trusted you."

She turned off the phone without allowing Piper to explain herself or make any more excuses. Then, hands trembling, she turned around and ripped the cord of her landline out of the wall. Afterward she burst into another crying fit that she assumed would last for days.

Three weeks later Carrie rubbed her rabbit's foot under the table in biology class as Mr. Dumas handed back the final exams. She had bought the trinket the day after losing her T, hoping to get some of her luck back, but so far it hadn't done much but be fuzzy and hang off her key chain. Today her stomach was tied in dozens of tight little knots. She had a bad feeling about this.

On the morning of the test not one but two black cats had run right by her as she locked up her bike in front of the school. That really did not bode well, especially with her lucky T on a whole other continent and the fabric of her life viciously unraveling yard by yard. Not even a rabbit's foot could combat that.

The last three weeks had been long, miserable, and lonely. Carrie had avoided Piper as much as possible at school, changed lunch tables, and given her the cold shoulder until Piper finally stopped trying to talk to her. Jason hadn't even bothered to try, which fueled her anger and kept her from mourning him too much. Still, every day was a struggle. Carrie had to concentrate to remember the new routes to class that would help her avoid both Piper and Jason. She had to keep her eyes peeled in the hallways so that she could spot them first and avoid eye contact. It was exhausting to the point that she hadn't been sleeping well or able to concentrate on studying.

But there was hope on the horizon. By this time next week the school year would be over. Then she wouldn't even have to get up in the morning. A depressing fact, but true nonetheless.

Mr. Dumas placed Marni Markenson's test on the table in front of her. Carrie sneaked a peek. Marni had gotten a B+. If Marni had pulled off a B+, that meant Carrie had to have gotten at least a—

D?

Carrie stared down at the paper that had just been dropped in front of her. There were red marks *everywhere*. It was as if Mr. Dumas's main heart artery had hemorrhaged while he was grading her test. The D had been circled and underlined and had arrows pointing to it, apparently indicating that her work was beyond *dismal* and *disappointing* and other negative adjectives beginning with the fourth letter in the alphabet. Carrie was absolutely shocked. She had never gotten a D in her life!

"See me after class," Mr. Dumas said before walking away.

Carrie slumped in her seat, tossing the rabbit's foot and her attached keys into her backpack in disgust. She should have known this would happen. The lucky T was shining its light somewhere else, and obviously the straight-A Carrie Fitzgerald was history.

That afternoon Carrie walked into her room loaded down with books for the extra-credit project Dumas had strongly suggested that she complete to bring up her grade. Immediately Carrie sensed that something was wrong—again. Then she saw it. The tiny, yellow, motionless body of Fido, her beloved fish, was lying on the floor in front of his aquarium. Carrie rushed over and dropped to her knees, but it was too late. Fido had jumped from his bowl. He had committed fish suicide.

"Carrie!" her mother called up the stairs. "I bought Fido some more fish food. Come down and get it."

Carrie let out an apathetic sigh, got up, and carried Fido into the bathroom. She wrapped him up in toilet paper and placed him in the bowl. Feeling numb, she stood back to say a few words.

"I'm sorry, Fido. If I had taken better care of my lucky T, none of this would have happened."

She reached for the flusher, then cringed and closed the bowl lid before sending him off to his watery grave. Carrie had walked back into her bedroom, feeling more alone than ever, when suddenly her cell phone began vibrating in her pocket. She pulled it out and looked at the caller ID.

It read: *Dear Ol' Dad.*

Even through her misery, Carrie's heart executed a little backflip, just as it did whenever her dad called. In fact, she was a bit more excited than usual. She was thinking about him seconds ago and he called her practically at the same time. That had to be a good sign. It was as if the planets in the universe were aligning again.

Carrie hit the talk button and smiled. "Hey, Dad!"

"Hey, Carrie Ann. How's everything?" he asked.

"Fine," Carrie lied. It wouldn't do any good to upset him with the weird and unsettling truth. "How're you?"

"Okay, but I have some bad news," he said.

Carrie sat down on the edge of her bed. *Of course you do,* she thought. *Is there any other kind now?*

"I know that we had plans for a father-daughter weekend, but a bunch of pilots have come down with this bizarre bird flu and the rest of us need to pick up the slack," he said. "So unfortunately I have to go to Tokyo instead."

"Tokyo?" Carrie was stunned. She hadn't seen her father in almost a year. And he had *promised* he would come to San Francisco for some quality bonding time. There might have even been a "no matter what" attached.

"I'm really sorry, kiddo," he said.

Carrie bit her lip. "But Dad, I—"

"I know, I know," her father said, cutting her off. "It's been a while, honey, and I miss you like crazy. I'll come out and visit as soon as I possibly can. I've just been having some really bad luck lately."

Carrie slid from the bed to the floor and closed her eyes. She knew all too well where her dad was coming from, but she couldn't bring herself to confide in him about losing the lucky T. She also couldn't bring herself to tell him how badly she needed him to be a more constant fixture in her life. Sporadic phone calls, letters, and e-mails just weren't enough. Carrie wanted a close relationship with her dad more than anything, and this distance seemed too difficult to overcome. If she let her emotions gush, she thought that she might feel a lot better and her dad might come around. But what if he didn't? She couldn't take that kind of rejection right now. So Carrie just sucked it up and said, "I understand."

This keeping-her-feelings-locked-up thing wasn't suiting her at all. Carrie's eyes began to tear up right after she'd spoken.

"I hate disappointing you like this," her father said. "I swear right after this Tokyo trip, I'll be on the next flight to California."

The tears were falling at geyser strength now. She felt so awful for not believing him.

"Ugh, they're calling my flight. I have to go," he said. "I'll call you as soon as I can. And remember, I adore you."

"I know, Dad. Fly safe," Carrie said, her voice cracking.

"Always," he said. "Good-bye."

Carrie hung up the phone and let out a heavy sigh. There was nothing good about "good-byes" at all.

On the final day of school Carrie began the dreaded task of cleaning out her locker. There were huge trash cans strewn about the hallway and her fellow classmates were taking great joy in dumping everything they had accumulated over the past year into the garbage. It was supposed to be this cleansing ritual/"summer's here" celebration, but Carrie wasn't looking forward to it. Going through her stuff meant having to remember how good she had it until recently, and there was nothing cleansing about that experience in the least.

Carrie's stomach churned as she rifled through three-ring binders and five-subject Mead notebooks. She came across some funny sketches that Piper had drawn of their English teacher, Mr. Purtell, in some R-rated poses. She found a crumpled-up piece of construction paper that had *Hey, what's up?* written on it. Yep, Jason and his astounding verbal skills just couldn't be matched. On the top shelf there was a pair of shorts she had borrowed from Piper when she forgot her gym clothes and a mix CD of cheesy disco songs, which Piper had made the day she figured out how to work her burner. And on the way bottom of her locker was a photo of her, Jason, and Piper at last year's Fourth of July Waterfront Festival on Pier 39. Jason was in the middle with his eyes closed. Piper was sticking her tongue out and pulling the tip of her nose up. And Carrie looked as if she hadn't laughed so hard in her life.

God, this is depressing, she thought. *Maybe I should down this whole bottle of expired Advil I just found and be done with it.*

But before she could OD on old ibuprofen, a familiar voice came out of nowhere.

"Hi, Carrie."

It was Piper.

Carrie turned around and looked into her best friend's eyes. She saw Piper was hurting, but with each step of her approach, thoughts about that awful day came rushing back into Carrie's head. It was too much to bear, so Carrie closed the door of her locker and began to walk away.

"Carrie, don't do this," Piper called out after her. "Please, you've been avoiding me for weeks."

Carrie was heading for the front door of the school, knowing that as soon as she hit the sidewalk, she was going to make a run for it. But she could also hear Piper closing in on her. Piper might not be speedy or athletic, but she was persistent as hell. There was no way she was letting Carrie get out of shouting range.

"You know I'm going to follow you all the way home and hold a candlelight vigil outside your door until you break down and talk to me," Piper said, reaching out to put a hand on Carrie's shoulder.

"Leave me alone, Piper," Carrie grunted, shrugging away from her. "I have nothing to say to you."

"I can't believe you're still mad. What did I do that was so awful?" Piper said, blocking Carrie's path.

This comment only made things worse. Of course she was still mad! Piper had let Carrie down when she needed her the most, and she didn't even know what she did wrong. What was up with this girl? Didn't she read *Cosmo*? Women have got to stick together!

"I can't believe how clueless you are," Carrie said sharply. "I'm angry at you because you ditched me for Jason!"

"No, I didn't," Piper replied tersely.

"Fine, whatever," Carrie said while rolling her eyes. "I'm leaving now."

"You're being so unreasonable. This isn't like you at all," Piper murmured.

"Yeah? Well, I was a wreck that night when Jason broke up with me. I thought you were going to come to my rescue and tell that idiot to get lost, but instead you were, like, his messenger or something," Carrie barked. "That wasn't what I expected you to do either, so if I'm not being myself, you should just deal."

"I wasn't trying to hurt you. This is all a big misunderstanding."

"No, I understand perfectly. You just can't admit that you screwed up."

Piper looked down at her feet. "Carrie, I don't know what you want me to do."

Then all the hurt Carrie was feeling inside came out in three short, harsh words: "Just go away."

"If that's what you want," Piper said sadly, her lower lip trembling.

Deep down, Carrie knew what she really wanted. To go back in time, save her lucky T, and undo this entire mess. But that was just a pointless wish, and before Carrie could take back what she'd said, Piper was down the hall, out the front doors of the school, and gone from her life. Possibly for good.

Chapter Four

"Like sands through the hourglass . . . so are the days of our lives. . . ."

Carrie shoved an entire Fudge-Covered Oreo into her mouth and chomped down as she bent over her left thumbnail with her nail polish wand. The familiar hourglass spun around against a blue backdrop. Carrie had never been big on soap operas. She'd always been a little too active to sit on her butt for an hour at a time and watch television. But in the last week, that had changed. Sometimes she could sit through an entire twenty minutes of one of these things without even flipping the channel. Sometimes twenty-five.

A commercial came on—some lady dancing across the screen like a whacked-out maniac with her mop—and Carrie moved on to her other hand. This was her third nail polish color this week. Another Carrie

Fitzgerald first. Nails had never been much of a priority.

"Well, this is depressing," her mother said, leaning against the doorway.

Carrie looked up, so brain dead it took her a second to process what was wrong with this picture. Then it hit her. It was Friday. She was supposed to be alone, just as she was most hours of her life these days.

"What're you doing home?" she asked finally, glancing at the clock.

"I thought I'd have lunch with my daughter today," her mother said, walking over and picking up the package of Fudge-Covered Oreos, the cereal bowl from that morning, and the empty Snapple bottle at Carrie's feet. "But I see you've already covered the four food groups—sugar, chocolate, caffeine, and more sugar."

Carrie blew out a sigh and rolled her eyes. Sometimes her mom could be such a *mom.*

"So, I'm wondering, are you planning on seeing the outdoors at all this summer?" her mother asked. She walked over to the bay window and with her free hand yanked the heavy curtains aside, thereby permanently blinding her one and only child. Dust bounced across the bright beams of light.

"God, Mom! Could you at least warn me?" Carrie asked, squinting.

Sunglasses, she thought. *I have to start bringing my sunglasses with me to the TV room.*

"When did you become so cranky?" her mother

asked. "I don't even know who I'm living with anymore."

"I'm Carrie. Nice to meet you," Carrie said flatly, her eyes on her nails.

"Oh, yeah. That's real funny," her mother said, flicking off the television. Carrie slumped her head back against the couch cushions. She was sending every signal she had in her arsenal. Couldn't her mother tell she just wanted to mope her life away? "Why don't you go to the pool?" her mom asked. "It's gorgeous outside."

"Because Jason's lifeguarding, Mom," Carrie said.

"Okay, so call Piper," her mother suggested.

"In case you haven't noticed, I'm not talking to Piper," Carrie said, trying to be patient. "Besides, she's at theater camp right now."

"Didn't you sign up for that too?" Carrie's mother asked.

Carrie's hands flopped to her sides, but she made sure to keep her wet nails free of the faux suede couch. "Yeah, but I didn't go because *Piper* is there, Mom!"

"Listen, I understand that this breakup with Jason hurts," her mother said, grabbing a few magazines and adding them to the load in her arms. "But your friendship with Piper, that's not something you want to give up on. Why don't you tell me what's happening with you guys? Maybe I can help."

Carrie swallowed hard. The thought about rehashing everything with her mom wasn't appealing, considering that she might spiral downward again. At least now Carrie

KATE BRIAN

was mad enough that she could hold it together without bursting into tears every hour on the hour. Talking about it would just take her two steps back in the recovery process. She was in the anger stage, and she liked it there.

"Mom, I just don't feel like talking. Maybe later."

Carrie's mom laid a gentle hand on her daughter's shoulder. "The least I can do is feed you some real food." Then her mom went into the kitchen and began going through the clutter of stainless steel pots in the cupboards over the sink.

Preferring to let her mind turn into mush rather than go into the other room and confide in her mom, Carrie grabbed the remote and turned the TV on again. Marlena was throwing some kind of fit in front of her kids. Carrie groaned. She hated Marlena. Why didn't they just kill the woman off already? They didn't seem to mind axing everyone else on these shows. One week of watching and she had already witnessed three murders—one guy died driving off a cliff after he found out his wife was cheating on him with his father, one lady bit the dust after being struck by lightning while being held hostage in a lighthouse by her cross-dressing ex-lover, and some doctor was shot by an angry husband who blamed him for messing up his mistress's brain transplant surgery.

Carrie pulled her eyes from the set and looked outside. The sky was a perfect, pristine blue. It was probably about eighty-five degrees out there. Carrie could just imagine the scene at the pool. Little kids jumping off the diving board, trying to make bigger splashes than their friends. Bigger kids were probably hurling themselves off the high dive in order to show off for the middle school girls. Abby Simpson and her posse were most likely in their bikinis, slathering on the suntan lotion, trying to get Jason and the other lifeguards to look their way.

Then suddenly all the negative thoughts started pouring into her brain. If she went to the pool, everyone would be talking about her breakup with Jason. They'd be watching them and whispering. Besides, if she had to watch Jason flirt with someone else, she just might go psycho in front of the entire pool-going community.

Carrie buried her head in the throw pillows that were on the couch. She held her hands outward because she wasn't sure if her enamel was fully dry yet. As she breathed in the calming scent of Febreze, her mind began to wander into Piper territory. Carrie reflected on what her mom said about how important their friendship was and that she shouldn't just let it go. Perhaps she shouldn't have been so hard on Piper. After all, people make mistakes. But before Carrie could really think about forgiving her, she remembered how awful she felt the night Jason broke up with her and how Piper had acted. It was something she just couldn't get past. Piper was supposed to be the one person in her life who never abandoned her.

And maybe if Carrie's lucky T hadn't been deported

to another country, things between her and Piper would be just as they were.

A couple of hours later Carrie was still in front of the TV, fast flipping through the news channels. She paused when she saw the word *India* scroll across the top of the screen. Carrie took a quick glance at the station ID in the lower-left-hand corner: the Travel Network.

"And now back to 'Calcutta: City in Crisis,'" the voice-over guy said.

Heart in her throat, Carrie hit the info button on her digital remote control. It was a two-hour-long special on Calcutta, India. Carrie stared at the images of the crowded streets, bustling marketplaces, and temples gleaming in the sun. Somewhere in this place was her most prized possession—the T-shirt that had been responsible for every big moment in her life.

Dropping the remote, Carrie pulled her foot up onto the couch to get to work on her toenails. She dipped the nail polish wand into the bottle a few times and then bent forward past her knee, sticking her tongue out in concentration. Just before touching polish to nail, she glanced up at the television to find a group of men and women pulling clothes off the back of a flatbed truck and placing them into boxes.

"Workers sort donated clothes to be shipped to vari-ous aid organizations around the city," the announcer said. *"This particular day's load will be sent off to a*

local women's shelter where single mothers are given the help they need to find work and—"

Suddenly Carrie dropped the nail polish and it spilled to the floor. It couldn't be . . . but it was! The woman in the center of the screen, smiling self-consciously at the camera, was folding her lucky T!

"Oh my God!" Carrie cried, clutching the sides of the TV set in a death grip. "Oh my God! Oh my God!"

She stared at the T-shirt as it was loaded into a box and sealed with brown tape. She watched the box as it was tossed to another aid worker and then loaded into the back of a van. And then the scene was gone, replaced by a bunch of schoolchildren in plaid uniforms, running down the street. It was almost like it had never happened.

But it had. Carrie had seen her T-shirt. She knew exactly where it was.

"Calcutta," Carrie said breathlessly. "A women's shelter in Calcutta."

This was truly divine intervention. It had to be. When did she ever watch the Travel Network? And what were the chances of her catching this very bit of the two-hour program?

Suddenly Carrie began dancing around the room, even though the happy music she was hearing was only inside her own head. She couldn't control her elation. In a split second Carrie went from being a step away from calling a teen hotline to being joyous over finding her lucky T. Well, she hadn't technically found it yet, but she knew its general whereabouts, which was a lot more than she knew before.

Now all she had to do was get to Calcutta . . . and Carrie Fitzgerald, luckiest girl alive, would be back in business once again.

The next morning was a beautiful, sun-drenched Saturday. Carrie walked downstairs, clutching a piece of wrinkled paper in both hands. She read her speech over for the fiftieth time, her lips moving as she attempted to commit it to memory. It was imperative that she sound sincere or else she wasn't going to get as far as the San Francisco city limits.

Dressed in the stretchy pants and oversized-T-shirt combo she always wore to Pilates class, her mother was hovering over the stove, whipping up a couple of egg-white western omelets. As always, the kitchen was the brightest and cheeriest room in the house. Carrie's mom spent most of her time here and had decorated it with that in mind. While the rest of the house was jammed with secondhand furniture—riddled with broken drawers, wobbly legs, and random stains— the kitchen was state-of-the-art. Silver countertops gleamed against cobalt blue tiling that rose from the floor halfway up the wall, where they gave way to light blue paint. Glass fish of all shapes and sizes swam along the top of the wall just below the ceiling, and every dish, bowl, and platter was another shade of blue or blue-green. Carrie's mother always felt most at peace near the ocean, so she had turned her work space into a tribute to the deep sea.

Carrie stepped into the room, hoping for the tranquility that her mother swore this kitchen brought her. Yeah, not so much. Her nerves were more frayed than the checkerboard throw rug in her bedroom. She took a deep breath and shoved the speech into the back pocket of her dark indigo DKNY jeans.

"Hey, Mom," she said brightly.

Her mother visibly jumped. "You're up early," she said, glancing over her shoulder. "And you're dressed. Are you on your way to snapping yourself out of this funk you've been in?"

"I'm trying to," Carrie said casually, slipping onto one of the stools at the counter. She leaned over and picked out an apple from the fruit bowl and began rolling it around on the marble countertop with both her hands. "I know I've been very moody lately."

"Moody is one way to describe it," her mother said, raising one eyebrow. Already Carrie could tell she was suspicious—and she knew why. Carrie rarely ever inferred that she was wrong and never had fully admitted to such. But she wasn't about to stop now. She was on a mission.

"So, Mom, I was thinking about things," she said, trying to sound casual. Her mother lifted the pan from the stove and slipped one of the omelets onto a plate in front of Carrie.

"And you wanted to talk with me about what's been bothering you?" she prompted.

"Uh . . . maybe."

Carrie didn't expect her mom to throw her a curve like that. Now she was all off-kilter. She tried to envision the written words in her mind. The page was burning a hole in her pocket.

Her mother eyed her expectantly as she served up another omelet for herself. She slid the other stool around to her side of the counter so she could face Carrie while she ate. "Maybe, huh? Well, I was really hoping you'd let me into that *cabeza* of yours. The easiest way to start this off is for you to tell me what's on your mind right now."

"I . . . uh . . . I think I'm getting a newfound appreciation for Indian culture," Carrie said, wondering if the speech was as moronic on paper as it sounded coming out of her mouth.

"Indian culture," her mother repeated. "Right."

"Well, India, India. Not American Indian," Carrie clarified. "You know, Gandhi and all that. So I was thinking maybe I could go to India with Celia and Doreen. I mean you keep telling me to get out of the house. . . ."

Her mother eyed her dubiously. "You want to go to India."

"Yeah," Carrie said, her stomach turning.

"With Celia and Doreen."

"Sure do." That was the part Carrie was least sure about, actually. Weeks on end with Dor-mean? Carrie would need to brush up on the art of verbal self-defense because that girl didn't know when to back off.

"And this has nothing to do with a certain T-shirt that was given away a month ago?" her mother asked.

"What?" Carrie's face turned bright red. "No! Why would you say that?"

"Carrie, I know you said that this shirt means a lot to you, but you cannot go halfway around the world to track it down," her mother said, chopping up her omelet, then scooping up the pieces with a slice of multigrain toast. "There are a billion people in India. Even if you went there, the chances that you'd find it are practically nil."

"But Mom, I—"

"I'm sorry, honey. It's out of the question."

"Wait, Mom," Carrie said determinedly. "You can't just say no like that. You don't understand. It's not just any T-shirt. It's . . . It's . . ."

Her mother stopped eating and waited, watching Carrie as she struggled to find something to say. Sure, she could tell her that the shirt was lucky, and she'd probably get the same response that she got from Piper, which was somewhere in between, "Aw, that's cute," and, "Are you freaking nuts?" But then her mom would wonder why she thought it had magical powers, and she'd have to invoke the evil palindrome: D-A-D.

"It's what, Carrie?" her mom asked. "What's so important that I should let my one and only daughter fly off on her own to a foreign country?"

"It's . . ." Carrie stared into her mother's eyes. She'd always been there for her. She was the only person Carrie could trust more than Piper. Maybe she could get away with telling her the truth. Maybe it wouldn't open up this Pandora's box in her mom's still-vulnerable heart. Anyway, wasn't it her mom's job to put whatever she felt aside so that she could help Carrie feel better? Wasn't that what mothers were supposed to do, listen to their kids, even when it might be difficult to hear what they had to say?

"Carrie, what's going on?" her mother prompted.

Carrie closed her eyes, crossed her fingers on both hands, and said it. "Dad gave me the shirt and told me it would bring me good luck. And he was right, Mom. It did. That's why I have to get it back."

When she opened her eyes again, cautiously, her mother was gaping at her. "What?"

"You don't have to believe me, Mom. You just have to trust me," Carrie said, moving forward on her seat. "You know that there is no way I would ask you to ship me off to India with Celia and Doreen unless it was really, *really* important."

Her mom shifted her weight on the stool as if she were uncomfortable. Then she ran both her hands through her hair. Carrie knew she was in trouble. The hands-through-the-hair technique was the major form of stress release for many of the women in her family.

"Carrie, I don't know what to say," her mother said, slumping forward so her elbows rested on the counter. "I can't believe your father would put a notion like this in your head. It's so typical of him."

The battle had begun.

"Mom, it's not a notion, and Dad didn't put anything in my head. I believe that it's real and that's all that matters, right?" Carrie replied, trying not to sound too bold but wanting to remain firm in her convictions.

"Of course it matters, honey. But here's the thing. Parents have to be responsible and make choices that are in the best interest of their children." Her mom took in a deep breath. "So I'm going to have to say no, Carrie. I don't like having to say it at all, but I feel like this is a bad idea."

Carrie felt her skin getting hot and prickly from the intense anxiety and she was almost knocking on the door of The T Zone. But she'd try one more rational argument before blowing up.

Deep breath.

"It's not like I'd be going by myself. I'll be with your best friend, who's a responsible mom in her own right. And besides, I'd get to travel and see the world."

Her mother pushed back from the countertop and wiped her hands on the napkin in her lap. "Just like your dad wants you to, I suppose."

"I'd like to think you both want me to be happy, and

this would make me happy," Carrie said while taking her mother's hand in her own.

Her mom was getting misty-eyed. "Sweetie, I want you to be happy. But I also want you to be safe. I just don't feel good about this trip—I'm sorry."

A well of anger rose up in Carrie too quickly for her to stop it. She let go of her mom's hand, got off the stool, and stood her ground.

"What you don't feel good about is the fact that this shirt means something to me and it means something to Dad. That's the only reason you won't let me go. You're just being spiteful and bitter," she said crossly. All she could think about was her T-shirt and her luck and how being without it made he feel very lost. "You're being so unfair. I wish that Dad was here instead of you!"

Ouch. Carrie felt the sting the second after the words were out.

"Yes, well, I wish he was here for you too," her mom said after a pause. "But I'm what you're stuck with. And the answer is still no."

Before she could say another unkind word, Carrie bolted up the stairs to her room, shut the door, and turned up her stereo loud enough so her mother couldn't hear her wailing like a little girl, which was exactly how she knew she was behaving. And that only made her cry harder.

Carrie spent the next two days hiding out in her room. She was too upset and embarrassed by the way she had acted to apologize to her mom. In fact, when she had escaped the confines of her bedroom to raid the refrigerator, Carrie ran right into her mom and wasn't able to do anything but mumble something that sounded like "whoopsexcusemesorry" and dash back upstairs. Needless to say, it was a small step toward forgiveness.

The more Carrie thought about it, though, the more she was glad that she had gotten a lot of stuff off her chest that had been weighing on her for a long time. But it certainly wasn't right to attack her mom for being . . . a mom! Did she really think she could fool her mom with some silly speech about the wonders of India? Like her mom would just say, "Hey, whatever. Fly to Timbuktu for all I care." Carrie couldn't even begin to come up with a way to make things right, and where could she turn for help?

The only thing that seemed to make her feel better was exercise-fueled endorphin rushes. Carrie did what seemed like a million push-ups over the course of forty-eight hours. After each session she was sweaty and warm and her heart was pounding. But those symptoms weren't solely from her workouts. Every second she wished her mother would walk in and tell her that things were going to be okay and she adored her, despite her sudden bout of insanity.

Then, whaddya know. Carrie got her wish.

"Hey."

Carrie looked up while in the middle of a push-up

and saw her mom leaning on the door frame. She was holding the cordless phone from the kitchen and smirking a bit. Carrie sat down on her yoga mat and crossed her legs. Her mom joined her on the floor.

"Mom." Carrie gulped so hard that it felt as if she was trying to dry swallow a huge multivitamin. "I am so sorry for what I said the other day. I was really out of line and . . . I don't blame you if you don't let me out of this house for the rest of the summer."

Her mother's smirk turned into a grin. "I know you're sorry, hon. And I know how hard the divorce has been on you. Your dad and I don't make things easier, either. There's still a lot of tension between us, and sometimes you get caught in the middle."

And with that, Carrie lunged at her mom and gave her the biggest bear hug of all time.

"Mom, I love you so much," Carrie whimpered.

"I love you too," her mom said, holding Carrie tightly in her arms. "And to prove it, I just spoke to your dad, and he loves you so much that he's getting you a free plane ticket to India."

Carrie froze. *What did she just say?*

Her mom pulled away from their embrace and looked at the deer-in-headlights expression on Carrie's face.

"I thought about what you said, how I might be preventing you from going out of spite. There may be some truth to it. But when you said that this would make you happy again, that's when I knew. If I let you go now, I might get my cheerful daughter back," her mom said while caressing Carrie's cheek.

"Mom," Carrie said with a sniffle. She was in tears yet again. "I want my old self back too."

"Well, okay, then. It's settled," her mom said as she rose from the floor and left the cordless phone on her dresser. "Call your dad and thank him. He's in Taiwan, so don't be too long."

"Did you tell him why I wanted to go to India?" Carrie said worriedly. She was concerned that once he heard the story, he'd want his daughter committed to the psych ward.

"I just said that you were going to find yourself," her mom said, and then winked.

One week later Carrie clutched her "lucky" rabbit's foot in both hands, wondering how she had forgotten that she hated flying. They had just taken off on the second leg of their trip, from London to Calcutta, and as far as Carrie was concerned, the ascent had been less than stellar. Granted, she hadn't been on a plane since last summer, when she had gone to visit her dad in New York for a week, but at least that pilot had known how to take off. None of these dips and bumps and even bigger dips. Didn't they know that the public had been trained to believe that most problems happened in the first five minutes of any flight? Wouldn't that inspire all pilots to do whatever they could to make those first five minutes as heart-attack free as possible?

It didn't help, of course, that they had stuck her in aisle 13. Planes shouldn't even *have* an aisle 13. But since they clearly had to have one, then there should be some rule on the books that allowed superstitious people to automatically switch seats with someone else. As it was, no one Carrie had asked had wanted to move. Now all she needed was for a flight attendant to kill a stow-away ladybug and Carrie would officially flip out.

Finally the plane seemed to level out and Carrie loosened her grip on the rabbit's foot and looked down at her notebook again. She had been working on a game plan for finding her T-shirt. Unfortunately, she didn't have much to go on. She still had the receipt number for the original package Celia had sent out to Help India, and she had compiled a list of women's shelters from the Web. Unfortunately, the list was about a mile long. So Carrie's course of action upon reaching Calcutta would be to go to the Help India headquarters and find out if they gave to specific shelters. Maybe she could narrow the list down a bit from there.

"I can't believe you're coming to India to find a shirt," Dor-mean said with a sneer.

"I can't believe how much food is stuck in your braces," Carrie replied.

"Shut up," Dor-mean spat.

"No, you shut up," Carrie replied.

"Listen, you have no idea what you're getting your-self into," Dor-mean said with an unappealing snort. "It's not like we're staying at some Hilton where everybody speaks English and waits on you hand and foot."

"I *know*," Carrie said. "I'm not expecting a four-star hotel." *Maybe two, two and a half,* she thought.

"That's surprising. I'm amazed that you didn't wuss out the minute you realized you'd actually have to work on this trip."

Carrie was offended to the core. "Hey, I'm up to whatever anyone asks me to do. So don't you worry about it, okay?"

"Whatever you say," Dor-mean said, eyeing her.

"Well, it's not like we're not going to have *any* free time. They're not going to have us toiling away twenty-four/seven, right?" Carrie said.

"Do you mind? I'm trying to read," Dor-mean huffed, and buried her nose in another *Let's-Go-India*-like tour book.

"Fine," Carrie said, sitting back in her seat, thinking about how everyone at home was at the pool soaking up harmful UV rays. "As long as I have a little time to get some kind of tan, I'll be okay."

Dor-mean snorted again into her hand. "Um, I don't think you'll be getting a tan," she said.

"Why not? Aren't we going to be outside working all the time?"

81

"Yeah, but it's monsoon season in Calcutta," Dor-mean said in her usual know-it-all tone of voice. "There's not gonna be much sun, Jockstrap." Then she placed the headphones on her Discman over her ears and hit play. The volume was cranked up so loud, Carrie could hear every word.

"The PhAAAAAAAAntom of the Op-er-a is there! Inside your mind!"

Carrie tucked her rabbit's foot into her pocket and opened the guidebook she had purchased at the London airport. As her wretched neighbor closed her eyes with a blissful smile, Carrie propped her tiny pillow between her head and the wall. She turned the book to the section on Calcutta ("recently renamed Kolkata," it read at the top) and curled up in as tight a ball as possible. At least she hadn't thought about the fact that she was on a plane for the past five minutes. If she could just read for a while until she fell asleep, she would be out for a few hours. And if she was lucky, she would miss three shows' worth of music and maybe a few turbulence pockets as well. Then when she woke up, she would be that much closer to her destination. That much closer to her lucky T.

And once you get your T-shirt back, everything will be fine, Carrie thought as Dor-mean started to whisper-sing along to the song. *Good things will start happen-ing again and you'll be the lucky Carrie you once were.*

Chapter Five

Eyes tired and bloodshot, throat dry, skin oily, and hair a raggedy mess, Carrie dragged herself off the plane behind Celia and Doreen. Gingerly she lifted her heavy, borderline-carry-on backpack onto both shoulders. After an entire day and night sitting in the same seat, her back ached and her muscles were wound so tight that she'd need an army of masseuses and chiropractors to get her feeling normal again. Carrie was so exhausted all she could think about was stretching out on a soft bed and getting some real sleep. The line of people paused at the end of the jetway, and Carrie looked out the window for her first view of India. The glass pane was streaked with rain, the coconut trees bending under the weight of the downpour, and the sky was the color of ink, even though it was the middle of the day.

"It wasn't raining when we landed," she said in astonishment.

"These storms, they come out of nowhere," said the small-framed elderly man who was shuffling along behind her.

Doreen grinned over her shoulder. "Told ya."

Don't kill her, Carrie thought. *If you kill her, you'll be sent to an Indian prison and you'll never find your T-shirt.*

The line inched forward and opened up into the small terminal, where families shouted and cheered and hugged the arriving passengers. A pack of women in bright saris—colorful, flowing garments with sparkling beads and glitter dangling everywhere—grabbed a skinny girl in a maroon UCSF sweatshirt into their many arms. A family in faded jeans and worn T-shirts greeted the old man who had been behind Carrie on line. A guy in a thoroughly wrinkled and sweat-stained white button-down shirt covered a beautiful giggling woman in kisses. Unfamiliar faces and rapid-fire foreign languages surrounded Carrie. Flight attendants and airport workers and tourists and families bustled around her. Everyone seemed to know where they were going and why. Everyone but Carrie.

Oh my God, I'm in India, Carrie thought, wishing she had Piper or one of her parents to hug. *I traveled a zillion miles from home . . . to look for a T-shirt. I am certifiably insane.*

"Oh! Nana! Nana-Ji!" a robust woman shouted, running at Carrie with arms outstretched. Carrie ducked out of the way, narrowly missing having her eye gouged out by the lady's super-long nails as she threw her arms around an excited middle-aged woman who was carrying a bunch of Disney World shopping bags and wearing a Goofy hat. This symbol of American culture plucked a vulnerable heartstring in Carrie's heart. *I want my mommy,* whimpered a small voice in her overwhelmed brain. Then she noticed that Celia and Doreen were hustling through the crowd at least ten yards ahead of her. She was not going to lose sight of the only people she knew in this place. Carrie adjusted her backpack and jogged to catch up, dodging and weaving around packs of people like the basketball star she was.

"Prandya!" Celia shouted, throwing her arms up and squealing. She raced toward a pair of women who stood at the edge of the crowd. "Prandya! Teensy! It's so good to see you!"

A stunningly exotic, voluptuous woman in a black tank dress hugged Celia as they jumped up and down. Her hundreds of silver bracelets jingle-jangled as the massive bun at the back of her head bounced. The second woman, a frail-looking older lady who flinched when Celia turned her ridiculous energy on her, barely managed a real smile. She had hypnotic dark eyes that Carrie could tell just by staring into them that years

85

ago this woman was probably the catch of her village.

"This is my daughter, Doreen," Celia said, turning toward Doreen.

"Nice to meet you," Doreen said. Then she pressed her hands together and bowed slightly. *"Namaste."*

"Namaste," Prandya and Teensy repeated, looking impressed. Of course, why wouldn't they be impressed with Doreen? Nobody ever really got to see her as "Dormean" except for Carrie.

"And this is our newest recruit. Carrie Fitzgerald, this is Prandya," Celia said, gesturing to the larger lady. "And this is Teensy," she added, pointing to the smaller one.

At least it will be easy to remember her name, Carrie thought, raising a hand in greeting.

"It's such a pleasure to have you all here," Prandya said, putting her arms around Celia, Doreen, and Carrie. "Come along. We'll get your bags and then we'll find you all some food. You must be starving."

Carrie's stomach grumbled audibly and they all laughed, even stone-faced Teensy. The plane food just hadn't cut it.

"This one, she needs a little *biranis*," Teensy said, patting Carrie's arm with a fluttering touch.

"I don't know what that is, but I would love a cheeseburger," Carrie said with a laugh.

Teensy stopped in her tracks and everyone's faces fell. Carrie blinked.

"What? What did I say?" Carrie asked, instant panic

seizing her. Had she already stumbled over the language barrier? Teensy turned and stalked off through the crowd without a backward glance and Carrie suddenly saw herself deserted by everyone in the middle of the bustling airport, left to fend for herself in a foreign land. She almost grabbed Celia's hand for a little security.

"Cows are sacred animals, loser," Doreen said under her breath.

Unfortunately, Carrie was too busy absorbing the fact that she had just made a mockery of this woman's religion, so she didn't have a witty retort ready to go.

"Not to worry," Prandya said, forcing a smile. "You'll find some of us take certain customs more seriously than others. Teensy, she never eats the sacred meat of the cow."

"Oh . . . sorry," Carrie said, swallowing hard.

In her mind, Carrie vowed to be more sensitive about her love of beef. Obviously it wasn't "what's for dinner" in this neck of the woods.

"It is all right. She will be praying for your soul tonight," Prandya said, patting Carrie on the back and nodding as if this was some kind of comfort. "Okay, let's get going."

Doreen looked over her shoulder, shook her head, and sneered at Carrie as if she was the biggest idiot on the planet. Carrie managed to stick her tongue out at Doreen, which was immature but effective because Doreen turned back around. Carrie glanced back at the gate, wondering what she'd gotten herself into and if there was any way she could get out of it. Between Dormean, quirky Celia, prickly Teensy, this new sacred cow rule, and whatever else that was ahead waiting to fall on her like a two-hundred-pound anvil, this was going to be one long summer.

Calcutta was mind-blowing. Carrie had never seen anything like it in real life. In fact, she had never seen anything like it in the movies, on television, or even in those random documentaries Mr. Phillips was always showing in world history. There were literally thousands of people. Pedestrians walked around in droves, pressing toward the windows of Prandya's tiny automobile, shouting to one another across the street. A trail of men carrying huge sacks of laundry stepped off the curb and traipsed right in front of Prandya's car, forcing her to slam on the brakes. While they were still stopped, a flock of chickens pecked their way in front of them from the other direction, pausing to take a poke around in the center of the muddy street.

All around Carrie were men in suits, guys in polo shirts and shorts, women in saris, and teenage girls in jeans. Little kids sported everything from crisp school uniforms to plain T-shirts. Never had Carrie seen so many different types of people crowded into one place, moving and talking and working and shopping and playing and laughing. Sure, there were all different races and economic strata represented in San Francisco, but Carrie rarely got to see so much diversity all at the same time. It was very cool, if a little overwhelming. She dug her digital camera out of her backpack and snapped a quick photo through the windshield. No one at home was ever going to believe this.

The rain had stopped before Carrie and the others made it to the car, leaving behind a whole network of ponds and streams. Children skipped through the river that had formed at the side of the road, which was dirty and full of random garbage—lettuce and paper wrapping and bits of multicolored gunk. Carrie bit her lip and felt her heart ache. Didn't these kids have playgrounds to run around in? Once she soaked up the atmosphere some more, she realized that a swing set and a slide might be hard to come by. Every inch of available space had been built up. These poor kids were lucky to have any sort of outside area to play in. Still, it made her want to take them all home with her and bring them straight to the pool, regardless if Jason was lifeguarding or flirting with some bimbo.

Even Dor-mean, Miss I Am the Authority on India and Everything Else in This World, had a look of awe on her face. She was jammed in between Carrie and Teensy in the backseat, rotating her head back and forth as if it were on a pendulum. A bus crammed with people rolled by, followed by a pickup truck with at least a dozen men in the back, gripping whatever they could to stay inside as the truck bumped along the road.

How can this many people fit in one city? Carrie thought, gaping around at the buildings that lined the street. The structures all seemed to be leaning this way and that, huddling against one another for support to keep from slipping into the mire the roads had become after the downpour. Laundry that had been hung to dry in an alleyway now dripped with water. Half the windows were covered only by faded sheets or cracked shutters. Colorful placard signs, some in English, some in the exotic symbols of the Bengali language, advertised theaters, Internet cafés, custom-made furniture, and TV repair. Makeshift stands lined the streets. There was a man selling bananas and mangoes from an open cart. Another man sat on the sidewalk surrounded by pots, stirring up some kind of concoction for the brave tourists who hovered around him. Nearby a pair of children sold sweets from a table, their mother hovering behind them as they made their sales.

"I can't believe how loud it is!" Celia shouted above the din on the street.

"I know!" Carrie agreed. "It's more crowded than the Halloween parade back home!" She leaned forward as far as she could without totally smushing Doreen. "Is there something special going on?" she asked Prandya.

"Something special?" Prandya asked.

"Yeah, like a parade or a huge sale or something," Carrie said.

Prandya looked confused for a moment, gazing out the windshield as a pair of old men with long beards tottered by with wooden canes. They were wearing nothing but sheets wrapped around them to cover the strategic areas. One of them looked up and smiled as he passed, flashing a single, yellow tooth.

"Oh, you mean because of all the people!" Prandya said finally, letting out a hearty laugh. "Oh, no, my dear. It is always like this. There are more than twelve million people in Kolkata."

"Wow. That's unbelievable," Carrie said, trying not to think about how difficult it would be to find her shirt among twelve million souls. She wanted to stay positive. Believing you could do something was half the battle. That was one lesson she had learned on the many courts she'd competed on.

As she looked out the window again, she spotted a group of about twelve women coming out of a cozy shop. They were all dressed in elaborate saris and wore rows of glittering bracelets and colorful *bindis* on their foreheads. They all looked so exotic and beautiful as they chatted together and walked down the street. Carrie looked down at her plain jeans and white tank top and wondered if she would ever be able to pull off something like that. Maybe she would have to do a little shopping while she was here—if there was time.

The car made another sudden stop and Carrie's

stomach lurched. Instantly all thoughts of international fashion flew out the window.

Oh, no, Carrie thought. *Please not now. Not on my first day here.* Carrie had always been prone to car sickness and between the sensory overload, her empty stomach, and the bucking of the car, she was suddenly extremely nauseated. She could only imagine what Teensy and Prandya would think of her if she barfed in their car. Not to mention the huge laugh Dor-mean would have at her expense.

Leaning back in her seat, Carrie breathed in and out slowly in an attempt to quiet her stomach, but it didn't help. The air was thick with humidity and a heady concoction of tangy, sour, and spicy smells that only made the sick feeling more intense. Suddenly there was no doubt in her mind that she was going to heave. The question was, would it be right here in the car, or would the gods be kind and let it wait until they got to the hotel?

Finally, mercifully, Prandya turned off the crowded street and onto a much less packed side road. As the car picked up a bit of speed, Carrie rolled down her window and stuck her head out, letting the breeze blow her knotty hair back from her face.

Suddenly the buildings started to come farther and farther apart and open air was again a reality. Prandya turned onto a wide, paved, tree-lined street and Carrie's jaw dropped. Where had *these* houses come from? They were huge and grand, made of real, solid brick and mortar with windows and flower boxes and paved pathways up to the doors. Carrie saw a maid in full uniform beating out a rug on one of the many verandahs. A gleaming Mercedes pulled up to a gate, which slid open automatically to let the car through. Carrie breathed deeply and smelled nothing but clean air and sweet flowers.

Wow, what a beautiful neighborhood, Carrie thought.

Prandya made another turn and the car splashed through muddy water before finally squealing to a stop in front of a tall, sorry-looking structure with windows that yawned open toward the street. A couple of skinny teenage boys kicked back on the steps, smoking cigarettes. The car backfired, sending a pack of birds squawking from the rooftop. Then the engine fell silent.

"Well, how is that for luck, huh?" Prandya said, turning in her seat. "We just made it!"

Carrie blew out a relieved sigh. Actually, the fact that she was able to avoid puking had to be the best luck Carrie had experienced in a while. Could being in the same country as her lucky T have some effect on her karma?

"Is this our hotel?" Carrie whispered to Celia as they got out of the car.

"This is a hostel, dear," Celia replied. "We're staying here with other volunteers. It'll have a rustic charm, I'm sure."

"Fine," Carrie said, nodding. "Great."

She had heard of hostels before. Carrie had always thought they sounded kind of cool and romantic in a way—like a dorm packed with kids from around the world, everyone roughing it together. Piper's collegiate cousin Maxine spent time backpacking throughout Europe last summer and came back with a ton of stories involving bathrooms shared with hot Irish guys and breakfasts of bread and hot chocolate eaten at huge tables with girls her age who were fascinated about America and wanted to test their English. There were huge parties where all kinds of languages were spoken, bad beer was swilled, and kissing games were an inevitable conclusion.

But this place took the phrase "roughing it" to the extreme. As Carrie yanked her bags from the back of the car, she looked up at the three floors of windows, some of which had been shattered, then duct-taped back together. Toward the base of the building, parts of the outer Sheetrock had crumbled away, revealing the bricks underneath. A couple of dogs scrounged through some boxes and trash bags in the alleyway, the sounds of their snarling and munching doing nothing to help Carrie's weakened stomach. She was fairly certain that no one she knew had ever stayed in a place that looked remotely like this one.

Suddenly a loud, wailing sound split the air and Carrie nearly jumped with fright. Across the street a pair of men paused on the sidewalk. They pulled rolled-up mats from their bags, laid them on the ground, and knelt down to pray. A pair of women who were walking and talking stepped around them, never pausing in their conversation.

"What is that?" Carrie asked, wincing against the sheer volume.

"That's the Muslim call to prayer," Prandya explained. "There's a mosque a block away and the call happens five times a day."

Carrie watched the men as they closed their eyes and bowed again and again, touching their foreheads to their mats. Five times a day? That took a level of devotion she could barely imagine. It took a lot of discipline and motivation for her to train for basketball and that was only once a day, sometimes even less than that. So far, India was completely foreign and utterly fascinating.

"Why aren't you praying?" Carrie asked.

"Oh, dear, I'm not Muslim. I'm Buddhist," she said with a smile. "We have all kinds of religions here, just like you have at home, I am sure."

"Come on, girls," Celia said, wrangling Carrie and Doreen, who was also intrigued. "It's impolite to stare."

Carrie tore her eyes from the praying men and shuffled toward the building, lugging her bags. One of the two teenagers stood, hiked his pants up, and clenched his cigarette between his teeth.

"Allow me to assist," he said, reaching for Carrie's suitcase.

"No, that's okay, I got it," Carrie said, wary of letting anyone take her bags. There was no way a pilot's daughter was going to ignore her "don't give your bags to anyone else" reflex. She'd hold on to her own stuff, thank you very much.

"Please. I can help," the guy said, smoke pouring out through his nose.

Carrie swallowed back a new wave of nausea. "No, really. I got it," she said, wondering where the nearest bathroom was.

"I see. Skinny American girl is too good for my help?" the guy said.

"No, it's not that at all. You see, my dad's an airplane pilot and—"

Without any warning, he took the cigarette out of his mouth and blew a stream of acrid smoke directly into her face. The smoke went up her nose, into her mouth, and gagged her for real.

Carrie felt the final heave. Her face burst into flame. This was it. This was where it was going to happen. She dropped her bags, slapped her hand over her mouth, and ran for the side of the stairs. Grasping at the wooden handrail, she leaned over, tried not to think of how mortifying this was going to be, and lost all three of her airplane meals into a tangle of weeds and trash.

So much for the being-in-the-same-country-with-the-lucky-T theory.

Behind her, she could hear the boys laughing, Prandya "tut-tutting," and Teensy muttering something in Bengali that cracked the guys up even more. The only thing missing from this humiliating moment: a tremendously loud cackle from Dor-mean. Too bad for her that Celia was standing right there, because otherwise she would have

96

given Carrie the beat-down of a lifetime. Instead Doreen just put her hands over her mouth to stifle the gargantuan guffaw that she was so close to unleashing.

"Oh, my dear! Are you all right?" Celia asked, laying a comforting hand on her back when she was finally through.

"I'm okay," she said, nodding. Her eyes were thick with tears and her throat hurt from all the gagging. "I could use some water, though."

"Of course," Prandya said. "Ali! Get her bags!"

The kid with the cigarette grabbed Carrie's stuff and followed her as they walked inside. Carrie didn't dare look him in the eye. She was embarrassed that she had thrown up right in front of him but even more so that after all her refusal, he had ended up carrying her bags anyway.

"They have to boil the water here," Doreen whispered to Carrie. "You never know what might be swimming around in it."

Oh, the humanity, Carrie thought, wishing her health-nut mom was around to rescue her. "Doreen, what did Teensy say about me just now?"

"How should I know?" Doreen replied. "Those tapes don't teach you how to understand the language when it's spoken at warp speed."

Ali leaned his head over Carrie's shoulder and grinned. "She said, 'That's what happens when you eat the sacred cow,'" he told her. Then he laughed all the way up the stairs.

"Ha!" chuckled Dor-mean. "That's a good one."

"Glad I'm here to amuse you," Carrie said.

Celia stayed behind on the first floor to meet a few people with Teensy while Prandya showed Carrie and Doreen to their room. She lumbered up the two flights of rickety stairs, arousing ominous squeaks and squeals from the floorboards. At the end of the surprisingly well-lit hallway on the third floor, Prandya opened a small door.

"This will be your room, girls," she said.

Doreen plowed straight in and dropped her bags on one of two small cots that were pushed up against the side walls. Ali had already deposited Carrie's things on the other cot, which was sagging in the middle—the head-board and footboard looked as if they were straining to meet each other over her bags. Carrie hovered in the doorway, unsure of whether she would actually fit in there along with Dor-mean, her crappy attitude, and all their stuff. The room, while clean and bright and equipped with a writing desk and one dresser, was roughly the size of Carrie's closet back home.

"What's that?" she asked Prandya, pointing to a contraption on the floor that looked like an oven burner.

"That is a mosquito coil," Prandya said. "We get a lot of bugs in the rainy season, so I suggest you light that before you go to bed."

"I brought tons of mosquito repellent," Doreen said with a proud little smile.

"Someone did their research," Prandya said brightly, causing the smile to widen.

Carrie rolled her eyes.

"Come along. I'll show you the bathroom," Prandya said.

Yes! That's exactly what I need, Carrie thought. *First I'll take a long shower and then I'll go right to sleep.* She didn't even care about eating anymore after watching all her other meals come back up.

Prandya opened a door at the opposite end of the hallway. The foul stench hit Carrie so hard she almost collapsed. She held her nose and backed up a few steps.

"Ali! Tell Gehra the toilet is backed up again!" Prandya shouted, slamming the door closed before Carrie even got a look at the shower. "I'm sorry, girls," she said. "The flusher goes out from time to time. It should be fixed very soon."

Stay positive, Carrie told herself. *Or more important, stay calm. Do not—I repeat—do not . . . freak . . . out. . . .* "That's okay," she said, still holding her breath.

"No problem," Doreen said brightly.

Carrie was surprised that Doreen hadn't studying plumbing in third world countries before the trip. How thoughtless of her!

"So, let's get you some water," Prandya said, wrapping her arm around Carrie's shoulders.

"Actually, I think I'm just gonna go to bed if it's okay with you," she said. "Jet lag and all that."

"But we will be having dinner soon," Prandya said.

Carrie felt weak, exhausted, parched, hungry, and sick all at the same time. But all she really wanted to do was go to sleep and recharge her tired, frazzled batteries.

"Save me something?" Carrie asked.

"Of course," Prandya replied.

"Thanks."

"Don't forget to light the mosquito coil!" Dor-mean called after Carrie.

"Yeah, yeah," she said under her breath. "Coil this!"

Carrie wasn't too concerned about the bug situation. Mosquitoes didn't bite her. It was one of those odd phenomena in her family. She and her mom could go hike the redwoods with ten people and come back without a single bite while everyone else was covered in them.

She walked into her room, threw everything on the floor, and rested her head on the small but soft pillow. Lately, when Carrie crawled into bed, she tossed and turned for hours. Thoughts of her lucky T, Piper, Jason, and her mom and dad would fill her consciousness, preventing her from dozing off. This time was different. Within fifteen seconds she was out.

That evening Carrie awoke from a deep, dreamless sleep, jolted awake by a loud noise. She blinked around in confusion. There was dark, grainy wood where her cream-colored wall was supposed to be, and the dim light coming in through the window was all wrong. In fact, the window was in an entirely different place. Where was she? Where was that singing coming from? Why was her face so close to the wall? What was that delicious smell?

"Hey. You're awake."

At the sound of Doreen's voice Carrie fully woke up and it hit her. *India. Riiiight.*

She rolled over, her cot letting out a zillion squeaks, and saw Doreen kicked back on her own bed, a magazine open in front of her. A single lamp was tilted toward her bed so she could read.

"What time is it?" Carrie asked, scratching an itch on her shoulder.

"It's about nine thirty," Doreen said. She gestured behind her at the desk against the wall. "Saved you some dinner. It's pretty good."

All at once Carrie's stomach grumbled and her head started to throb. She was happy to note that the yummy smell seemed to be coming from the food Doreen had brought her, although there was a fifty-fifty chance it might be laced with anthrax. But at this point Carrie was so hungry she decided that she'd give her archrival the benefit of the doubt and prayed that the only thing Dor-mean had done was spit in it.

She pushed herself out of bed and sat down at the desk. She poured a glass of water from a full pitcher and took a long drink. The cool liquid wound its way down her throat and into her empty stomach. Then she lifted a cloth napkin from the top of the plate and was greeted with a mound of rice, chicken, and vegetables in some kind of spicy-scented brown sauce. She grabbed the fork and dug in.

The first bite sent an explosion of hot flavors through her mouth, throat, and nose. It was as if the entire dish had been soaked in jalapeño pepper juice. Carrie grabbed her water and took another long gulp.

"Too spicy for ya?" Doreen asked.

"No," Carrie said, coughing up her left lung. "It's good, actually."

Even though every one of her taste buds was on fire, there was no way she was going to crack in front of Doreen. She'd eat every last morsel even if it killed her.

As Carrie ate each forkful of food, she downed a huge gulp of water, which barely extinguished the flames in her mouth. After a while the burning sensation on her gums subsided, which made her relieved at first, but then suddenly her lips went numb: could she have suffered permanent nerve damage from Indian food? Knowing her luck without the T, most likely.

The only good thing about singeing the inside of her mouth was that it kept Carrie's mind off the persistent itch on her leg. After the novocaine effect set in, she was really able to focus on how irritated her skin was. She scratched at her upper arms and her inner thighs. When the center of her back started to angrily cry out for her fingernails, she dropped her fork and decided to see what the heck was going on. When she looked down at her legs, she almost screamed. They were covered with red bumps.

"Oh my God!" Carrie said.

"What?" Doreen asked.

"What *are* those?"

Doreen lifted her chin and looked over with minor interest. "Mosquito bites, duh," she said.

"But I don't *get* mosquito bites," Carrie cried, scratching at her arms.

Doreen screwed up her face in false sympathy. "Should've lit the coil before you went to sleep."

"How about I light the mosquito coil under your butt?" Carrie snapped. The pain from her bites was so severe, she was afraid it might push her to homicide.

"Aren't we sensitive," Dor-mean said mockingly. "Too bad you didn't bring any of this."

She pulled a bottle of Skin-So-Soft out from under her pillow. "I really wish I could spare some."

Yep, this girl is going down! Carrie thought. *She is evil and must be destroyed.*

"Doreen, give me the Skin-So-Soft or else," she said, standing up and putting her hands on her hips.

"Or else what, Jockstrap?" Dor-mean said, getting off her bed and crossing her arms in front of her nonexistent chest.

Okay, Carrie hadn't really thought things through beyond this point. Yes, she was taller than Doreen and she had more muscle. But something told Carrie that if she were betting on this fight, she would put all her money on her opponent. The girl had enough rage in her to fuel a Mack truck. If they were to go at it *Kill–Bill* style, Doreen would probably be the last one standing.

"Or else . . ." Carrie said, hoping that something really smart would come out next. "I'll tell Celia."

That would have been smart if she were five years old.

Dor-mean laughed so hard she was red in the face. "So you're going to tell my mommy on me?"

Then after a few more hearty chuckles, she plopped back down on her bed and got back to her magazine.

Outside in the alley a dog barked and then howled, sending a chill straight through Carrie. A howling dog meant death was near, which at the moment seemed perfectly fitting. If Carrie and Doreen were going to be roommates for a good part of the summer, someone was certainly getting carried out of there in a body bag.

After Carrie made her way to the bathroom and saw her reflection in a severely broken mirror (why not tack on another seven years of bad luck?), the answer was obvious. Carrie hardly recognized the person looking back at her. Her skin was sallow, her eyes were droopy, and her hair was dirty and frizzed. She looked like she had walked out of a Wes Craven movie. Carrie splashed some cool water on her face and then looked up again. Lovely. Streaks of mascara were now running down her cheeks.

Just then Carrie thought of Piper. Her heart turned around and around in her chest. This whole trip would have been a lot more fun if she were here. Piper would have saved her from Dor-mean on the plane, would never have let her barf in front of complete strangers (or at least would have told them off for laughing while Carrie was too weak to do so), and would have made even the bug bite situation seem hilarious somehow.

Don't think about her, she told herself. *Just remember why you're here. You have to find your shirt and get your life back. . . .*

Trying to put the aggravating itch, Piper, and Dor-mean out of her mind, Carrie returned to her room, lay down on her squeaky cot, and pulled the sheets over her head. The cool fabric felt good against her raw skin. Carrie finally drifted off to sleep once again. This time she did dream. She dreamed that she was in the backseat of a tiny auto. Outside the car, on the teaming streets of Calcutta, a million people walked and shopped and shouted and laughed. And every last one of them, every man, woman, and child Carrie saw, was wearing her lucky T. But no matter what she did, no matter how hard she stretched out the window, she couldn't touch any of them, and no one seemed to notice she was even there.

Chapter Six

Carrie woke up to another prayer call and this time the bright morning sun was streaming through the window of her tiny room. She sat up and stretched, feeling well-rested, refreshed, and determined. Today she was going to get out there and start her search for the lucky T. Today was the first day of the most important mission of her life.

Doreen's bed was already made. (Whoop-de-do.) On the desk were a few flyers with the Help India logo on them. Carrie scanned through the first one and found the address for the organization's Calcutta headquarters. Then she pulled out one of the guides Doreen had "lent" her and checked the map. The address was only eight blocks away from the hostel. Sweet! Already things were picking up.

Carrie stuffed the flyer and the guide into her backpack, grabbed her toiletry bag, and was about to head for the bathroom when a brilliant thought lit up her mind. She lifted Doreen's pillow so that she could snatch the bottle of Skin-So-Soft and slip it into her own bag. But all that was there was a handwritten note from Dor-mean that read, *Nice try, loser!*

Grrrrrrr . . . Carrie thought. *This girl is practically the first cousin to Ursula, the nasty octopus in* The Little Mermaid. But Carrie shook it off very quickly. Doreen wasn't going to ruin her resolve.

After taking a shower in the now smell-free bathroom (God bless whoever fixed the toilet), throwing on a pair of jean shorts and a pink racer-back tank top, and wrapping her hair up in a soggy bun, Carrie grabbed her backpack on her way downstairs and stashed it in the corner by the front door. She was planning on waiting for the moment when everyone was distracted and then slipping out to the Help India headquarters. Since she had no idea when that moment might come, she figured it would be best to have her stuff within grabbing distance.

"Good morning!" Carrie said as she traipsed into the dining area. Sunlight filtered in through three large windows. The wooden floor was dotted with multicolored rugs in various states of wear and tear. Celia was pouring tea into faded china cups at each setting and Doreen was folding mismatched napkins.

"Someone's in a good mood," Celia commented with a smile.

"What can I say? I slept well, I'm clean, and I'm no

longer puking," Carrie replied, knocking on the nearest wooden chair.

She took a seat at the large communal table. Celia and Doreen joined her as a pair of men in their mid-thirties delivered the food from the kitchen through swinging doors, depositing heaping bowls and trays on the table. There was a huge platter of yellow rice that appeared to be mixed up with onions, a plate full of doughnuts and fluffy biscuits, and some kind of brown stew that smelled amazing.

This was going to be a good day. Carrie could feel it. She was taking charge and she hadn't felt this optimistic in weeks. Maybe that meant she was going to find her T-shirt today. She felt as if it were already in her grasp.

Celia stopped the two men on one of their many trips back to the kitchen. "Sanjee, Dan, this is Carrie," she said, smiling in her direction. "Sanjee and Dan run the hostel. They wanted to meet you yesterday, but by the time I brought them upstairs, you were already napping."

"Sorry. It was kind of a long flight," Carrie explained. "But it's nice to meet you."

"And you," Dan said. "Hope you like *puris.*"

"And if not, we have cornflakes," Sanjee added with a wink before they disappeared again into the kitchen.

"What's *puris*?" Carrie asked Celia.

"Here," Celia said, placing a biscuit from the bread platter onto Carrie's plate. "They're delicious. But don't eat yet. Wait until everyone's seated."

Carrie smiled. Her mother would have said exactly the same thing. She started thinking about what her mom might be doing at that very moment. A wave of homesickness crept over Carrie as she filled her plate. She was glad that her mom had always experimented with recipes and raised her as an adventurous eater. She was also glad her mom had called up her dad and arranged this whole trip. Carrie had been thinking a lot about what her mom did—how she reached out to her ex-husband, even though she rarely ever talked to him— just so that her daughter could go off and chase a T-shirt. Carrie would have to bring back the best souvenir ever, like a huge sparkling bejeweled *bindi* dot or something.

"Ooh . . . I see you've taken the *usal* and the *pohe*," Prandya said, eyeing Carrie's plate as she sat down across the table. "Good choices. Very hearty. They will help you work hard."

"*Usal* and . . . *pohe*?" Carrie repeated, the words strange on her tongue. "Which is which?"

"The *usal* is potato-and-lentil stew and the *pohe* is rice and onions," Doreen replied.

"Very good," Prandya said, clearly impressed.

"Doreen read every book and looked at every Internet site she could find before we came here," Celia said, giving her daughter a proud squeeze.

"I recognized the cornflakes," Carrie joked.

Other workers started to trickle in and Celia introduced Carrie, who had been the only one of the new arrivals to sleep straight through dinner the night before.

"This is Amelie and Alfred from Amsterdam," Celia said with a smile as a buff, blond couple sat across from Carrie at the table. "You've already met Ali and his friend Sanjay." Carrie sneered at the two scrawny boys from the day before. Then four older and gruff-looking men lumbered in, taking the last seats at the end of the table. "This is Taj, Satish, Ravi, and Paul," Celia said. "Everyone, this is Carrie."

"Hello," Carrie said, smiling brightly.

One of the men nodded at her, but the others just talked among themselves. They didn't seem to be the most social group of guys, but that was okay by Carrie. They weren't even close to her age, so she wasn't going to be too upset if they didn't feel like making friends.

"Eat, everyone! We are all here!" Dan announced, coming out from the kitchen.

Carrie smiled. This hostel thing wasn't so bad after all.

After finishing off the spicy, garlicky *usal*, some *puris* and *pohe*, and a bowl of cornflakes in seriously sweet milk, Carrie helped the rest of the crew clear the table. Whenever someone left the kitchen, she glanced around, wondering if anyone would notice if she bolted. She was helping Sanjee scrub pots in the sink when everyone else started to trickle out.

"Let me finish here," Sanjee said. "The others will be meeting in the back room to hand out assignments."

"The back room?" Carrie said.

"Right through that door and to the left," Sanjee said, taking over the scrub brush.

If everyone was in the back, she could definitely get out the front. This was her chance.

"I think I left something in the dining room," she said, then turned and quickly pushed through the swinging door. The dining room was empty. Heart pounding, Carrie tiptoed through the room and into the hall. She could hear voices coming from the back room. Ali's nasal voice boomed, followed by Celia's belly laugh. Perfect. They were all occupied.

It's just for the morning, Carrie told herself, staving off any guilt that might try to push its way into her consciousness. *You'll be back by lunch. They'll never even notice you're gone.*

Creeping quickly to the doorway, Carrie grabbed her backpack, held her breath, and slipped out the front door, closing it quietly behind her. Wispy white clouds raced one another across the sun high above. Carrie had packed her umbrella, but it didn't look as if she would need it. This was a perfect day for some T-shirt hunting.

"Where you go?"

Carrie's heart thumped, but she set off anyway. Maybe whoever had spoken wasn't talking to her. She had no idea where she was going—the maps were still tucked away in her pack—but when she heard footsteps scurrying behind her, she quickly crossed the muddy street. As soon as her foot hit the sidewalk on the other side, Teensy appeared in front of her. The woman's tiny face was pinched into a million wrinkles as her sharp eyes glared up at Carrie. Unreal. No one that old should be able to move that fast.

"Where you go? You here for to work!" she said, pointing a finger at Carrie's chest.

"I was just—"

"No. No 'was just,'" Teensy said. She grabbed Carrie's arm in a surprisingly strong grip, her bony fingers cutting into her skin. "You here for to work. You come back. Work!"

Carrie opened her mouth to protest. This was ridiculous. She wasn't in some kind of prison camp! This random woman couldn't tell her what to do. But before she could even say anything, Celia appeared at the front door of the hostel, shaking her head and laughing.

"Trying to get away so soon?" she said, wrapping her arm around Carrie's shoulders. "Don't worry, sweetie. This is going to be *fun!*"

"You are supposed to be hammering," Ali said as he walked by, hauling bricks.

Carrie sneered at his back as he crossed the floor of the loosely framed house. The support beams stretched up and open against the blue sky and workers hung out above, lifting boards for what would one day be the roof. The floor underneath was coarse, grainy wood and all around the base of the house the men from that morning were pouring cement.

Carrie stared at the wooden board and beam in front of her. She had less than no idea what she was doing. Prandya had handed her a can full of nails and a hammer and told her to secure the board to the wooden beam. Already she had hammered in five nails. She was sure that was enough, but she didn't know what she was supposed to do next, so she just stopped and waited for instructions. That was until Ali came by. Now she was just hammering for the sake of hammering. The last thing she wanted was to have both Doreen and that guy on her bad side.

"Can I have another stack of wood, please?" Doreen said, tossing another perfectly measured and sawed-off board onto a pile. Carrie glanced at the mound that represented Doreen's last hour of work. Each board was shorn straight and true and each was exactly the same size as the last. Who was this girl's father, Ty Pennington?

"Why don't you pace yourself, Doreen?" Carrie said, tucking a stray lock of hair behind her ear as she continued to hammer. "You're making the rest of us non-construction-inclined volunteers look bad."

Doreen straightened up from the next board she was measuring. Then she slid some L-shaped tool down to the end of the board and secured it. Carrie didn't even know what the thing *was* and here was Doreen moving it around like a pro.

"Well, I don't see anyone else having any problems," she said, sniffing superiorly as she slipped the pencil out and drew another line. "Just admit that you suck at this."

"Ha! I can hammer rings around you, girlfriend," Carrie said, turning toward Doreen. Between the heat and Dor-mean's wisecracks and the confusion and the fact that she was here in India but was still being kept from her T-shirt search, Carrie had one nerve left, and it was being trampled on big time.

"Is that some sort of challenge?" Doreen asked, peering over her shoulder to make sure her mom wasn't in hearing range. "Because I'll kick you to the curb faster than Jason did."

Okay, a low blow.

"Oh, you did *not* just say that," Carrie growled, clutching her hammer as if it were a weapon.

"I didn't just say it, Jockstrap," Doreen snarled. "I *meant* it."

"You wanna go? Let's go!" Carrie yelped.

But before she could swing the hammer around like a samurai's sword, it slipped out of her hand and landed square on her flip-flopped foot.

"Ow! Oh, man! Owowowowowow!" Stars exploded before Carrie's eyes—a phenomenon she thought only occurred in cartoons. She was sure her big toe was going to explode. She jumped up and down, clutching her left foot with her right hand.

"Ow! Ow! Ow!" she cried out. Even though she was in pain, this exertion of pent-up energy felt sort of good. She brought her foot down again and Doreen's eyes widened.

"Carrie! Watch out!"

KATE BRIAN

Carrie's foot hit the leg of the supply table behind her. The leg collapsed and the table buckled sideways, the top becoming a perfect slide. Every nail, screw, hammer, wrench, saw, and all the other nameless tools slid right down the tabletop, off the foundation of the house, and directly into the freshly poured cement outside. The whole thing made a loud crash, punctuated by a dozen thick plops.

And then there was silence. Carrie looked at Doreen. Doreen went pale. For a moment nobody moved. But only for a moment.

"Who did this?" a deep voice bellowed. "Who did this to the cement!?"

One of the scary guys from breakfast that morning climbed directly into the house, swinging up by the beams. The guy had muscles in places Carrie had never even thought of before. His face quivered with rage and his eyes were about to pop out of his head.

This time Carrie really did see her life flash before her eyes, and it was way too uninteresting for her to die now. She backed up quickly, limping on her foot a bit.

"Who is the genius that dumped a hundred nails into my freshly smoothed cement!?!"

The man whirled around and peered at Carrie. He looked just like the Hulk. Only not green, and his shirt wasn't ripped to shreds.

"It was you, yes?" he demanded, getting right in her face.

116

"Stupid prissy American girl! Why are you even here!?"

Tears of fear sprang to Carrie's eyes. She backed up again and then froze. Then she looked up and gasped. A ladder. She was standing under a ladder.

"Oh, no," she said quietly. "Oh, nonononono."

She stared at the Hulk. This was it. This was definitely how she was going to die.

"And now she is going to cry, is that it?" the man demanded. "Go ahead, prissy girl! Cry!"

"Now, now, now, Taj!" Prandya called out, hustling over and getting in between Carrie and Mr. Crazy McScarington.

Celia was there momentarily as well, stepping protectively in front of Carrie.

"I'm sure the girl didn't mean it," Prandya said.

"Who cares if she meant it?" he shouted, snapping Carrie out of her ladder-of-doom thoughts and back to her present situation. "She did it! Hours of work are ruined!"

"Carrie, you know how you wanted to get out of here this morning?" Celia whispered, tilting her head back toward Carrie.

"Yeah," Carrie said breathlessly.

"I think you should maybe do that," Celia said.

Taj broke away from Prandya and lunged in Carrie and Celia's direction, teeth bared. Carrie let out a terrified shout.

"I think you should maybe do that *now*," Celia added.

Carrie didn't need any more prompting than that.

She turned and jogged like a gimp through the house-in-progress, catching looks of dismay and disgust from all the other workers as she went.

"Excuse me! Do you speak English?" Carrie asked a pair of women walking toward her on the street.

"We are in a hurry," the taller woman replied, scurrying by.

"But I just have a quick question!" Carrie shouted desperately.

The women ignored her and disappeared into the thick crowd. Carrie jumped in front of a couple of businessmen, who were talking in rapid-fire Bengali. She walked backward to keep up with them.

"Do either of you know where I can find—"

The men brushed her off and walked quickly away. Shoulders slumping, Carrie spotted an elderly woman in a rust-colored sari sitting on a bench by the side of the road. And she was smiling right at Carrie. Her heart gave a hopeful leap and she walked over to the woman.

"Hi! Do you know where AJC Bose Road is?" Carrie asked.

The woman shook her head, still smiling, and replied in Bengali. Carrie sighed. *If only Doreen wasn't such a tool, I could have brought her along to help me understand everyone.*

"Thanks anyway," she said, then turned away. It was amazing how with all the people walking around, it seemed impossible to find someone who would stop long enough to help her.

The search had started out promisingly enough. The lady at Help India had been very resourceful, printing out a list of all the women's shelters they were affiliated with and not even asking why Carrie needed it. At first the ten addresses hadn't seemed too overwhelming, but as soon as Carrie had hit the street to try to find the first one, she realized she might have underestimated the difficulty of this task. Some roads had two or more street signs and others had none at all. Carrie continually consulted her map, but whenever she thought she had figured out where she was, the next street had an entirely different name than it should have according to the grid. Figuring it all out while navigating the mayhem on the street and trying not to look too helpless and confused was a lot to handle.

Carrie came to the corner of a wide road where traffic was flowing by. Everyone around her stopped to wait for the light to cross and Carrie welcomed the sudden pause in the commotion, looking around for a street sign.

"Shakespeare Saranai," she whispered, happy to note that it sounded familiar from her many scourings of the map. *Saranai* seemed to be another word for "street"— that much she had picked up on. And a lot of the roads were named for famous figures like Shakespeare, Lenin, and Gandhi. She yanked out one of her maps and, thankfully, found the road. But the second she did, the light changed and the pack of people moved her into the street. Carrie struggled toward the edge of the crowd, still favoring her sore left foot, trying to stay on the corner so she could plot her next move. She was jostled and elbowed and bumped around but finally emerged near a glass-walled phone booth and leaned back against it. She took a deep breath and looked up. The sky was rapidly darkening. Not a good sign.

Carrie looked around desperately for a place to stand out of the way. Then she spotted a tiny café with a picture of a teacup painted on the window. The awning was listing to the side and had a few holes in it, but the lights inside were bright and welcoming. It wasn't Starbucks, but it was good enough.

Carrie ducked inside, leaned back against the wall, and took another deep breath. There were about a hundred people per square foot of space in this city. It made San Francisco look like a ghost town.

"American, correct?"

Carrie glanced up. The older man behind the counter was smiling at her from behind wire-rimmed glasses. His brown skin was wrinkled and leathery and his gray hair was shaggy around his ears.

"How can you tell?" she asked.

"The confused look on your pretty face," he said.

Carrie smiled. A nice guy who spoke English! Eureka!

"Can I help you with something?" the man asked.

"Actually, I'm looking for AJC Bose Road," Carrie said, unfolding her list of shelters. "Do you know where that is?"

"I know exactly where it is," the man said. "The next block that way."

He pointed in the direction Carrie had just come from and her brow furrowed. "But . . . I was just there," she said, now uncrumpling her map. "That's . . . Lower Circular Road."

The man laughed lightly and shook his head. "I always feel bad for the tourists. The government, they have been changing the names of the roads for a few years now but not always changing the signs. You most likely saw one of the old signs, but Lower Circular Road is now AJC Bose Road."

"Thank you!" Carrie said giddily, shoving the map back into her bag. "Thank you so much!"

"My pleasure," the man called after her.

Carrie came to the corner and turned onto AJC Bose Road, noting that the sign did, in fact, also read Lower Circular Road. The question now was, which way to go. She looked around for building numbers to give her an idea of where she was but saw none. Like many of the other streets she had walked along today, AJC Bose seemed to defy definition. To her left was an upscale-looking furniture shop with a red-and-gold divan in the window. Across the street was a tall, gleaming apartment building with a small, run-down-looking Laundromat right next door that had a makeshift hut leaning against its outer wall. The building on the opposite corner was a modest brick building with an elderly couple lounging on the steps.

Back home there were wealthy neighborhoods, middle-class neighborhoods, lower-class neighborhoods, enclaves of college kids, and whole blocks filled with ex-hippies. Wherever you were in San Francisco, you could pretty much predict the types of people you would see. But here everyone was mixed up together, living side by side.

It was actually kind of cool.

Okay, focus, Carrie told herself. *Where are we going?*

People brushed by her, walking fast, talking on cell phones, and going about their business—everyone with a destination, everyone looking as if they knew exactly where they were going. Carrie wished she could be one of them. She needed a sign. Some kind of clue as to where to begin.

Just then something on the ground to her right caught her eye. A coin lying on the sidewalk. Carrie grabbed it up in her palm. It was round and copper with some foreign writing on it. Obviously not a good luck penny, but close enough. Carrie pocketed the coin, feeling instantly more secure, and moved off to the right. It was as good a sign as any.

A few steps more brought her to an alley, the end of which was littered with cow dung. Scrunching up her nose, Carrie was about to jump over to the other side when she heard a little girl's screech. She glanced right and saw five girls in the middle of the alley, running around, playing tag.

"I'm going to catch you!" one of them shouted.

Carrie smiled. They spoke English and they obviously

lived in this neighborhood. Maybe one of them could tell her where to find the shelter.

"Um . . . hi," Carrie said.

They all stopped instantly and looked up at her, wide-eyed. Suddenly Carrie realized that like any other kids in the world, they were probably trained not to talk to strangers.

"I'm not scary, I swear. I just need some help," Carrie said.

The tallest girl, also clearly the oldest, eyed Carrie warily. "Help with what?"

"Do any of you know where I can find number—"

Suddenly Carrie heard a small spatter. Something wet hit the back of her neck and for a moment she thought it was raining, but then the little girls looked up and started to laugh. There was a slight pressure on Carrie's backpack and she glanced over her shoulder, confused.

Ew! There was some kind of white-and-brown spatter gleaming and fresh right on her bag. Carrie followed the girls' line of sight and saw it. A monkey—a small, pink-faced monkey—was sitting on a rusted pole that stuck out from the side of the building above—and it was pooping.

"Oh God!"

Carrie turned to flee and slammed right into someone who hadn't been standing there moments before. A tall, solid someone. As Carrie lost her balance and fell, her mind was filled with only one thought:

Here goes my very last shred of dignity. . . .

Chapter Seven

"Are you all right?"

Wow. That was some voice. Deep, sexy, *British.* Carrie looked up into the brightest hazel eyes she had ever seen. Apparently the person she had bumped into was a tall, dark-haired, brown-skinned hottie with a way cool accent.

"I'm . . . I'm fine," Carrie said, surprised to find that it took her a moment to process her thoughts. She looked around at the dirty alley floor for a spot to press her hands down, but before she found one, Mr. Gorgeous had offered her his hands.

"Allow me," he said.

Carrie smiled, her heart fluttering around like a butterfly, and gave him both her arms. He easily hoisted her up and held her hands for a moment longer than was strictly necessary. His black locks were slicked back as if he had just showered and his preppy red polo clung to his shoulders and chest, then hung loosely to his waist. He wore a single, blue braided bracelet on one arm along with a black sports watch. When he slipped his strong, callused hands from hers, brushing her skin, a warm charge sizzled over Carrie's skin and at that moment a crack of lightning flashed overhead.

"I am Deepankhar Sharma," he said, holding out his hand again. "Everyone calls me Dee."

"I'm Carrie," she replied, shaking his hand.

"A monkey pooped on her!" one of the girls announced helpfully, causing the group to burst into laughter again.

Dee's smile blew Carrie away—it was a perfect grin that took over his whole face, dimpling his cheeks and crinkling his eyes at the corners. He was, hands down, the handsomest guy she had ever been in the presence of in her life. And her mouth was hanging open.

"On my backpack," she said, recollecting herself. She pointed behind her and he stood on his toes to check it out. "Bird poop is supposed to be good luck, but I don't know if I can say the same for monkey poop."

Dee chuckled. "Well, it's not too bad," he said. "Let me help you get cleaned up."

Hmmm . . . maybe all animal excrement is good luck, Carrie thought.

"That'd be great," she said. "Thanks."

"Come on." Dee tilted his head toward the end of the alley. "My cousin has a stand near here."

Thunder rumbled overhead as Carrie followed him

back to the packed street. None of the ten thousand people walking, sitting, lying, shouting, playing, and working all around her seemed remotely disturbed by the fact that the sky was about to open up above them. At that moment Carrie wasn't all too disturbed herself. She was too busy wondering if she had any food wedged between her teeth or a bad case of rank breath.

If only I had remembered to pack those Oral-B Brushups, she thought.

"So, Carrie, what are you doing in India?" Dee asked as he sauntered down the street. He walked with his shoulders back, his posture perfect, looking comfortable among the chaos, as if he had lived here his entire life. He exuded confidence with every step and Carrie couldn't help but feel light-headed when he'd place his hand on the small of her back as he guided her through the crowd.

"I . . ." *Do not tell the truth. It'll sound crazy,* her mind warned her. "I'm working with Help India."

Dee turned to her, his slightly bushy eyebrows raised. "Really? That's great," he said. "I'm volunteering as well, at the Calcutta Children's Shelter."

"Oh?" Carrie said. "Is that like an orphanage?"

"Yes. Exactly," Dee said. "I work there every summer."

This guy was insanely cute, preppy in a J.-Crew-catalog kind of way, chivalrous to victims of guerrilla monkey poop attacks, and philanthropic. Could it get any better than this? Was he the long lost prince of some remote island country, set to inherit a fortune?

"This is kind of a long way from home, isn't it? I mean to come every summer," she said.

"How do you mean?" Dee asked.

"Well, you're from England, right?" she asked. "Your accent?"

Dee smiled again, practically putting Carrie in some sort of hypnotic trance. "Actually, I'm from Calcutta. I'm studying in England now, at Cambridge. I'll be going back for my second year in the fall."

"Oh," Carrie said, trying to shake off this weird halo effect that Dee had on her.

"You'll find a lot of us have English accents in this city," Dee said. "We were under English rule for a very long time and there are still a lot of British patriots here."

Carrie flushed. Dee had a brain, too. She might have to get close to that body of his and make sure he wasn't bionic or something.

Another ominous rumble of thunder sounded above. The sky was practically black now.

"So, where did you come from back in the alley?" Carrie asked. "It was like you appeared out of nowhere."

"That's what superheroes do," he said with one of those Colin Farrell half smirks that could make a girl fall down on her knees and beg for mercy. "I come to the rescue of beautiful women all the time."

Beautiful women? Carrie thought with a smile. Ha!

Mr. Gorgeous was flirting with her. "Saving them from monkey poop?" she asked, smiling shyly.

"Precisely," Dee said with a laugh. It was a great laugh. Full and happy and accompanied by that "take me, I'm yours" smile. "Ah!" he said, looking up. "Here's Raj."

Precisely. I love it! No American guy would ever use the word precisely, Carrie thought giddily. She loved the way Dee talked, using *however* instead of *but* and *precisely* instead of *totally, man.* It made him seem so mature and sophisticated—not at all the type of guy who would dump a girl so he could watch basketball with his friends.

Dee stepped up to a small fruit stand on the side of the street. The front looked like a makeshift lemonade kiosk a kid might make in his garage back home. Written across the top placard was a list of fruits and their prices, and the goods were displayed in crates on a slanted shelf in front—everything from bright orange mangoes and deep purple plums to ripe red guavas and hairy-skinned kiwis. Behind the counter stood a tall, broad guy in a wife beater who looked a lot like Dee, only chunkier and with a mustache. He was wiping out a bowl with a white rag.

"Hey, Dee Dee!" He grinned at them as they approached and stretched out his hand.

"Will you ever stop calling me that?" Dee said, slapping hands with him.

"Nah, I enjoy irritating you too much," Raj replied.

His eyes traveled over to Carrie and his smile widened. "And who's this?" he asked.

"This is Carrie," Dee said, opening a hand toward her. "Carrie, my cousin Rajeesh. Don't pay any attention to him."

"Got it," Carrie said with a laugh.

"Please," Raj said, shaking hands with her. "He's the one you should pay no attention to. What good is he with his college and his volunteering? If there's anything you need while you're here in Calcutta, you come to me. I got my hands in every business there is."

Carrie's smile widened. "Good to know," she said. "But for now, we're just looking for a wet rag."

Raj looked at Dee with confusion.

"Monkey excrement," Dee said. Carrie turned to display her stain.

"Ah," Raj said, nodding knowingly. He looked up at the sky. "Well, Mother Monsoon is about to take care of it for you, but let's see what we can do."

He dipped his rag into a bucket on the counter behind him and handed it to Dee. Carrie turned her back to him so he could go to work on her backpack. She smiled as he rubbed and scraped away, loving the attention and the chivalry. Maybe this was what passed for romance in Calcutta—a guy taking care of your monkey poop situation. "Good as new," Dee said finally, handing the rag back to Raj, who threw it on top of a dirty pile on the floor.

"You guys hungry?" Raj asked. "I got some fresh mango in this morning."

"Sounds great," Carrie said, her stomach grumbling.

"Coming right up." Raj grabbed a few mangoes and turned to his counter to slice them.

"So, what are you doing with Help India?" Dee asked, leaning his side against Raj's stand. A few feet away a man sold steaming hot, spicy-scented meat out of a pot, heaping it into pita-like bread for his customers. Next to him was a newsstand selling everything from bottled water to Popsicles to condoms and breath mints. People bustled around, pausing to make purchases or bargain with the hawkers. As the sky darkened, all the colors around Carrie seemed to fade to gray and brown. The noise seemed to dull her ears as the very air around her thickened.

"We're building houses for needy families," Carrie said, glancing warily at the sky as it rumbled again. "Actually, I'm not building much of anything. All I did today was injure myself and ruin a whole mess of cement."

Dee snickered and brushed back the bangs of his shiny black hair with his hand. "Not much of a craftswoman, then?"

All Carrie could think was—*Cute . . . boy . . . overload!* But she managed to say something normal and not stupid.

"I'm afraid not," she replied. "But maybe I just need a little practice."

"Everything in life takes practice," Dee agreed.

Carrie smiled. Jason probably would've just said something lame like, "Yeah, that sucks." In fact, she had only known Dee for a total of ten minutes and already he was calling to attention every one of Jason's flaws. She began drawing a mental chart that had Dee's pros in one column and Jason's cons in the other. Dee was a conversationalist who was involved with charitable causes. Jason's idea of a stimulating chat was shouting, "I totally just housed you!" when playing NCAA College Basketball 2K3 on his Xbox. Dee seemed generally interested in Carrie and asked her questions about her life. Jason's inquisitiveness could be characterized by these two sentences: "What time is it?" and "Do you have any gum?" Dee appeared to be worldly and mature. Jason's primary news source was *SportsCenter* and he loved scatological humor.

Wow, looks like there's no comparison, Carrie thought.

"Your fruit, miss," Raj said, handing her a paper towel full of ripe mango slices.

"Thank you," Carrie said. She bit into the first piece and closed her eyes as the sweet taste filled her mouth. There was one thing she had to hand to India: The food was amazing.

"Listen, I'd hate to steal away a volunteer, but if you're really that horrendous at building, maybe you should come work with me," Dee suggested, a sly look in his eyes penetrating Carrie to the core. "One of our floor monitors is leaving and I'm looking for a replacement. Are you interested?"

Was she interested? Was he *kidding?* Working with a hot, sexy, *older* guy who was totally the anti-Jason instead of working alongside Dor-mean the Wonder Witch and the band of jerky men? Chilling with a bunch of kids instead of toiling away in the sun? No contest.

"Yeah. I'm definitely interested," Carrie said. *And maybe I could squeeze in a little cuddle time between playing with the kiddies. And finding my lucky T, of course. Wow, if he can distract me from my mission this easily, he must really be the superhero he says he is.*

"Great," Dee said, smiling.

Carrie bit into another piece of mango just as a few big, fat raindrops started to fall. She and Dee huddled under Raj's makeshift metal roof with him and helped him throw a plastic tarp over his fruit. Within seconds the rain had turned from drizzle into full-on downpour. Suddenly Carrie couldn't even see the throngs on the street for all the rain. It slammed into the metal over their heads, making enough noise to drown out a Slipknot concert.

"This should pass quickly," Raj shouted, glancing up. "Not too bad."

"Are you kidding me?" Carrie asked, laughing at the sheer volume.

Dee grinned. "Foreigners."

The three of them backed farther away from the edge of the roof as it quickly sprouted a splashing waterfall.

Steam rose up from the street, creating a thick fog that danced in the rain. Puddles formed almost instantly all around the stand and water splashed up on Carrie's ankles as the huge drops pounded into the little lakes. Carrie had to squeeze up against Dee to stay dry. Beneath his thin shirt she could feel just how solid and strong he really was. Dee smiled down at her and placed his hand on the counter next to her hand. A warm tingle rushed up her bare arm as both their pinky fingers barely touched.

Oh, yeah. She could get used to this.

"It sounds like a wonderful opportunity," Celia said later that evening when asked if she'd be able to do without Carrie's services. It almost seemed as if she were trying to hide her relief.

Carrie, who was dotting on some ant-itch cream she had bought at the newsstand, furrowed her brow as Celia stood up from her cot, where she had been rubbing her ruddy feet. This wasn't exactly the response she had been expecting. Doreen, who was hanging out in her mother's room, sighed audibly and leaned back into the wall.

"Really?" Carrie said.

"Of course! Working with children?" Celia said. "It sounds just perfect for you!"

"Based on what?" asked Carrie, who had never so much as baby-sat in her life.

Celia paused, blinked a few times, and then shrugged elaborately. "Based on a gut instinct," she said, clapping Carrie on the shoulder. "Just call your mother and let her know what you're doing. I'll have to meet this boy who recruited you, of course, but as long as that all works out, then . . . Godspeed!"

As Celia left the room, Carrie turned to Dor-mean, who was still working on perfecting the dirty look on her face.

"The workers really don't like you," Doreen offered as an explanation. "They were praying to Vishnu to be delivered from evil all afternoon."

"Oh," Carrie said, mortified. Well, that hardly seemed fair. One little mistake and they were all against her?

"Don't look so devastated, Jockstrap," Doreen said, getting up and pausing next to Carrie in the doorway. "You're outta here, right? Isn't that what you wanted?"

Carrie stepped aside to let her pass. For once Dor-mean had a point. Celia couldn't have made it easier for her. And now she was going to get to spend her summer with Dee the Hottie. Maybe he would even help her in her T-shirt hunt. After all her work that day Carrie had found only one shelter—the one on AJC Bose—and the director there had told her they hadn't received any clothes from Help India in months. A full day of hiking around the city and she had come up empty. If she was going to survive this search, she was going to have to be more efficient. A guy like Dee could be a lot of help. He grew up in Calcutta. Maybe he could help decipher the street-name changes and show her how to get around.

"By the way, I saw you talking to that guy," Doreen said, still hovering in the hallway.

Carrie was utterly flabbergasted. Had Doreen gone off the deep end?

"Are you stalking me, weirdo?"

"Yeah, right. Then I'd actually have to give two craps," Doreen snapped. "My mom sent me out to look for your sorry butt because she was worried about you."

Carrie rolled her eyes. "I can take care of myself, thanks."

"We'll see about that," Doreen said suspiciously, then turned and walked downstairs with a slight spring in her step. Carrie narrowed her eyes after her.

That girl was up to something for sure.

Chapter Eight

That evening Carrie and Celia whipped through the streets of Calcutta in an auto-rickshaw, squeezed into the backseat with Carrie's bags on their laps. Prandya had told them that the tiny, three-wheeled vehicle was the fastest way to get around town, and now Carrie understood why. Because it was so small, the driver was able to zip in and out of traffic, cutting off slower-moving vehicles and taking corners at hyper-speed. Carrie felt as if she were racing in the Indy 500, zooming from lane to lane, edging out the competition. The driver laughed as he dodged a cow, ran a light, skidded around a corner, took out a garbage can, and slammed on the brakes, just avoiding getting blindsided by a car that looked as if it was right out of the 1950s.

Carrie glanced at Celia and cracked up laughing. The woman looked as if she was ready to throw herself from the car, which she could have done quite easily. The "doors" were actually just openings and both Carrie and Celia had their feet pulled in as far as possible to prevent injury.

"Well, this is . . . bracing," Celia said as the motor roared to life again.

"I think it's kind of fun," Carrie said, grinning.

"Kids," Celia muttered under her breath.

Carrie looked out the small window to her left, trying to take in the sights, but it was all very bumpy and blurry. Normally a ride like this would have made her carsick instantly, but the wind whipping at her face from the open door kept her stomach in check and the smile on her face.

Finally the cabbie was forced to slow down as he pulled onto a wide street so jammed up with traffic that even *he* couldn't find a spot to slip through. On the other side of Carrie's window was a surprisingly wide-open space—something she hadn't seen since she arrived in India. It was a huge park that might have been pretty in the daytime with its many trees and bushes and huge lawns. But now, as the sun went down, everywhere Carrie looked were men, women, and children in rags, claiming benches and bits of grass and curling up to stay the night. A pair of little boys held out paper cups to passersby. Whole families huddled together under trees. A few women stood by the curb, wringing out clothes that had been soaked in that day's rainstorm. It was like a campground for the homeless.

"Omigosh," Carrie breathed, her heart squeezing tightly.

"Overwhelming, isn't it?" Celia said. "It makes you wish we could build a dozen houses a day."

A little girl stood by the fence, her face streaked with dirt, her clothes two sizes too big, staring out at the traffic. For the first time Carrie really thought about what Celia and Doreen were doing here. They had given up a big chunk of their summer so that some of these people might have a roof over their heads. Suddenly she felt absorbed by guilt for giving up so easily and chasing a cute boy across the city.

"Maybe I should bag this whole CCS thing and come back with you," she said, swallowing hard.

"You're just as needed where you're going," Celia said with a comforting smile. "Don't worry about it."

Up ahead the traffic started to move and the auto-rickshaw was soon zooming away. Carrie kept her eyes on the little girl for as long as she could, wishing she had a suitcase full of lucky Ts for her and her family. Finally she sat back in her seat again and sighed, thinking of home. Whether or not she ever got her shirt back, at least she had her mom and her house and her friends. Well, some of her friends, anyway. At that moment Carrie realized that she felt pretty lucky for the first time since before she lost her lucky T.

The driver turned the auto-rickshaw and entered a neighborhood that looked just like a middle-class area from back home. The streets were lined with stucco homes with real windows and yards and driveways. Orange and yellow flowers blossomed everywhere. Huge trees with massive leaves dripped excess water onto the sidewalks.

Another turn took them onto a street packed with large apartment buildings. People lounged on front steps and gathered on corners. Music blared from somewhere inside one of the buildings. Christmas lights twinkled on a few of the rooftops. Carrie was just taking it all in when suddenly she heard the squeal of brakes and she was thrown forward. If the duffel bag on her lap hadn't acted as a buffer, she would have broken her face on the back of the driver's seat.

"You are here," the driver said.

Carrie looked out the window and saw Dee standing right next to the auto-rickshaw. He was wearing a denim shirt and madras shorts, his hair flopping over his brow. He had his hands in his pockets and unleashed the super-duper hot half smirk as soon as Carrie's eyes met his.

Viva la India, she thought.

"Welcome to CCS," Dee said, taking the bag from her lap and offering her a hand out of the auto-rickshaw.

"Thanks," Carrie said, all bubbly and giddy. She couldn't believe how she acted like the president of Ditzville whenever she was in front of him.

Celia said something to the driver and then came

around to size Dee up. Dee held out his hand to take the bag she was carrying as well. Carrie couldn't help grinning as she watched him. Dee was such a gentleman! Jason would never offer to help carry her stuff. In fact, he usually walked alongside Carrie while she struggled with her books, backpack, and basketball gear, chatting on his cell with nothing else in his hands, clueless as ever.

Dee was definitely summer crush worthy.

"So, you're the guy who's stealing our Carrie away," Celia said, eyeing him.

"I hope you can spare her," Dee replied, brushing his hair away from his face.

"Well, at least she's still donating her time," Celia said diplomatically. "She came here to help and that's what she'll be doing."

"Um, she's standing right here," Carrie said, raising one hand.

Celia and Dee both laughed.

"Our director, Lalit Banarjee, is out on an errand at the moment, but he told me that if you have any questions about our program, you should feel free to call," Dee told Celia. "But I assure you my parents would not allow me to be here if this was anything other than a reputable organization and a safe environment."

Wow. Dee sounded very official and . . . old. Carrie turned to Celia with a confident smile, but on the inside she couldn't help but feel like this guy might be completely out of her league. He was a student at

Cambridge! Hello! He got to hang out with international babelicious coeds who had seen the world and experienced life. Up until now Carrie hadn't been too far out of San Francisco and didn't know the first thing about being cosmopolitan. What if Dee only saw her as a pesky little kid? What if she had already fallen into the dreaded "friend/sister quadrant"? What if she had to leave India without tackling Dee in a fit of passion?

Then a pang of guilt came over Carrie again. She was at a children's shelter. She should be thinking about being altruistic and helpful, not about her own tragic plight!

"I'm sure it's all fine. Carrie, just give me a call if you have any problems," Celia said. She gave Carrie a quick hug. "Take good care of her or you answer to me," she said to Dee with narrowed eyes. Then she got back in the auto-rickshaw and with a squealing of tires, she was gone.

"So, want to see where you'll be staying?" Dee asked.

"At this point as long as it's got a bed, it's gold." Carrie stopped herself. "It does have a bed, right?"

"With a mattress and everything," Dee said.

A sudden flash of a PG-13-rated daydream pulsed through Carrie's mind. She and Dee were lying in a hammock in the forest furiously making out when Carrie shook her head a bit and got back to reality.

"Hey, you never know," she replied as she followed him across the sidewalk, avoiding the many cracks along the way.

*　　*　　*

"This is your room," Dee announced, walking in and placing Carrie's bags on the floor.

The tiny chamber had plain white walls and faded pink curtains on the single window. A twin bed stood against the wall across from a small dresser and lamp. A pole hung behind the door for clothes and a clean mosquito net was draped over the bed. Carrie had never seen a more welcoming sight in her life. Let the mosquitoes try to get her now.

Dee had just taken her around the entire facility—the dining area, the classrooms, the dorm rooms, where the kids were already asleep for the night—talked with her about her responsibilities as floor monitor, and went into detail about the children's schedule, which seemed a bit like overkill to Carrie. Breakfast was at 8 a.m., and then the primary kids had class while the older kids had free time. At eleven it switched so that the older kids had class, which was usually arts and crafts or reading, and the younger ones had free time. After that lunch was served, then nap time, then study hours, then dinner, and then they usually had a nighttime activity. Lights-out was at 8:30 p.m. sharp. It seemed to be a tighter itinerary than what she had when she was an eleven-year-old camper at Sunny Bunny Summer Academy. What about organized games of King of the Mountain, archery lessons, and kite-building sessions? Carrie understood that these kids didn't have a lot of resources or opportunities—that was apparent from the run-down look of the place—but still, why didn't they have any time to play?

Dee shifted her focus back to the room. "Well, what do you think?"

"It's perfect," Carrie said, relishing the thought of a night without . . .

Then her eyes hit the small mirror on the wall and she screamed out loud.

Carrie had seen Dor-mean's reflection.

"What's wrong?" Dee asked frantically.

"Look behind you!" Carrie shouted.

It was like a teen slasher film gone terribly awry.

Dee turned around and jumped back slightly when he saw Doreen and her braces-filled smile. "Hi, who are you?"

"I'm Doreen, one of Carrie's friends from back home. And I might have known, Carrie, that *this* was your situation." She nodded at Dee.

"Oh, well, any friend of Carrie's is a friend of mine," Dee said courteously but confusedly.

"What's up, Doreen?" Carrie asked through clenched teeth. "Did I forget something?"

Doreen smirked. "As a matter of fact, you did. Remember that list . . ."

Oh, no, Carrie thought. *She wouldn't dare.*

"The one with the women's shelters on it. You left it in our room," Doreen said while waving the paper around in the air. "I brought it over because I thought you'd need it to find your—"

"Thanks, Doreen!" Carrie hastily interrupted her and yanked the list out of her hands. Obviously Doreen had sneaked into her bag and swiped it before Carrie had left for CCS.

Dee seemed rather intrigued. "Wow, you were looking for women's shelters too?"

Carrie scrambled to say something and push Doreen out the door simultaneously. "Uh . . . yeah. I was hoping to volunteer there in my spare time. We get spare time around here, don't we?"

Dee blinked. This clearly wasn't a question he was expecting.

"Yes. One day a week. It's usually scheduled by myself or our director, Mr. Banarjee," Dee said. "I really can't believe how committed you are, Carrie."

Doreen let out a belly laugh as Carrie tried to nudge her out of the room, into the hallway, and then out the front door where she could kick her butt all across Calcutta. "She's committed all right, committed to—"

"Helping others less fortunate than me. Exactly, Doreen. Now, shouldn't you be going?"

"No, your friend doesn't have to leave," Dee said. "You two can hang out and I'll head back to my room."

Oh my God, he's so sweet and nice. And Doreen is seconds away from blowing it, Carrie thought.

"Nah, I better let Carrie get her rest. She has a big day of T-shirt hunting to get to, don't ya, Carrie?" Doreen said with a satisfied grin.

And there it was.

"T-shirt hunting?" Dee asked. "I don't get it."

"Oh, she didn't tell you?" Doreen went on as Carrie just stood there in shock. "The actual reason Carrie came to India was to find this T-shirt of hers. Her mother gave it away by mistake. My mom, Celia, took it for Help India and shipped it over here like a month ago and now it's somewhere in this city and she's on a mission to find it."

For a split second Dee looked at her as if she had just started speaking backward. Carrie was as frozen as Joan Rivers's face. And Doreen?

"Would you look at the time? I've gotta run," she said while glaring at Carrie. "See you guys around."

Then Doreen flounced out the door.

Carrie, on the other hand, was beyond devastated. The story sounded so stupid and idiotic coming from her severely chapped lips, as if Carrie was this complete flake who'd travel all the way to India to get a T-shirt back. Well, that's pretty much what happened, but whatever, Doreen made it seem so much worse than it was.

Then Dee broke the awkward silence and laughed, breaking into the wide grin that sent the butterflies in her stomach spinning.

"What?" she asked with a smile. "What's so funny?"

"You! You're kidding, right?" Dee said. "Although it's kind of an elaborate story—coming halfway across the globe to search for a T-shirt. Who would do that?"

Carrie snapped her mouth shut. "Um . . . I would."

Dee stopped laughing and took a step back, looking at her out of the corner of his eye. "Come on . . . seriously?" he asked.

"Very seriously," Carrie said, starting to grow hot under his gaze.

"So, you came to India not to volunteer, but to track down a shirt that your mother gave to charity and that you want back," Dee said.

"Look, the way Doreen explained it, it all sounds a little weird . . . okay, a lot weird, but I swear there's a really good reason—"

"A really good reason you came all the way here for a shirt or a really good reason you passed yourself off as someone who actually wanted to help?" Dee asked, the amused expression completely gone now.

Carrie felt as if she had just been slapped. She *did* want to help. At least she did now that she was here. But she wasn't just going to give up on the idea of finding her lucky T. As far as she was concerned, she could find time for both.

"That's not fair," Carrie said. "I'm here, aren't I?"

"Yes, for now. What happens if you find this shirt of yours?" Dee asked, crossing his arms over his chest. "What then?"

"Well, then I . . ." Carrie paused. She hadn't really thought about it. If she found her T-shirt tomorrow, would she stay in India or go right home?

"Look, I thought you were a serious volunteer," Dee said. "But if you're not serious about being here, then you shouldn't stay."

"You're kicking me out?" Carrie asked.

"That's kind of up to you," Dee replied. "The moment those girls meet you, they're going to become attached. It's what children do. So if you're just going to up and leave in a couple of days, I'd rather know now."

"I . . . I didn't say I was just going to up and leave," Carrie replied. "I mean, before Doreen even brought it up, I had decided that I was going to ask if you could help me look for it."

"Me? Are you joking? I'm sorry, but I have better things to do with my time than search Calcutta for a lousy T-shirt."

Somewhere in the neighborhood the final prayer call of the night started up, but nobody in this room was falling to their knees anytime soon.

"Hey! It's not a lousy T-shirt," Carrie said sharply. "It's very important to me. My—"

"Important to you?" Dee said, his voice rising. Then he looked around and lowered the volume to a harsh whisper. "Do you realize that some of these kids have never even owned a single piece of new clothing? They don't have parents and you're worried about a T-shirt? I'll wager you have a dozen others packed in your huge suitcases. What's wrong with you?"

Carrie's face turned red with indignation. "You have no right to talk to me like that," she snapped.

"Excuse me, but I have every right," Dee said, his handsome face creased with anger. "You know what? I've changed my mind. It's not up to you. I think you should go. I'd rather these girls not have a shallow, self-obsessed floor monitor to influence them."

"What?" Carrie said.

"You misrepresented yourself to me," Dee said. "You said you were a volunteer."

"I *am* a volunteer!" Carrie shouted, having entered The Temper Zone in the same way someone is shot out of a cannon.

"No, you're not. You're a fraud," Dee replied.

Carrie was momentarily at an uncharacteristic loss for words, thinking back to the homeless girl in the park—to her realization that until today she had never really thought about how much help was needed here. Was he right? *Was* she a fraud? While Celia and the others had been genuinely excited about getting to work, she had tried to sneak out. And no matter how moved she had been by that little girl, she definitely wouldn't even be here if it weren't for her T-shirt. Maybe Dee had a point. A really awful, horrific point.

But however right he was, there was no way she was going to let him judge her without knowing much about her. Besides, at that moment she was doing a good enough job of judging herself.

"You know what, if I had realized you were going to be such an jerk, I would have just stayed with the crazy house builders," Carrie said finally. "At least they weren't mean!"

Not most of them anyway, she thought.

"Well, like I said, you should just go back there," Dee shot back while heading out to the hallway.

"Well, fine!" Carrie replied.

"Fine!" he shouted in response.

Carrie whirled around and slammed the door to her room. She was about grab her stuff and hoof it back to Help India when it hit her. She didn't know how to get back there. And if she called Celia right now to come and get her, the woman would freak, considering she had probably sent Doreen out in the auto-rickshaw so that she could give Carrie the list that she had "left behind." Plus Carrie would look like a doofus, changing her mind so fast.

She sat on the bed in the single room. She thought of how quiet and peaceful it would be to fall asleep there. Her back ached, her feet throbbed, and she was eyeing that mosquito netting like it was made of diamonds.

Carrie zipped back over to the door and opened it quickly. Dee was out in the hallway pacing and muttering to himself. She cleared her throat to get his attention. He turned toward her and threw her a nasty look.

"I'll just crash here for the night and I'll be out at the crack of dawn," she told him.

"Whatever you say," he replied, walking down the hallway to the stairwell. "Nice knowing you."

He took the stairs to the third floor, where the boys stayed, and Carrie stood in the hallway for a moment, feeling angry and stung and shocked. She couldn't believe this was happening. She had thought that Dee was intelligent and mature and giving and chivalrous and kind, and while she was afraid of how he might react if he knew the truth, she had no idea he'd be that bent out of shape about the whole thing. If it weren't for Dor-mean, Carrie could have gone for months without seeing Dee's imperfections. Oh, she'd have to get that girl back with a vengeance. Too bad Piper wasn't around to help her hatch a master grudge match.

Carrie groaned under her breath and headed back into the dormitory. So much for summer romance—and so-called friends—and luck.

Chapter Nine

Something was pulling on Carrie's hair. She woke up, startled, and found that the mosquito netting had been pushed away. Standing over her was a slim girl about ten years old with huge brown eyes and curly black hair. With a look of intense concentration, the girl tied off a braid that she had worked into Carrie's hair, let it drop, and then started on another.

Carrie sat up straight and the little hairdresser took a few steps back. Behind her were two more girls about her age, pulling clothing out of Carrie's open suitcase at random. One of them had Carrie's 49ers baseball cap covering half her face. The other was wearing her favorite turquoise necklace and the flowered shirt she had bought at BCBG just before leaving on her trip.

"What're you doing?" Carrie blurted, still blinking the sleep from her eyes.

The little braider girl shrugged her small shoulders. "Playing," she said. "Who are you?"

"I'm Carrie."

Two of the girls eyed her, trying to size her up. The third couldn't because her eyes were effectively blinded by the red-and-gold baseball cap. The silence was deafening, and Carrie felt the distinct need to break the ice. She reached over and pushed the cap back on the girl's head to reveal light, almost golden eyes looking back at her uncertainly. Carrie's heart warmed and she smiled.

"Playing dress up, huh?" Carrie asked. She and Piper had done the same thing many times themselves, raiding their mothers' closets for costumes. The thought of Piper instantly made Carrie's heart squeeze with homesickness. It was so odd to think that the person who she had shared almost everything with since kindergarten hadn't talked to her in weeks.

The little girl nodded. "You have nice clothes."

"Well, I'm sure we can find you something more glam than that hat," Carrie said, trying to distract herself. It was too early in the morning for serious thoughts.

She pulled a light blue, brushed-cotton sweater out of her bag, took the cap off the girl's head, and pulled the sweater on. It fit her like a muumuu, the V-neck reaching down to her belly button and the sleeves and hem trailing almost to the floor, but the girl hugged herself and grinned.

"What's your name?" Carrie asked her.

"Asha," the girl replied with a shy smile. She thrust out her hand with the sleeve hanging down and pointed at the braider. "That's Manisha and that's Trina," she said, jabbing toward the other girl.

"Nice to meet you," Carrie said with a quick nod. "Here. Let me help you with that," she said to Trina, who was trying to shove her arm through the neck hole of the flowered shirt. Carrie gently maneuvered her arms through the right places and pushed the girl's straight hair behind her ears. "It's very you," she said.

"I want to wear something too!" Manisha announced, clutching her hands together.

Carrie laughed. "Okay, let's see." She pawed through the tangle of clothes the girls had created and came out with a red tank top that had colorful beads sewn all along the neck and straps. "How about this?" she said, holding it up.

"Ooh. What is it made of?" Manisha asked.

"Cotton mostly," Carrie said with a shrug. "Here. Lift your arms."

Manisha did as she was told and Carrie slipped the tank top on over her faded blue T-shirt. Manisha looked down and ran a fingertip lightly along the beadwork.

"I like this shirt. Where did you come from?" she asked.

"Uhhh . . . California?" Carrie said. "It's in the United States."

"Oh, we know California," Manisha told her. "It's where the movie stars and the models live. Are you a movie star?"

"No," Carrie said, laughing. This girl was big with the questions. "And I'm not a model either. But you guys are ready for a fashion show." Carrie leaned back to admire them. "Can you walk like models?"

"Like this!" Asha announced. She put her hands on her hips and then sashayed around in a circle, knees high, hips wagging back and forth. She even pursed her lips in a haughty expression and raised her chin.

"Nice!" Carrie said with a laugh. The moment she approved, Trina and Manisha broke into their own catwalks, copying Asha's poses. Carrie was almost doubled over with laughter and the girls were dissolving into giggle fits as well. It was like a pre-breakfast fashionista party.

A sudden rap on the door caught them all by surprise. Carrie looked up to find Dee poking his head into her room. She saw his eyes go directly to her chest and she grabbed her sheet off the bed, holding it over her thin tank pajama top. Her face flushed crimson while Dee let out a few coughs and began rubbing his eyes frantically. It was as if had gotten a whiff of some strange pollen, but Carrie knew all too well he was trying to distract her from the fact that she had just caught him checking her out.

"Training them for a life of consumerism?" he asked after he got his composure back.

Carrie's eyes flicked to the graphic on his T-shirt. "You're one to talk, Abercrombie boy," she said.

She tried not to grin too widely when her comment

wiped the condescending smirk right off his face. So much for the high-and-mighty, "I'm so self-sacrificing, I must be a descendant of Gandhi" act. Dee straightened up and crossed his arms over his chest, hardly covering the big A&F.

"She has better clothes than Rasheeda did," Trina said matter-of-factly.

"Thanks," Carrie replied.

"And she's prettier," Asha added, grinning.

"That's nice of you to say," Carrie said, smiling right back. Rasheeda must have been a substandard floor monitor.

"Well, I just came to tell you girls that you're late for breakfast," Dee said. "Let's give Carrie her things back and head downstairs."

The girls quickly struggled out of their costumes and tossed everything toward the open suitcase. Carrie clutched the sheet to her and looked at Dee, at a loss for what to do or say. She had told him she would be out of there at the crack of dawn, and from the brightness of the sun streaming through her window, it was way past that hour.

"I arranged for Raj to give you a ride back to the Help India hostel," Dee said, his expression unreadable. "You can have breakfast with us and then he'll be here to pick you up."

Somehow Carrie was stung by this news. Her indignation from the night before had been slightly quelled by a good night's sleep and the impromptu fashion show. But clearly Dee was still angry and really wanted her out. Well, if that was the way he was going to be, then she didn't want to be here either.

"Fine," Carrie said, lifting her chin defiantly.

"Great," Dee said gruffly. Then he turned and was gone.

Carrie threw down the sheet and stood up. *How did I ever think he was sweet?* she wondered, tossing her things back into her bag with frustration.

He was totally and completely infuriating.

"So, you're one of those *fickle* American girls, huh?" Raj joked.

"Hey, it's not just me," Carrie said. "Your cousin doesn't want me here either."

"Dee? Yeah. That boy has had a point to prove since the day he was born," Raj said, reaching down from the dirty flatbed of his old, semi-rusted truck to lift Carrie's bags.

Carrie laughed. "Really?"

"Oh, yeah," Raj said. "Heaven forbid you should step one foot out of line in front of the golden boy." He paused, dusting his hands off on his colorful Hawaiian shirt, and looked down at her. "He told me about your fight."

Carrie flushed. "Did he tell you how shallow and self-centered I apparently am?" she asked.

"No, but he did tell me he felt bad for freaking out," Raj said.

"He did?" Carrie was shocked. This guy had a conscious? Go figure.

Raj jumped down from the flatbed, his sandals kicking up a cloud of dust. "Listen, Dee may be wound a little tightly, but he's not all bad to have around. He's a good guy. Kept me out of more trouble than I care to divulge," he added with a wink. "It's just sometimes he lets his whole I'm-so-moral thing get the better of him. If you stick it out here, I bet he'll grow on you."

Carrie looked back at the CCS building. "I don't know. He seemed pretty serious about wanting me gone."

"Well, before you two fought, he seemed pretty serious about wanting to get to know you," Raj said with a shrug. "The afternoon before you came, all he could do was keep asking me what I thought of you."

Carrie's flush deepened. "What did you say?"

"I said you seemed like a fickle American girl," Raj joked, grinning.

Carrie whacked his shoulder and Raj laughed, walking over to the driver's side door. "So are you going or staying?" he asked.

There was no way Carrie could sort out the tangled ball of emotions she felt at that moment. Two seconds ago she thought Dee hated her, but from what Raj had said, it wasn't that black and white. Did he really feel bad about shouting at her last night? If so, she might be able to forgive him, especially considering he had been right about a few things. Part of her didn't want to stay and deal with him, but a bigger part of her wanted to find out if something was there—if there was any salvaging that initial attraction she had felt for him yesterday. And part of her had already gotten attached to those little girls. And she *really* didn't want to go back to Help India with her tail between her legs.

As she stood on the street, contemplating her fate, Carrie heard a sudden shout, followed by a round of laughter. There, at the back of the yard, were half a dozen kids, throwing a basketball haphazardly toward a net-less hoop. One of them ran to pick up the ball and dribbled it clumsily back toward his friends. It hit his toe and bounced off, smacking one of the girls on the knee.

Something stirred inside Carrie's chest—a familiar twinge of excitement. The backboard and hoop looked like home to her. The kids running and jumping and slapping the ball away from one another suddenly looked like potential best friends. When was the last time she had touched a basketball? When was the last time she had even exercised?

Carrie turned and grinned at Raj over her shoulder. "I think I'm staying."

Raj laughed and came around again to help her pull her things down. "You sure this time?"

"Hey, from here on out you can call me Carrie the Fickle," Carrie said, slinging her backpack over her shoulder. "Thanks, Raj."

"Like I said, anything you need here in Calcutta, I'm

your man," he replied with a smile. Then he hopped into the truck and took off.

"Well," Carrie said to herself. "Here goes nothing."

The last thing she wanted to do was go back through the building and risk bumping into Dee, so instead she made her way around the corner, looking for a break in the fence. Toward the back, right near the basketball hoop, was a gate with a meager latch. Carrie popped it open with her elbow and made it through with all her bags. The boys and girls stopped playing and looked at her curiously as she dropped her stuff.

"All right," Carrie said, clapping. "Who wants to really learn how to shoot?"

"I do!" Trina announced, running up to her.

For the first time Carrie realized how tall the girl actually was. She had at least a head on most of the boys around her and she looked stronger, too.

"How old are you guys?" Carrie asked.

"I am twelve years old," Trina said.

"I'm eleven!" Manisha announced, walking over. "And I want to shoot too."

"Girls can't shoot," the tallest boy of the bunch said. He was holding the ball to his side in the crook of his arm and looking at her as if he were some kind of basketball god and she were just an amateur. There was nothing Carrie loved more than a challenge.

"Oh, yeah?" she said, strutting up to him. She held out her hands and, looking dubious, he handed the ball to her. Carrie turned and without so much as a pause shot the ball. It swooshed right through the hoop.

Two points, she thought with a grin. The boys all whooped and laughed while Trina and Manisha stuck their tongues out at the tall, cocky boy. The ball hit the ground and bounced off toward the fence as Carrie gave her audience a little bow.

"You guys want to do that?" she asked them.

"Yeah!" a couple of kids yelled.

"Great," Carrie said with a grin, retrieving the ball. "Let's get to work."

As the game wore on, Carrie took a step back to admire the kids' progress. It was unbelievable, actually. Just a couple of hours ago they had been the most pathetic lot of players she had ever come across. And now . . . well, they weren't perfect, but there had been a drastic improvement. On an impulse she went to her backpack and fished out her camera. She hadn't taken many pictures since arriving in India because she had been so busy and overwhelmed. This game, however, was totally photo worthy.

Carrie squeezed off a few shots, catching Dash, the cocky boy, as he went for a layup and Trina as she grabbed the rebound. She was just refocusing her shot when through the viewfinder she saw Dee and an older Indian man step out the back door of the shelter.

Carrie swallowed hard. The moment she had been

dreading earlier that morning had arrived—Dee had finally discovered that she hadn't actually left as he had wanted her to. Together he and the light-skinned, serious-looking man seemed to be examining the proceedings and discussing something grave. Were they talking about her? Was she really going to get in trouble for hanging around?

Turning off her camera and placing it back in her bag, Carrie decided she might as well take the bull by the horns here. She wasn't going to wait for them to come over and read her the riot act. She would go to them.

Carrie wiped her suddenly sweaty palms on her jeans, crossed her fingers, and walked around the basketball court toward the two guys. Dee caught her eye as she approached. For a split second she could have sworn she saw him smile. Was it admiration? Appreciation? Or was it just amusement because he knew she was about to be chucked out on her butt?

"Hi," Carrie said as she reached the door. An ominous grumble of thunder sounded overhead. She waited for Dee to introduce her, but he said nothing. "I'm Carrie," she added.

"*Namaste,*" the man said, placing his palms together and bowing slightly. "It is an honor to meet the basketball star who has been entertaining our children this morning."

Carrie smiled. "Thank you."

"Carrie, this is Lalit Banarjee," Dee said. "He's the director of CCS."

"Nice to meet you, Mr. Banarjee," Carrie said. Then, because another brief silence fell, she put her hands together and mimicked the older man's bow. *"Namaste."*

Fortunately Mr. Banarjee smiled. "It is always a pleasure to meet a person with such energy. I believe the children are taken with you. Asha is inside with some of the other girls and she has not stopped talking about you all morning."

Carrie blinked. "Really?"

"She's driving one of our floor monitors, Miss Tara, mad in the arts and crafts room," Dee informed her.

"What's she saying?" Carrie asked.

"Oh, that you are beautiful and smart and have the most lovely hair," Mr. Banarjee said.

Carrie's hand flew instinctively to her ponytail. She couldn't believe anyone would say that about her frizzy mop. She glanced at Dee, who was staring at her, and he quickly looked away.

"We have some investors coming tomorrow," Mr. Banarjee said. "I'd love for them to meet you."

"Uh . . . sure," Carrie said uncertainly. She wasn't even supposed to be here now, let alone tomorrow.

"It is nice to have you aboard, Carrie," Mr. Banarjee said. "You are obviously an asset to CCS."

Carrie's heart twisted as the director smiled and moved off. Part of her wanted to correct him—to let him know that she wasn't sticking around. But he had seemed so sincerely pleased, she just couldn't find the words to do it.

Dee smiled down at her and shook his head, clearly impressed with the praise she had garnered. Carrie smiled back. Could it be that all was forgiven? Maybe Raj had been right and Dee now regretted last night's freak-out. Carrie hoped that was true because at this point she knew she would much rather stay at CCS playing with the kids and getting praised than hammering at a wall and getting dirty looks.

"I thought you were leaving," Dee said finally, attempting to contain the smile.

Carrie looked at him uncertainly, trying to discern what he was thinking. Did he want her to leave or did he want her to stay? His words and his body language—arms crossed over his chest again—seemed to say the former. But his smile and his eyes . . . they seemed to say the latter. It was nearly impossible to tell. Carrie had no experience with mysterious guys. Jason had been easier to read than a Captain Underpants book.

"Miss Carrie! Watch this!"

Carrie and Dee turned to see a tall, gangly boy named Akhtar shoot a perfect three-pointer from almost half-court. Everyone on his team cheered as Dash picked up the ball and dribbled it back. Then Akhtar did some sort of celebration dance that seemed like a cross between break dancing and the hokeypokey.

"Sweet!" Carrie shouted.

"Come on, Carrie!" a smaller boy named Shiva

called out, running over to grab her hand. "The team of Akhtar is kicking the butt of the team of Dash."

Dee and Carrie both laughed.

"Maybe tomorrow," she said over her shoulder to Dee as Shiva dragged her away. At that moment there was no rush. Carrie was right where she wanted to be, and as she played with these kids, her lucky T was pretty far from her mind.

Chapter Ten

The next day Carrie handled some crisis situations around CCS. There was a big water pipe fiasco first thing in the morning, and Carrie led the other floor monitors in the quest to prevent the entire facility from flooding. Mission accomplished. In the afternoon the movie projector ate the second reel of *Lassie,* so Carrie put on a shadow puppet show that had the kids roaring with laughter. Then Mr. Banarjee cornered her and told her how much she impressed the investors, who had been around all day to witness her quick thinking. He thanked her so profusely that Carrie couldn't possibly even think about deserting the guy and the rest of the staff. If Dee wanted her to leave, he'd have to take it up with all of them.

Speaking of which, later that evening Carrie was on her way upstairs to tuck in the girls when Dee emerged from Mr. Banarjee's office holding a box wrapped in brown paper. A skitter of excitement raced through Carrie as she paused on the third stair. This guy even looked amazing in 200 percent humidity.

"This came for you today," Dee said, holding a medium-size box in his Shaquille-O'Neal-size hands. "I thought I would wait and give it to you tonight so that you would have time to open it."

She would recognize that box anywhere. Her mother sent her one just like it every summer when she was at Sunny Bunny.

"Thanks," Carrie said, barely able to contain the urge to rip it open right there. *Hooray for care packages!*

"Do you have a minute?" Dee asked, putting the box underneath his perfectly toned right arm.

"Sure, what's up?" Carrie replied coolly. She was try-ing to act aloof because of how badly Dee had treated her, but it was pretty difficult, considering that she really wanted to grab him and nibble on his left earlobe.

"I want to apologize about blowing up day before yester-day. I really don't know what came over me. Sometimes my temper gets a bit out of control and I say a bunch of stuff I don't really mean. Does that ever happen to you?"

Carrie smiled knowingly. "Yeah, once in a while."

"Anyway, I feel as if I jumped to conclusions about you and that was very unfair. Maybe I can get to know you really well and then judge you?" he smiled with the last part.

"We'll see what happens," Carrie said matching his smile.

She reached out to take the package into her hands, but Dee playfully pulled it away.

"Nope, I'm not handing it over until you tell me I'm forgiven," Dee said with a sly smirk.

Carrie laughed again. "So you're holding my mail hostage? That's supposed to be an incentive?"

"Who knows what could be in here? Maybe a million dollars. Perhaps a month's supply of candy," Dee said while giving the box a few shakes and listening to the contents shuffle around.

"Okay, okay. You're forgiven," she said in submission. "Now hand it over."

Dee moved up to the stair below her so that they were at eye level. Carrie could see the flecks of brown in his hazel irises. Dee put the package in her hands, his fingers gliding against her skin very slowly. They both stood there for a few seconds, completely motionless. Then Carrie broke out of her trance.

"I better go," she said softly. "I have to kiss some little girls good night."

As Carrie scampered up the stairs, she thought of one hundred different ways she'd like to get to know Dee, and all of them involved lip-to-lip contact.

About a half hour later, when Carrie turned off the lights in the ward and stole back to her room, she realized she hadn't thought about her shirt once today. She sat down cross-legged on her bed. As quietly as possible, she tore open the brown paper wrapped around the box. Inside she found one of the small white crates her mother always received her fruit-of-the-month in and she grinned. Her mom had packed a bunch of stuff in there— half a dozen granola bars, a few bags of trail mix, two editions of *Shape* magazine, some samples of organic makeup and skin care products, a book about superstitions and phobias (ha!), a small package wrapped in colorful birthday paper, and two envelopes. The first was unmarked. The second had Carrie's name written on the front—in Piper's loopy handwriting.

Carrie's heart seized up at the sight of the familiar script. Piper!

With a shaking hand, Carrie placed Piper's letter aside and opened the other envelope. She was praying that it wasn't from Jason because then she might combust before getting to ride off into the sunset on a camel with His Majesty, the prince of some yet to be determined island country, Dee.

Thankfully, when she saw the handwriting, she realized it was just a note from her mom. She exhaled a sigh of relief and continued on.

Dear Carrie,

I hope you've settled in at your new place! Thought I'd send you a few things to make it feel more like home. You'll see I've included a coupon book for McDonald's because I'm sure there's one of them tucked away someplace secret. (Actually, I did my research and there's not one anywhere near you. Ha!) Also, Piper dropped by to see you when she got back from camp and she almost died when she heard where you were. She insisted I include this note from her. She seemed really sad that you weren't here, Carrie. I hope you two can work out whatever is wrong between you. Piper is a sweet, sweet girl and you have been friends for too long to let it all go now.

Okay, enough of the parental lecture. I miss you THIS MUCH! Can't wait to have my baby girl home again.

Love ya!
Mom

P.S. DO NOT OPEN THE PRESENT UNTIL YOUR BIRTHDAY! And don't think I won't know if you do it early. Mothers always know.

Carrie felt tears prickling at her eyes. She missed her mother so much she could practically smell her Lilac perfume. And sure enough, with a second dig through the box Carrie found a coupon book entitling her to free fries and ninety-nine-cent Big Macs. Her mother must be lonely and slightly off her rocker to actually encourage her daughter to binge on not just fast food, but *foreign* fast food.

How could I have thought that being without my lucky T for my birthday would be worse than being without my mom? Carrie wondered, her heart so heavy it was weighing her down. *What's* wrong *with me?*

171

Shoving the booklet back down underneath the other contraband, Carrie took a deep breath. She was not going to sit here and regret her decision. She refused to wallow. Especially when there was nothing she could do about it. Instead she turned to the second envelope and tore it open. She had no idea what to expect, but whatever was in Piper's letter, it couldn't make her feel worse than she already did.

Dear Carrie,

INDIA!? What, are you kidding me? I know you're mad, but c'mon, did you have to go all the way to another country to keep avoiding me? I came over to your house all nauseous and nervous and ready for another big blowout fight scene and your mother tells me I've gotta wait another few weeks. But I couldn't. So I'm just going to tell you here how I feel.

I miss you sooooo much, Carrie. I know I've said this before, but I never meant to hurt your feelings. All I was doing that night was hanging out with The Prego Posse (it's what my brother's group of friends are calling themselves these days—can you believe it? They say the name was inspired by the Sopranos, but all it really does is make me think of spaghetti). I was as shocked as anyone else when Jason walked in. You've got to believe that when I talked to you, all I really wanted to do was to help you feel better. Clearly I must take some remedial courses in Consoling Your Friend because now I see where I failed you. I should've been more sensitive and left for your place as soon as I knew what happened. I should've been supporting you when you were feeling low, but instead I was careless, which just made things worse.

But you've gotta know that if anyone ever kidnapped me and said I had to choose Jason over you or else they'd kill me, I would choose you, even if it meant disembowelment or some other grisly, torture-filled death! You're my BEST friend and my platonic other half. Remember when we were eight and we used to play Power Rangers? I let you be the pink one EVERY TIME, that's how much I loved you then, and I still love you now. Besides, chica, when it comes down to it, we're really fighting over a GUY! A smelly, egotistical, Maxim-reading STEAK HEAD! We made a pact never to do this, and somehow here we are. . . .

I hope you can realize that I was just trying to make the best of a crappy situation and that I'm so sorry for hurting you.

PLEASE write me back and/or call me as soon as you get home. I will not start my junior year with us not talking. I REFUSE!

Take care of yourself, and I really hope you find that special shirt of yours.

Always,
Piper

P.S. If it makes you feel any better, Jason went camping with Doug and got a major case of poison ivy on his butt after going to the bathroom and wiping with the wrong type of leaves. Of course, Doug forgot the tp along with the tent poles, but that's a whole other story altogether.

Carrie laughed so loud and hard that she began to cry. Huge splats of water hit the page and blurred the words *REFUSE* and *Always*. It was amazing how Piper could bring her so much happiness in the strangest of circumstances. Carrie felt SO badly for not talking to her friend for weeks and then shutting her out on the last day of school. She was *lucky* that the girl even *wanted* to speak to her again. She wished Piper were there right then so she could just hug her and make everything that happened go away. And before she could really do anything to stop it, Carrie was sobbing uncontrollably.

Care package! Carrie thought, tossing the whole thing aside as she tried to get control of her crying. *This might as well have been a pipe bomb. It would have hurt a hell of a lot less.* A severe, dull ache traveled throughout her body, then set up camp in the pit of her stomach. It was the same feeling she got when she first realized that her lucky T was gone. Today was the first day she had truly felt lucky without it, and now that feeling was lost too.

"I have to get out of here," she said, standing up with conviction. She folded up the notes and replaced them in the box, then shoved it all under her bed. She would open it again in the morning when she wouldn't feel quite so raw. But for now she just had to take a break from all the emotions those letters had stirred up.

Carrie tiptoed out, closed her door quietly, and headed for the basketball court, wondering if somewhere, all the people she loved were missing her as much as she missed them.

Lights from the buildings around the CCS yard cast a dim glow over the court, just enough for Carrie to see the ball in front of her and her white New Balance sneakers down below. She dribbled a few times, hoping the noise wouldn't rouse anyone from inside, and shot. Obviously her focus was off. The ball slammed against the backboard and ricocheted back at her, almost taking her nose with it.

Physical activity had always helped Carrie clear her head, but on this warm, clear night—the least humid she had experienced in India yet—it just wasn't working. Carrie walked over to the basketball, sat down on top of it, and put her head in her hands. What the hell was she doing so far from home? What had she been thinking, chasing her T-shirt all the way here? Why was she always making such rash decisions and flying off the handle so much?

"Are you all right?"

Carrie jumped up at the sound of Dee's voice and wiped her hands under her eyes. The basketball rolled and bumped across the court until he stopped it with his foot. Carrie watched him looking her over, hoping that it was dark enough out so he wouldn't see her reddened eyes and tearstained cheeks.

"I'm fine," she said, her voice cracking, indicating otherwise. "I was just . . . thinking."

"About what?" Dee asked, grabbing up the ball and walking slowly toward her.

Carrie's breath caught in her throat at the sight of Dee out here in the shadows with nobody else around. His gorgeous face, which she could see more and more clearly as he approached, seemed to be wracked with concern. Carrie noticed how his plain white T-shirt showed off his perfect shoulders and arms. She noticed the big hands again as he palmed the ball and how succulent his mouth was. . . .

Oh God, Carrie thought. *I'm in lurve.* This was a phrase she and Piper made up last year when Carrie was trying to describe how she felt about Jason. "Lurve" was definitely bigger than liking a boy but somewhat shy of loving that boy. And now that she had another guy to compare her feelings to, Carrie was convinced that she didn't "lurve" Jason at all. "Lurve" was how she was feeling about Dee, even though they had only just met.

It was his passionate personality that had caused him to shout at her on the first day they set eyes on each other. Carrie knew what that was like. Watching Dee for the last few days, she realized that he had only exploded because he really cared about CCS and the kids that lived there, which was just so cool. None of the guys Carrie knew from home cared about anything other than food, sports, and Lindsay Lohan's boobs.

"What is it?" Dee asked. He had this sultry deepness to his voice that Carrie just wanted to record and listen to on her iPod player for all eternity. "Are you homesick?"

She was so homesick, there were times she had actually thought of fashioning some sort of raft that would take her to safety à la Tom Hanks in *Castaway*. Suddenly Carrie wanted nothing more than to feel Dee wrap his arms around her and hold her close to him for the rest of the night. But instead she took a small, protective step back. Dee probably had a line of hot, brainiac English chippies waiting for him back at Cambridge. Even if he didn't, did they really have a future? There was that little problem of him living on a whole other continent.

But he's here now, a little voice in her head told her, sending a thrill of excitement through every nerve ending in her body. Carrie smiled slightly. Her emotions were so all over the place she was scared she was going to have to check herself into India's equivalent of the nuthouse.

"Yeah, I miss home a lot," she said finally, thinking of her mom making some healthy but weird concoction in a blender, Piper pretending to be a waffle in acting class, and her dad catapulting across the sky somewhere.

"Do you want to talk about it?" he asked.

Carrie gazed into his eyes once more. *Oh God, it's definitely lurve.*

"To be honest, if I talk about it, I think it might make it worse," she replied.

"I know exactly what you mean," Dee said. "I was a mess the first time I left home. But it's going to get better, trust me."

If by "trust" you mean "marry," Carrie thought, *I am all over that.*

"You know, when I was feeling this way, I tried to do something distracting to get my mind off my troubles," he said.

Like making out under a waterfall? Carrie wondered.

"Do you play just for fun or professionally?" he joked, popping the ball out of his hands and spinning it on the tip of his pointer finger.

"You're looking at the only sophomore on the varsity team at my high school," Carrie said.

"Well, well. You up for a little one-on-one?"

"Absolutely," Carrie said. Already the sadness was starting to become a dull memory. "But I should warn you, I play like a girl."

Dee smiled. "Let's make it interesting, then."

"What did you have in mind?" Carrie asked, tilting her head flirtatiously.

Dee reclaimed the ball and dribbled a few times from hand to hand, moving between Carrie and the net. "If you win, I will help you look for your T-shirt tomorrow."

"Really?" Carrie said, practically jumping at the thought of having a little help. "And if you win?"

"If I win, you let me show you my Calcutta," Dee replied. "The places I really love."

Nothing like a win-win situation to put a smile on Carrie's face. "Bring it on," she said, bending at the waist.

"We play to eleven, one point per basket," he told her, tossing the ball to her.

She tossed it back. "Prepare for a butt kicking."

Dee dribbled the ball, faked left, and then went right around Carrie. She made a lame attempt at trying to block him, letting him think it was her best move. He executed a little spin, throwing in a bit of fancy footwork, and hit a layup over her head. Carrie jumped and swatted at the ball with her hand, but she knew she was too late to block it. It sailed through the hoop and dropped to the ground.

"Yes! That's one-nothing," Dee cheered, throwing his hands in the air.

"Nice one," Carrie said.

"There's a lot more where that came from," he replied, grinning.

Carrie tried not to burst out into a giggle fit. He was so gullible. Didn't he realize she was just feeling him out? Trying to get a bead on his best stuff so she would know how to attack? Dee was in for the shock of his life.

"This game is going to be a cakewalk," he chided her, moving his weight from side to side like he was stretching out his thighs.

Carrie was about to prove him right because she was close to fainting from the mere sound of him trash talking. Still, she couldn't wait to wipe that cocky expression off his face.

"Ready?" she asked, bouncing the ball to him.

"I'm always ready," he replied, bouncing it back.

Carrie dribbled to the right, took it up a few steps, then stood right in front of him and shot a perfect three-pointer right over his head. It slapped onto the ground and bounced off into the darkness. Dee's face actually fell.

"What was that?" he asked.

"That, my friend, is called a buzz kill," she replied with sugary sweetness. "Your ball."

Dee grinned mischievously and Carrie laughed, tipping her head back toward the sky. This was the most fun she'd had since her lucky T went MIA.

The rest of the game was serious, fast, and sweat inducing. But all the running, dribbling, and shooting didn't give Carrie half the cardio workout Dee's proximity did. Each time he brushed by her to make a shot, touching skin to skin, her pulse went into overdrive. When he got up right behind her to try to smack the ball away, practically every inch of his body making contact with hers, she had to stop herself from melting into a puddle of goop.

"Take it out," Dee said, bouncing the ball back to her after hitting a fadeaway that made it ten-six in Carrie's favor.

She dribbled to half-court while Dee walked over, stood in front of her, and lifted up the hem of his shirt to wipe his face. Carrie practically salivated at the sight of his perfect six-pack abs.

She shook her head in an attempt to clear her thoughts. *Okay, get a grip. You have game point here.*

She tried to dribble past him, but Dee faked her out and snagged the ball, shooting an easy layup.

"Yes!" he cheered, throwing his fists in the air.

If his defense strategy was distract-and-confuse, he definitely had his moves down pat.

"I'm catching up," Dee told her, retrieving the ball and passing it to her.

"It's still game point," Carrie informed Dee, bouncing the ball back and forth from one hand to the other. He watched the ball with both eyes, wagging his head back and forth slightly as if he was a spectator at a tennis match.

"I know," Dee replied. "But you're never getting past me again."

He's cute even when he's delusional, Carrie told herself.

Without warning, she charged right into Dee and he staggered back a few steps, flailing his arms for balance. He dove at the ball, trying to whack it away, but Carrie spun out of his grasp, ran for the hoop, and hit a spectacular shot just as Dee's body vaulted into view again. He was far too late, and by the time his feet met the ground, the ball was already bouncing away.

"Aw, yeah!" Carrie cheered. "Take that, big man!"

Dee put his hands on his hips and laughed, trying to catch his breath. "You're a sore winner, Carrie," he said.

To illustrate his point, Carrie threw her arms up and did her version of the Akhtar celebration dance while Dee shook his head at her, amused. Carrie caught his eye and watched as a come-hither smile slowly crawled across Dee's face.

Holy cow, she thought. *I think he wants me. Maybe I should stop dancing around like a lunatic before he changes his mind.* "Hey, good game," Carrie said finally, acting all cool and collected.

"Yeah. I'll get you next time," Dee said in a typical I'm-a-guy-who-just-lost-to-a-girl fashion.

Then, much to her surprise, Dee came over and held out his hand. Carrie smiled and went to slap palms with him. When she did, Dee grabbed hold of her hand and held on to it for a few seconds. And then he let go very gently, each finger tracing an invisible path on her soft skin.

Dee was growing more and more perfect by the second.

"So, what time do we set out in the morning?" he asked, lifting up the hem of his shirt to mop his brow again and causing Carrie to foam at the mouth like before.

"Actually, even though I wiped the court with you," Carrie said, looking at him slyly, "I'd still like to see your Calcutta."

"Really?" he asked, his face brightening.

"Most definitely," she replied.

Dee checked his watch. "Well, the night is still young," he said.

Carrie grinned. "Just give me fifteen minutes."

*   *   *

When Carrie walked out of the front door of CCS and into Dee's view, all he could say was, "Whoa."

In fourteen minutes and thirty-nine seconds Carrie had transformed herself from sweaty WNBA wannabe into a freshly scented, elegant young woman. She was wearing a yellow tube top that accentuated both Carrie's "positives," a long, flowing white skirt, and the strappy gold sandals she'd thought she was crazy for packing in the first place. Instead of wearing her blond hair up in a loose bun like usual, Carrie opted for the tousled look and added a delicate pink flower barrette for the finishing touch. Her makeup was very minimal—lightly bronzed cheeks and glossed lips—except for the smoky eye effect that she and Piper had perfected last summer. If only her best friend could see her now.

"So, do I look okay?" Carrie asked.

Dee was so taken aback, he put his hand over his heart. "You look . . ."

Beautiful? Lovely? Drop-dead gorgeous?

"Absolutely stunning," he said.

Carrie grinned from ear to ear. "Thanks. You look amazing yourself."

Dee looked down and smiled. "All I did was put on a fresh shirt."

"I know," Carrie said coyly. They stood there awkwardly for a moment, taking each other in. Then Carrie snapped them out of it. "So, where are we going?"

"I'm taking you to a party," he said. "Sort of."

"I've been dying to go to a sort-of party," Carrie joked.

"Glad you're so easy to please," Dee said. He hadn't stopped smiling since she had walked outside.

They walked for a few blocks, past boarded-up houses, businesses with their metal gates drawn, and an alley in which a pack of dogs were attacking a garbage can. With each step the music grew louder and louder. Carrie wondered if Dee's friends were going to be at this party and if so, would they accept her? She had this big fear that she'd embarrass him somehow and then Dee would lose interest. Whatever she did, Carrie promised herself not to act like a moron. If she was wearing her lucky T in this situation, she wouldn't be worried in the least.

Dee led her around a corner and Carrie was so stunned by the sights, she almost tripped. The courtyard she had walked into was clearly a marketplace by day. Kiosks covered by tarpaulins and tied up with rope and twine had been pushed back against the walls of the bordering buildings. Awnings had been collapsed and shelves of clay pots, bowls, and artwork shoved away. The square itself, however, was full of life. People jammed every available inch of space, milling around, chatting, and drinking from teacups and glasses. Twinkle lights were strung up in the far-right corner and a band played beneath them, pounding out a dance beat on the drums while a woman in traditional Indian garb sang in Hindi. The sight was very

India, the voice was very Bengalese, but the song itself was very club worthy.

"Wow," Carrie said as Dee wove his way through the crowd. "This *is* a party."

"These people work hard all day," Dee called over his shoulder. "At night this is how they unwind. Would you like to dance?"

Carrie looked out at the swirling crowd. The women were so graceful, a blur of raised arms and swinging hips. It was incredibly intimidating but fabulous nonetheless.

"I don't know," she said, biting her lip. "I'm not really a dancer."

"I don't believe that for a second," Dee said. He grabbed both her hands and pulled her toward him.

"No, really. This is a *bad* idea." Carrie resisted, trying to pull her arms away, but Dee's grip was too strong for her. She soon found herself right in the center of all the whirling colors.

I hope he likes a girl who can humiliate herself in public, Carrie thought, looking around her uncertainly. *Otherwise I'm dead.*

Dee started to dance and Carrie was unsurprised to find that he had rhythm. There didn't seem to be many things that Dee wasn't good at. But for now she was focusing on his hips. His hips, which were swirling around in this grinding motion . . .

"Come on! Try it!" Dee called out, taking her wrist and pulling her toward him again.

The music pounded in Carrie's ears as she studied the women around her. Slowly she started stepping from one foot to the other, hoping she was on beat. The dancers seemed to have one move in common—they kept raising their arms over their heads, one, then the other, in a C shape as they spun and twisted and swirled. At a loss for another plan, Carrie lifted one arm, then the next, mimicking their moves. But while the other women looked exotic and fluid and gorgeous, she felt as if she was pantomiming a monkey.

Carrie moved in jolting gestures for a few beats, then caught Dee laughing and gave up, dropping her arms.

"Forget it! I suck!" she shouted over the music.

An older woman in a purple shawl took pity on Carrie, came up behind her, and gently held her arms. Carrie's first instinct was to move away, but the woman smiled at her and raised her arms. Using her hands to deftly bend Carrie's elbows and jut out her hip, the woman moved Carrie like a doll into a perfect pose. Then she got right in front of her and demonstrated a few moves, nodding at Carrie to copy her.

Carrie glanced at Dee, who smiled his encouragement. She held her breath and did her best to follow the woman. It was slow going, but eventually she found the beat and was able to make a passable go at a simple dance. Dee stood aside and watched her as she started to get into it, smiling and joining the other women, all of whom seemed more than happy to have her there.

Toward the end of the song everyone just started to spin and spin and spin. A hundred skirts and shawls whipped at Carrie's legs and arms, sliding silkily over her skin, tickling her everywhere. Carrie giggled, twirling as fast as she could. Before long she forgot how out of place she was. She forgot that she looked different and dressed differently and moved differently. And for a minute she thought of the time when her dad tried to teach her the box step before her eighth-grade dance and how he took her by surprise in the end with a humongous dip. The memory only made her smile on the spinning dance floor, where everything in her life melted together and seemed so beautiful.

With a crash of cymbals the song came to an end, but it took Carrie a moment to stop twirling. When she did, the world continued to spin around her and she laughed, grabbing on to Dee for support.

"Are you okay?" he asked.

"Yeah, I'm . . . I'm fine," she said, trying to find a fixed point to focus on and locate her balance again. Her eyes passed over the undulating crowd toward the buildings that bordered the square. As she gazed at the blue door of one of the businesses across the way, it opened, and Carrie's knees went out from under her.

There was a woman with a laundry basket. Clothes folded. Glittering green star. Right on top.

Oh my God, it's right there! My lucky T-shirt is RIGHT THERE!

Carrie pushed herself up. She had to get to it. She had to stop the woman with the basket.

"Whoa!" Dee said, mistaking her near fall for more dizziness. "Let's get you to a chair."

Carrie staggered into the crowd a few steps, still getting her footing. The woman loaded the basket onto the front of a moped. She climbed onto the seat. Dee turned away in search of a chair and there was no time for Carrie to explain. She dove into the crowd and ran as fast as she could.

Chapter Eleven

"Carrie! Carrie, where are you going!?"

Ignoring Dee's cries, Carrie shoved her way through the melee of arms and legs, saris and turbans, chairs and tables and benches. Over the incredible din she could hear the rev of an engine and the sound of the moped coughing to life.

"Stop! Please stop!" she shouted.

A dozen pairs of eyes turned to look at her, confused, disturbed, curious, but not the right ones. Not the eyes of the woman on the moped. Her eyes were trained dead ahead, and just as Carrie reached the sidewalk, the moped lurched and the woman sped away.

Oh, no. Not like this. I am not going to come this *close and lose it all over again!* Carrie thought.

She tore after the moped, sprinting outright just as she did on the last half lap of every race. The woman

189

headed for the mouth of the marketplace and Carrie's already panicked pulse took it up to a fever pitch. If the woman made it to the main street, Carrie would lose her for sure. She jumped over a garbage bag in the middle of the sidewalk, spun around a brown saried elderly woman who sat with her dog on the curb, and turned it on again. Up ahead the crowd parted for the moped to get through and then closed all too quickly to bar Carrie's way. She jumped up onto a stoop, vaulted over the handrail, and landed out on the street she and Dee had strolled down just moments ago.

"Stop!" Carrie cried, near tears as she ran right in front of the moped.

The woman's eyes widened and she slammed on the brakes. The T-shirt was right there, hurtling at Carrie in the darkness. Suddenly all the details around her were HDTV vivid. The birthmark just above the woman's lip, her tiny nose ring glinting in the dim light, the one bent bar on the front of the moped's metal basket. All this she took in, but she barely even registered the fact that she was about to get run over. The T-shirt would save her. It always did.

And then at the last second the moped swerved, just missing Carrie's shin. The woman tottered in her seat and almost went over but regained her balance and looked back.

"Crazy *gehra!*" she shouted.

Then she revved the engine again and sped off into the night.

"No!" Carrie wailed, chasing after her. "Come back!"

But it was no use. At the corner the woman turned right and disappeared into traffic, leaving Carrie doubled over, gasping for breath.

Oh God, it was there. It was right in front of me! Carrie thought desperately. Still bent at the waist, she started to sob, choking for air. Maybe this had been her one and only chance to get it back and she had missed it.

Carrie dropped down on the curb and buried her face in her hands. She heard Dee's footsteps pounding up the pavement and only sank her head lower. The last thing she wanted was for him to see her like this. The second-to-last thing she wanted was to have to explain.

But then Carrie heard the familiar sound of the most annoying voice ever to hit eardrums.

"I can't believe you're actually on the basketball team. That's as fast as you can run?"

When Carrie looked up, she saw Dor-mean towering over her. She was holding a huge, half-eaten turkey leg and looking rather smug.

Didn't this girl have a single sensitive, compassionate bone in her body?

Doreen took another bite and starting chomping loudly. "Looks like you're having a bit of bad luck, eh, Jockstrap?"

"Well, now that you're here, that's putting it mildly," Carrie said with a sneer. "And where did you come from anyway? Aren't you supposed to be behind Teensy, kissing her butt?"

"My mom brought me to this as a reward," Doreen replied proudly. "I helped build five houses in one day. That's a Help India record."

"Who cares?" Carrie sighed.

"Too bad you didn't get the license plate number on that moped," Doreen said, and then wiped her greasy mouth off with the back of her hand. "You'd be able to trace it to the owner and get an address."

Carrie knew Doreen well enough to know that she only said things like that when she had the goods on someone. She got up from the ground and met Doreen eye to chin.

"You memorized it, didn't you?"

"Maybe I did, maybe I didn't." Doreen snickered.

"I'm not fooling around. You better tell me what it is," Carrie demanded.

"Oh, if I'm going to tell you what it is, you're going to have to make it worth my while," Doreen said slyly.

Don't do it, a little voice in Carrie's head shrieked. *It would be like making a deal with the devil!*

But what choice did she have? She came all this way for her lucky T and nothing should get in the way of her finding it.

"Fine. What do you want?" Carrie asked tersely.

"Get me a date with that guy you were dancing with."

Carrie shook her head, thinking she misheard. "Uh, what?"

"I want to go out with that guy you work for," Doreen said.

"I see," Carrie said calmly, right before screaming, "ARE YOU OUT OF YOUR MIND?"

"Hey, one date with the hottie gets you the license plate number. Take it or leave it."

Carrie decided to counterattack. "How do I even know you really memorized it?"

"How do you know I didn't? Are you willing to take that risk?" Doreen barked.

Carrie thought about how desperately she wanted the shirt back and heaved a heavy sigh. "Okay, I'll do it."

Doreen looked very satisfied with herself. "Good. I'll come by CCS tomorrow night."

Carrie couldn't do anything else but glare at her.

"See you later, loser," Doreen said before blending into the crowd.

A millisecond later Dee was there to the rescue.

"Carrie! What happened? Are you okay?" Dee asked, breathing hard as he placed his hand on her back.

"I just want to go home," Carrie heard herself whimper.

"*Home* home or back to CCS?" Dee asked in a comforting voice.

Much to her surprise, Carrie let out a strained laugh, brought on by sheer desperation and helplessness. "Both, I guess."

Dee wrapped his arm around her and started walking. Clearly sensing she didn't want to talk, Dee didn't ask her a single question during the fifteen-minute stroll back to CCS. It was the nicest thing anyone could have done for her.

And how would Carrie repay him for his kindness? Tomorrow she had to turn him over to the ghastly Dor-mean.

The next day Carrie and Dee stood in the laundry room at the Indian Christian Women's Coalition, picking through bags and bags of clothes. Dee worked quickly and methodically, pulling out only red items, checking them for the star Carrie had described, then folding them into a pile. Carrie, meanwhile, was barely paying attention as she listlessly pulled out shirt after sweater after ill-conceived vest.

"You know what? This is pointless. It's not here," she said finally, collapsing into an orange plastic chair. The gray sky outside cast the whitewashed room in a bleak shadow that the one fluorescent bulb couldn't combat. Rain slid down the thin windowpane behind Carrie as the soft purr of the dryers provided a fittingly dull and lulling hum.

"I thought we decided to be positive about this," Dee said. "The woman you saw last night probably works at one of these shelters. It might be this one."

That morning over breakfast Carrie had explained her

bizarre behavior from the night before to Dee. His jaw had dropped slightly as he realized that she had, in fact, seen the T-shirt she had come here to find—that it was even possible that she was in the same section of the city as the shirt. Seeing how upset she was, he had taken it upon himself to pep-talk her into renewing her search. However, Carrie had yet to tell Dee that her "friend" Doreen might hold the key to the entire mystery and that in her weakened state she had sold him out for access to that key. She felt so awful about agreeing to pimp Dee out for the night and had been trying to come up with a way to get out of the whole thing. But at this point no brilliant ideas had come to her, and the day was half over.

"I don't think so. Why would someone with a laundry room right in her own building be out doing laundry?" Carrie asked as the two industrial-size washing machines swished away. "That doesn't make any sense."

Dee sighed and sat down across from her. He laced his fingers together and his biceps flexed. Even in her depressed state Carrie had to channel all her willpower so that she didn't throw herself on top of him.

You can't give this guy up to Doreen, a little voice inside her said. *Go back and tell her to stuff it, then find the T-shirt yourself.*

But even though Carrie knew this was the wiser thing to do, she couldn't help feeling beaten down by the universe. With Doreen's help she could get to the lucky T faster and then life would be normal again.

"You still haven't told me why this T-shirt is so important for you," Dee said while inspecting a few more red T-shirts.

Carrie looked at him, at his soulful hazel eyes so open and patient. For a split second she heard herself telling him about the lucky T's connection to her father. How the moment she realized it was really gone, it felt as if her dad was gone as well. But she felt strange confiding this type of intimate information when she might just turn around and give him up as a sacrificial lamb hours later.

Think about what you're doing, Carrie, the little voice piped up again. *Just look at those kids back at CCS. They think the world of Dee. Would they ever forgive you for hurting him?* Carrie took a deep breath and leaned forward. It didn't matter how many times her inner voice chided her. Just then she decided to swallow all her morals and make good on her word to Dor-mean.

"The T-shirt is good luck," she said finally. "I need it back because it's always brought me good luck and ever since I lost it . . ."

"You've had bad luck?" Dee asked.

"Something like that," Carrie said, thinking of Piper and Jason, then Fido and her bio test and her dad going to Tokyo. "Actually, I'm as superstitous as they come."

"Ah, so that's why you shuddered when I opened an umbrella indoors last week."

"Yeah, and the reason I almost cried when Manisha crossed two kitchen knives when she was setting the tables," Carrie said with embarrassment.

"Well I don't believe in superstitions or luck," Dee said matter-of-factly.

"You don't?" Carrie asked, taken aback. To her that was like someone saying he or she didn't believe in trees. Luck was just a fact of life.

"No. I believe we make our own luck," Dee said. "It's all in how you look at things."

Okay, Carrie thought. *It's now or never.*

"That's true. I'm not as unlucky as some people," Carrie said, wondering where this was going to lead. She hadn't quite thought it through.

"Absolutely," Dee said. "There's always someone else out there with bigger problems to face."

Carrie smiled, her heartbeat giving an extra-hard thump. Dee obviously was one of the kindest guys on the planet, which was why she felt like a ogre for what she was about to do.

"Right, like Doreen," Carrie blurted.

"What's the matter with Doreen?" he asked.

A good question, Carrie thought. *With so many possible answers.*

"Uh—well—you see," she stammered. *Think fast. He's waiting.* "She's . . . kind of . . . like . . . dying."

"Oh my God," Dee said, completely shocked.

Did I just say she was dying? I am SO going to hell.

197

"She didn't look sick to me at all," Dee added.

"Yeah, uh, she's a tough one. Fighting it every step of the way, that Doreen," Carrie said, gulping hard.

"What is she fighting?" Dee asked with concern.

Carrie realized that even Dee's inquisitive nature was charming. So far he only had one flaw, and that was being overly zealous about volunteering. As for Carrie, she was hitting a new low with this Dr.-Death-vs.-Doreen story.

"Oh . . . um . . . it's a rare . . . brain . . . tissue . . . abnormality." Carrie stumbled over each and every word as if she were on a racetrack, jumping over the hurdles blindfolded. "I can't really pronounce the medical term because it has a lot of consonants."

Dee looked perplexed. "Wow, that sounds awful."

Hell. I am going straight to hell.

Carrie tried to make the situation a little brighter. "Well, she's here with a group who makes wishes come true for sick kids, so she's really happy."

Once she said it, she knew what was going to come next.

"Really? Coming to India was her wish?" Dee sounded impressed.

"Uh-huh," Carrie replied nervously, and wrung her hands together. "But there's something else, too. And you can help."

"Sure. What can I do?"

Carrie closed her eyes and paused. This was the most

inane thing she had ever done (except for flying to India to get her lucky T-shirt back, of course).

"Take her out on a date?" she mumbled.

"I'm sorry, did you just ask me to take her out?"

"Yeah, uh . . . she really would love a romantic evening here, you know, before she . . ." Carrie made some sort of face that was supposed to indicate "kick the bucket."

"I see," Dee said pensively.

Is there a place worse *than hell? If so, I might be heading there instead,* Carrie thought.

Dee sat quietly for a moment, thinking about whether or not to take a terminally ill teenage girl out for a nice evening. Carrie sat there thinking about her dad and how disappointed he'd be in her right now, even if all this was just part of the plan of getting her precious T-shirt back. Her posture slumped forward as if a baby grand piano had been just set on her shoulders.

Then Dee took her by the hands, which she hadn't stopped wringing, and spoke while looking longingly into her eyes. "Carrie, I know it must have been awkward to ask me this favor, but you did it because you care about your friend. So I'll do it because it means something to you. Okay?"

Carrie's heart sank down into her feet. "Okay."

"Good. Should I call her up or something?"

"No, I'll talk to her and tell her to come by tonight. Is that okay?" Carrie said as enormous pangs of guilt beat her up inside.

"Yeah, that's fine," he said.

"Oh, just one thing. She's very secretive about the whole brain thing, so don't let her know you know, okay?" Carrie couldn't wait for this lie fest to be over.

Still holding her hands in his, he pulled her up from her chair so that they were standing inches apart from each other. Then he leaned over and whispered in her ear, "It'll be our little secret."

A few hours later Carrie rested her chin on her hand and propped her head up as she lay facedown on her bed. She tried to concentrate on the India guidebook in front of her instead of checking the clock every five minutes and running to the window to see if Dee's bike was out front, which would mean he was home from his date with Doreen. Right now Carrie was hoping to distract herself by reading the section on birthdays. Since hers was coming up soon, she thought she might find something cool for her—and maybe Dee—to do, that is, if he hadn't fallen madly in love and run off with her nemesis to get married. She also thought it might take her mind off the fact that she wouldn't be home for the traditional party and shopping spree with her mom. But it was so hot and humid in her room that Carrie couldn't seem to concentrate. She had read the same sentence at least ten times and had stripped down to a tank top and her Hello Kitty panties.

"In India it's traditional for the birthday girl or boy to give presents rather than to receive. . . ."

Carrie had this image of herself handing out presents to the kids at CCS on her birthday. She'd be like Santa Claus for a day and see their happy smiles. Perhaps she'd also be able to get rid of the horrible taste of shame that had been in her mouth since yesterday. Here she was, scheming and lying to a good guy for the sake of her lucky T, and there were all these children that she should have been paying attention to. From now on she would be all about prioritizing and putting other people's needs first.

Just as she made that mental vow, she heard a sound coming from outside, like a chain had just been locked. Carrie hurried over to the window and saw Dee's bike. Then she raced over to her door, opened it up, and ran down the stairs to greet him. She had to know right away how it went. Hopefully Doreen hadn't given him the worst night of his life.

Carrie called out to Dee as he was going up the stairs to the third floor. "Hey, how'd it go?"

Dee spun around, looked at Carrie, and smiled widely. "It was fine."

"That's it? Just 'fine'?" she asked.

Dee started chuckling really hard now.

Okay, weird.

"Yes, Carrie. Everything is fine," he said, smirking.

"What's so funny?" Carrie said, crossing her arms in front of her chest. "Were you and Doreen making jokes about me all night or something?"

201

"No," Dee said, smiling mischievously. "I just hadn't pegged you as a Hello Kitty person, that's all."

Carrie gasped in horror. Then she glanced down at herself just to make sure.

Yep, she was standing in front of Dee . . . in her underwear.

This is not bad luck, Carrie thought. *This is karma.*

Now she had two choices: (1) run back to her room squealing as if she had just seen a rat and lock herself in her room for a few days or (2) stand there and act completely unashamed. After all, they were both grown-ups, sort of, and it was just underwear.

Carrie decided to do a combination of both (1) and (2).

"Yeah, Hello Kitty. She rocks," Carrie said in this odd, I'm-trying-to-be-cool-when-I'm-obviously-mortified tone of voice. "Wish I could stay here and chat, Dee, but I'm beat, so off to bed I go."

"Sure, Carrie. Whatever you say," Dee said, flashing her another one of his heart-stopping grins.

And with that, Carrie dashed off to her room and beat herself over the head with her India guidebook for a few minutes. Then she sat on her bed and smiled. Tomorrow Doreen would give her the license plate number, she'd get her lucky T back, and it seemed that Dee had had a good time, so no one would be getting hurt. This might have worked out after all.

Carrie woke up in the middle of the night to a tap, tap on the window. Instead of feeling afraid, she was annoyed.

She was in the middle of a pretty stellar dream that involved Dee wearing Hello Kitty underwear, and whoever was trying to get her attention had completely interrupted her. Carrie stomped over and threw open the window, after which a few pebbles hit her in the face. She looked down and saw a shadowy figure on the ground below.

It was Doreen. As far as Carrie could see, she was wearing this very pretty, shimmering purple dress and her hair was done in an upsweep. Apparently Doreen cleaned up real good.

"Carrie, I need to talk to you," she whispered.

"Can't this wait until tomorrow? I could get in trouble for this," Carrie said softly.

"No, get down here now!" Doreen said more intently.

"Okay, okay. I'll be right there."

Carrie walked over to the door, grabbed her robe this time, and headed out to meet Doreen. When she came face-to-face with her, Carrie could hardly believe her eyes. Doreen had this wine-colored lipstick on and her lashes were thick with mascara. She was beautiful, even though she was crying.

"Why . . . did . . . you . . . do . . . this . . . to . . . me," she said between heaving sobs.

"Doreen, what happened?" Carrie said. She had never seen the girl shed a tear in her entire life, which made Carrie really worried.

"You . . . told . . . Dee . . . I . . . ." Doreen continued to gush. "That . . . I . . . was . . . DYING?"

Oh God, Carrie thought. *Think damage control.*

"What? Where would he get an idea—"

"He said you told him!" Doreen snapped.

Okay, Dee's second flaw is that he's horrible about keeping secrets.

"It's true. I did," Carrie confessed, not wanting to drag this out any further. "I'm so, so sorry, Doreen. I don't know why I said those things."

"You didn't think he would go out with me unless I was some charity case," Doreen cried.

"No, no. That's not what I think at all," Carrie said, reaching out to comfort her with an outstretched hand.

But Doreen backed away. "Yes, it is. That's why you and Piper hung out with me in the first place, out of pity. Then you ditched me when you got tired of it."

In a split second Carrie thought about the hundreds of hurtful things Dor-mean had said and done to her over the years, and for some reason, none of it compared to the humiliation and pain Carrie had caused her. Doreen had been jealous of her and Piper for such a long time, and all she wanted was for Carrie to be envious of her for once. Sure, Doreen had bribed Carrie and forced her into this mess, but did she have to make up that ridiculous story? Why didn't she just tell Dee what really happened? He would have helped her out regardless. Just then she searched her soul and came up with a theory. Maybe deep down, Carrie hoped that

Doreen would get a taste of her own medicine. Only now it hardly seemed worth it.

"Doreen, I don't know why we grew apart, but Piper and I hung out with you because we liked you. I swear, we thought you were really fun to be around," Carrie said.

"Well, why aren't we friends anymore?" Doreen asked, squatting down and putting her head in her hands.

Carrie knelt down next to her. "I wish I knew. Technically I'm not even friends with Piper anymore."

Doreen looked up in surprise. "Really? You're not?"

"No, we got into this fight before I left," Carrie explained. "But I plan on making up with her. And if you'll let me, I'd like to make up with you too."

Carrie put her arm around Doreen and she didn't shrug it away.

All of a sudden Doreen started to giggle. "You know, the whole night I played along with Dee. I was really mad, but not because you pulled this stunt on me."

Carrie was a bit curious to hear why. "What were you mad about?"

Doreen smirked. "That I hadn't thought of it myself."

Carrie put both of her arms around Doreen and hugged her. "You need help, you know that?"

"Nah, you're the one who needs help, right? A stupid T-shirt must be found."

"You were bluffing all along, weren't you?" Carrie asked, grimacing.

"Yeah, I was," Doreen said meekly. "Are you pissed?"

Carrie thought about it carefully. Doreen could have tattled on Carrie to Dee, but she didn't. And that could have been an utter disaster. Now was the time for forgiveness all around. "I'm not pissed, but I could use an extra hand trying to track it down. You in?"

Doreen smiled. "I'm in."

"Good." Carrie stood up and brushed herself off. "So, are you going to tell me about the date or what?"

"Well, one thing's for sure. That guy is completely hung up on you. It was Carrie this and Carrie that all night," Doreen said while standing up and walking toward the building with her old friend.

"Come up to my room," Carrie said. "I can't wait to hear all the details."

Chapter Twelve

The next morning Carrie lay on her stomach on the floor of the lounge, coloring with Asha and Manisha. Big, fat drops of rain slapped against the windowpanes and the sky outside was as dark as pitch. The fact that it was overcast and dreary made Carrie even more tired than she already was. The night before Doreen had ended up staying over, and she and Carrie had talked until the sun came up. They covered lots of ground and got reacquainted with each other. They laughed, they cried—there were some Kodak moments. But most important they started anew, which Carrie was quite happy about. Now if only she could find her lucky T, get lucky with Dee, and fix the mess she left back home, everything would be great.

"What're you drawing?" Manisha asked, adjusting her elbows and craning her neck so she could see.

"I'm drawing me," Carrie replied. She turned the page toward Manisha.

"Oh! It looks just like you," Asha said, running her fingertip over the blond frizzy hair Carrie had created. "I like the shirt."

Carrie sighed and looked down at the green star she had drawn on the cartoon Carrie's chest. "Yeah," she said. "Me too. You know, this T-shirt is actually lucky," she added, figuring the kids would find this interesting.

"Really?" Manisha asked, eyes wide. "But I've never seen you wear it."

"That's because I lost it," Carrie told them.

"You lost a good luck shirt? That's bad," Asha said, making an exaggerated face as if she was appalled.

"I know, but I'm going to find it," Carrie said, laying the picture aside. "Even if it kills me," she added under her breath.

"We'll help!" Manisha offered. "I find all kinds of things in the city. Pennies and necklace chains and candy wrappers . . ."

Carrie laughed and gave Manisha a small hug. "Thanks."

"Wait, who are those people in the corners?" Asha asked.

"That's my mom standing next to our house in California," Carrie answered. "And that's my dad. He lives in New York, but he's an airplane pilot, so he travels all around the world."

Manisha looked perplexed. "Your mother and father don't live together?"

Oh, great, how do I explain this? Carrie thought.

"Well, sometimes parents don't get along very well and they have to live apart in order to be happy," she said, hoping that she wasn't confusing them.

"That would make me sad," Asha said with a frown.

"It made me sad for a while. Sometimes I still feel sad. But I know that both my parents love me very much," Carrie said reassuringly.

"Does your father miss you?" Manisha asked with concern.

This was the first time someone had ever asked her that. Sure, lots of Carrie's friends and even her mom would ask her if she missed her dad after he moved out. They'd ask if she was okay with everything and if she was feeling hurt. But until now nobody ever asked her if she thought her dad missed her. If she really thought about how unavailable her father had been over the past few years—how many basketball finals and school plays he missed, how many visits he canceled, how many phone calls were cut short for one reason or another— she might tell Manisha no, he didn't seem to miss her at all. But on the other hand, there were the countless letters and postcards sent from around the globe, the hundreds of photos he had e-mailed her, and the thoughtful gifts she received via FedEx, including one special item that she had cherished so dearly.

All of a sudden Carrie's eyes welled with tears. "Yes, he misses me very much."

Carrie cleaned herself up after the coloring crying jag and decided to take her half-hour break on the front steps of CCS. She buried her nose in her guidebook. Currently she was studying a map of the area, scouting out the next few places she would look for her lucky T. Her resolve had definitely strengthened and she was more determined than ever to get her hands on it. Finding the shirt meant finding the way back to her old self. But then again, Carrie had already began to feel as if she was changing a little bit each day. She was learning new things about the world; her perspectives were shifting. What if by the time she found the T, she was a completely different person altogether? And what if she changed so much that she and her dad wouldn't be able to connect at all?

Carrie's thought patterns were interrupted by the sound of Dee's hurried, clomping footsteps. She actually heard him approaching from the back of the house and her heart started to pound. Now she was only able to think about what Doreen had said about Dee liking her and her entire body began to tremble with excitement.

"Hey," Dee said, seeming a bit uncomfortable.

"Hey," she replied.

Dee sat down next to her. Inside, a million nervous Ping-Pong balls danced around in her stomach, but outside, she was the picture of calm. She didn't want to let him see how much he had gotten under her skin.

"I'm sorry for acting like a creep yesterday," Dee said plainly.

Carrie's heart skipped a few surprised beats. What the heck was he sorry for?

"I should have mentioned your indecent exposure as soon as I noticed," Dee said, flushing slightly. "But you looked so cute."

Carrie's jaw dropped. "Really?"

"Yes! Is it so hard to believe that I think you're cute?" Dee asked.

"No, actually," she quipped.

"Well, it's good to know that you're humble."

They both leaned back against the steps and stared straight ahead. Carrie's palpitating heart had gone from sickened pounding to happy flutters in less than two minutes. Everything she found out about Dee just made her like him more. A guy who was bold enough to tell her to her face that he thought she was cute? Had Jason said anything like that to her—ever? Well, once he complimented her shoes, but that isn't even remotely the same.

Without much warning, Carrie's conscious kicked in. Suddenly, her remorse for lying to Dee about Doreen's fake terminal illness was in overdrive. There was no way she could justify her behavior and not confessing was making her feel more guilty every minute that passed by with Dee still in the dark. It was now, or never.

"Uh, Dee, I've got to tell you something," Carrie began. "And once you hear what I'm about to say, you might not like me anymore."

"I find that difficult to believe," Dee said sweetly.

Yikes, this is going to be REALLY hard.

"Well, you see . . . the thing is . . . hypothetically speaking, of course," she stammered.

"C'mon, out with it, Carrie," Dee said, eyeing her curiously.

"Right. Okay," Carrie said before inhaling and exhaling deeply. "I made all that stuff up about Doreen so you would go out with her because she promised that if you did, she'd give me information about where my shirt might be."

Dee didn't even blink. "Yeah, I figured as much."

Carrie was completely stunned. "What?"

"Did you really think that I'd fall for that story? I mean, a brain tissue abnormality with an unpronounceable name?" Dee asked with a slight chuckle.

"Shut up, it could exist," Carrie said, trying to hide the emerging smile on her face. "If you knew I was lying, then why did you go along with everything?"

Dee shrugged his shoulders. "I don't know. I suppose I was interested in seeing what might happen next."

"So you find me interesting, too, huh?" Carrie replied.

"Yes, I do," Dee said, grinning. "Besides, it was obvious from the other day at the marketplace that something was going on between you and Doreen. It seemed like it needed to be resolved, which is why I blew your cover during my dinner with her."

Oh my God, this guy is as perceptive as Oprah. And if he can overlook my temporary insanity, he's definitely a keeper.

Carrie blushed. "Well, it seems as if you can read me like a book."

"Maybe. But I still think you have some surprises up your sleeve," Dee quipped.

"I just might," Carrie said.

An uncomfortable pause surfaced. Carrie had the urge to surprise him right then by tackling him to the ground and covering him with kisses, but before she could even entertain the notion, Dee cleared his throat and spoke up.

"So, you're reading up on India, I see."

"Yeah," Carrie said, holding up the book. "Refining the T-shirt-finding strategy."

"Great," Dee replied.

"Actually, I also read something in here yesterday and it started me thinking. . . . My birthday is this Friday and—"

"Is it? Why didn't you say anything?" Dee asked.

"I don't know. I wasn't sure what I wanted to do, but then there was this whole section in here about birthdays in India and . . . now I think I know."

"Do you?" Dee asked with a smile.

Carrie smiled back.

"I do," she said. "But I could use your help again."

"You know how it works, Carrie. Your wish is my command."

"You don't have to do this, you know," Dee said as Carrie led him down a skinny aisle at a toy store the following evening. "That's a lot of children to buy presents for."

"I know I don't have to. I want to," Carrie said, picking up a small tin drum. "Besides, it's my birthday. I've been in India for a while already and I haven't had the chance to do anything traditional."

"Oh, you have—you just don't realize it," Dee said, pausing in front of some model airplanes.

"I don't know if eating *puri* every morning counts," Carrie joked.

"Well, think about it: you've been eaten alive by mosquitoes, you've been pooped on by a monkey, you've danced in the marketplace, you've survived an auto-rickshaw ride, and you've been caught in at least a dozen rainstorms. These are all very traditional Indian experiences."

"There's never a dull moment around here, is there?" Carrie said.

"Never," Dee replied, grinning.

"Well, anyway, I have all this spending money and I haven't needed much since I've been here," she added, giving the drum a little rap. "I mean, except for anti-itch cream and the occasional bottled water. Might as well spend it on the kids."

Dee's grin widened as Carrie continued along, taking in the displays of colorful kites and balsa wood airplanes, the shelves of porcelain elephants decorated with colorful headdresses and blankets lined up next to familiar bright pink Barbie boxes.

"I should get one of these for my niece," Dee said, picking up a little beaded change purse. "She's just starting to learn the value of saving her allowance."

"Here," Carrie said, pulling out the lucky coin she had found on the street during her first T-shirt search. She had been keeping it in her pocket with her rabbit's foot ever since, but somehow she didn't mind parting with it, especially for Dee. She plunked it into the purse and snapped it closed.

"Thanks. What's that for?" Dee asked.

"It's bad luck to give someone a purse with no money in it," Carrie explained.

Dee rolled his eyes. "Do you have a whole book on this or something?"

Somewhere in the store a child whined and cajoled, begging his mother for a puzzle.

"I told you, Medha. You can get one thing," the mother said in soothing tones. "You already picked out the spaceship."

Carrie's heart panged and she smiled slightly, thinking of her mom. This shopping excursion was very different from her usual birthday outing. By now Carrie's mother would have been so tired from hitting every store between Pacific Sunwear and Hollister Co., she would be dragging Carrie to the food court for a Häagen-Dazs break.

"Where did you go?" he said, coming up behind her.

The slight whisper of Dee's breath tickled her earlobes and sent goose bumps all down her arms.

"Huh?" she asked, blinking as she turned to him.

"You were gone for a second there. Where did you go?" Dee asked, his incredible hazel eyes searching hers.

"Oh . . . uh . . . home, I guess," Carrie said. Then, embarrassed by her confession and the closeness of him, she turned and quickly walked the rest of the aisle. At the back wall she spotted a box of soft, felt dolls. They had dark cotton skin and wore saris of pink, blue, or green. Each doll had a sweet smile, a single *bindi* on its forehead, and long yarn hair wrapped into a braid down its back.

"Ooh! These are so sweet!" Carrie exclaimed. "We don't get to wear anything as cool as this back home," she added, fingering the soft material.

"No saris in The Gap?" Dee teased.

"Not exactly. I'd probably look totally awkward in one anyway," she said.

"I highly doubt that," Dee told her. "You look lovely in just about everything. Or barely anything."

Carrie smiled at his sexy comment and then began counting out the dolls like she hadn't heard what he'd said at all. "What do you think? They'll like them, right? And they're soft so they can sleep with them."

"They're good for the girls, but I don't think the boys will be as appreciative," Dee said.

"That's true," Carrie replied, gathering a couple dozen dolls up in her arms and following Dee down another aisle. "All right, what do boys play with around here? Is there some kind of cool Indian toy I can get them like a toy rickshaw or a plush monkey or maybe those drums? Although that could give the rest of us permanent headaches."

"I've got it!" Dee said, turning around with a small box in his hand.

Carrie looked at it and her eyebrows came together. Not exactly the Indian toy she'd been imagining. "Matchbox cars?" she said dubiously.

Dee nodded, his eyes gleaming with excitement. "Trust me," he said. "Matchbox cars."

Damn, he's gorgeous Carrie thought, raising one eyebrow while admiring the snug fit of Dee's jeans as she followed him to the cash register.

Two days later, on Carrie's sixteenth birthday, she stood back and smiled with Dee, Mr. Banarjee, and the other members of the CSS staff, watching as the boys crashed their toy cars into one another and the girls kissed and hugged their dolls. On the table in the cafeteria were half-eaten plates of sweets and cake, which Carrie and Dee had purchased from a local bakery. The walls were trimmed with hot pink and gold paper streamers hanging down from the ceiling and covering every surface, while a string of paper lanterns crisscrossed the room. That afternoon Dee, Dash, and Akhtar had strung white Christmas lights everywhere after Dee had cleared the extra electricity usage with Mr. Banarjee. It was the most beautifully decorated birthday party Carrie had ever seen, and it had kept her mind off thoughts of home and how much she missed being there for her birthday. She had spent most of her money on the party, but it was absolutely worth it.

Plus she had blown out every candle on her cake in one try, guaranteeing her wish—to find her lucky T— would come true.

"This is a nice thing you've done," Mr. Banarjee said. "We don't have many birthday parties like this around here."

"Well, I'm glad I could give them one," Carrie said, fingering the green beaded bracelet that had arrived that morning—a present from her father that, according to his note, he had purchased on a trip to Cambodia. She was also wearing the new digital sports watch her mother had sent her. It had two readouts on the face, one programmed to local Calcutta time, the other giving her the time in San Francisco.

Her parents might not be with her for her sweet six-teen, but she was glad they had each sent her something she could wear—things that made them feel as if they were close.

"Well, we should be going," Dee said over her shoulder.

"Going? Where?" Carrie asked.

"Dee has requested the evening off for the two of you so that you might continue the birthday celebration on your own," Mr. Banarjee said with a kind smile and a wink. Behind him two of the other floor monitors, Tara and Kelly, widened their eyes and smiled suggestively.

When Carrie turned to Dee, he was grinning. He walked out into the hall and Carrie followed, dying of curiosity. As soon as they were alone, Dee reached out and took both her hands in his. Carrie's knees almost gave out.

"There's something I'd like to show you," he said, his hair falling adorably over one eye. "Something special. Will you come?"

His thumb moved back and forth along her palm as he stared into her eyes.

"Sure," Carrie said with a smile. "I'm intrigued."

"Great. I just have to grab something and we'll go," he told her. Then he turned and bounded up the stairs, taking them two at a time.

Carrie waited until he was gone, then leaned back against the wall, catching her breath. He had a whole plan for her birthday? But he had only found out about it a few days ago. Where was he taking her? What were they going to do?

If Carrie guessed right, she would be in need of gum and lots of it. She dug through her purse in the search of spearmint Orbit and hoped that even though she wasn't wearing her lucky T, her birthday would be magical.

"So this random building is the special place you wanted to show me?" Carrie asked as she climbed to the top of the fire escape on the side of the brick apartment complex Dee had brought her to. "Somehow I find that hard to be—"

The word died in her throat as she emerged out onto the roof. The view took her breath right out of her. The sun was just starting to dip toward the horizon, illuminating the turrets and steeples of the many temples that dotted the skyline. The bubbly roofs of the mosques sparkled in the sunshine. A building in the distance that looked as if it was covered in gold blinded her with its beauty. On a rooftop a few blocks away a couple dozen men conducted some sort of game that looked like golf, the sound of the ball smacking against the bat reverberating out over the city. The shouts of the players rose into the air, and at the same moment church bells clanged off to the west as if they were signaling the sun's descent.

Carrie looked at Dee, her heart completely full. He was watching her intently, enjoying her reactions to the many sights around her.

"I take back what I was about to say," Carrie told him. "I find it very easy to believe."

This must have been what her father was talking about all those times when she was little—back when he used to tell her how enchanting the world was. He must have been talking about sights like this. Carrie touched her new bracelet and sighed, wishing she could tell him in person that she understood now. But as usual they were apart and Carrie had no idea when she'd be seeing him again. "Come on," Dee said, bringing her back to the moment. "We'll watch the sun go down. It's better than any play or movie you've ever seen."

All right, snap out of it, Carrie told herself. *You're supposed to be having a romantic birthday moment with the hottest guy in the Eastern Hemisphere. Lighten up!*

Dee slipped his backpack off his shoulders and took out a blanket, which Carrie helped him spread on the dusty roof. They sat down together and Carrie leaned back on her hands, taking a deep breath of the sweetly scented air. She could hardly believe it was her birthday. Without her parents, without her friends, without the party and all the presents, she expected that it wouldn't be a good birthday. Still, even though she missed her mom and dad and Piper and the ritual of it all, Carrie thought it was a good idea to focus on the positive. Her first birthday on her own was looking pretty good, all things considered.

Another crack of the bat pulled her attention away from her thoughts and back to the cricket game.

"Why are they playing on the roof?" Carrie asked.

"Well, there aren't a lot of open spaces in this city, but the obsession with cricket around here far outweighs the population problem," Dee said. "People will play wherever they can find open space. And that includes rooftops."

Dee told Carrie all about himself—what his childhood was like in India, how he got along with his parents, what his best subjects were in school, what college life was like—and Carrie couldn't have been more captivated. She watched his lips move with every word and imagined what it would feel like if they were pressed up against hers. And she laughed out loud when Dee told her a story about him getting caught breaking curfew. His parents snagged him while he was sneaking back into the house after going out with his friends to see a late-night viewing of *The Texas Chainsaw Massacre*, which was playing at a run-down theater in Calcutta.

"You know it really happened, right?"

"Yes, I'm a Leatherface believer," Carrie said through another belly laugh.

"Hey, it was the only thing I ever got grounded for, and it was worth it. One hundred twenty minutes of pure gore, thank you very much." Dee chuckled.

"So have you ever broken another rule?"

Dee shook his head. "No. Not that I know of."

Carrie whistled. This guy *was* as straight as they come.

"Ah, but you misunderstand," Dee said, turning to her, his eyes dancing. "I said I never broke another rule, but there are many things my parents never had rules about. Bungee jumping, for example. Or . . . going away to England for school, or . . . taking strange but completely adorable American girls onto rooftops at night."

Carrie flushed. "You are bad to the bone," she joked.

"Oh, look. Here's the best part," Dee said.

Carrie tore her gaze away from his handsome profile and gazed out at the sun. It was a huge ball of burning gold dipping down quickly now, its rays reflecting prisms off the golden spirals of the temples and the glass skylights that dotted the city. The sky exploded with streaks of color—pinks and purples and mixed-up hues Carrie had never seen before. In minutes the sun was gone, but the colors remained, bathing the city in their spectacular rosy warmth.

All over the city the call to prayer rang out, the lilting song wafting up into the atmosphere. Leaning her head back, Carrie let the glow wash over her and breathed in deeply. For the first time since she had arrived in India, she felt totally relaxed. And it was all thanks to Dee.

"Thanks for bringing me here," Carrie said with a sigh. "This was the perfect ending to my birthday."

"It's not over yet," Dee said. "I have a gift for you."

Carrie's eyes popped open. "But I'm not supposed

to get gifts," she pointed out, smiling nonetheless.

Dee scrambled to his feet. "You may be in India, but you are still American. That means you get a gift." He reached into his bag and pulled out a large purple box tied with a sheer gold ribbon. "I hope you like it," he said, holding it out to her.

Touched at his thoughtfulness and giddy with anticipation, Carrie slid the ribbon from the box and lifted the lid. A tiny gasp escaped her throat. There, folded up neatly beneath bright pink tissue paper, was the most beautiful turquoise sari Carrie had ever seen. The edges were decorated with silver and gold beading in haphazard swirls. When she lifted it out, the smooth, silken fabric made a lush swooshing sound as it unfurled.

"Dee. It's gorgeous," Carrie said, holding it up against the pink sky.

"You like it?" he asked, grinning happily.

"I *love* it," Carrie said. "Can you help me put it on?"

"Well, the *choli* and the petticoat are in the box, but you can't exactly change into them here," Dee said, glancing around at the windows of the buildings nearby.

"The *choli* and the petticoat?" Carrie asked.

"That's the shirt and the skirt that go underneath," Dee said. "But I guess I can teach you how to wrap it over your jeans and T-shirt if you want."

"Yes, thanks," Carrie said, holding the fabric up to her body. She couldn't wait to feel Dee's hands against her skin.

Lucky T

Dee took the sari and unfolded it, standing on the blanket so the fabric wouldn't touch the silt-covered roof. At one end were four wide gold stripes, running horizontally across the sari.

"This end is the *pullao*," he said, holding it up. "This part will hang down your back when we are done, so you want to leave this off to your left."

Carrie nodded and Dee stepped behind her, reaching up and over her with the sari. The fabric billowed up, tent-like, enveloping her briefly in a shroud of turquoise light, then fell in front of her, held around her by Dee's strong arms. Carrie's heart started to race at his closeness, his breath on her neck, his skin brushing hers.

Okay, calm down. He's dressing *you, not* undressing *you,* Carrie told herself.

"At the top-right corner you make a knot, like this," Dee instructed slowly, his voice at her ear sending a rush of heat straight through her. He tucked one corner through a twist of fabric and tied it, then moved in front of her and stood just inches away, so close she could see the faint line of stubble on his chin.

"What next?" Carrie asked, her voice coming out a near whisper.

"Next you . . . you tuck the knot into your waist-band."

Carrie looked down at her jeans and her pulse raced. Dee flushed and smiled, then cleared his throat.

"Here," he said, handing her the knot. "Tuck it right in the middle."

Carrie swallowed hard and did as she was told. Everything inside her was alert, on edge. She could practically feel Dee's heart pounding as well, just inches away beneath his thin T-shirt. He stared into her eyes, she stared into his, and for an instant she was certain he was going to kiss her, but he pulled back, breaking the spell.

"Now you wrap it around once," he said, his fingertips brushing her stomach as he grasped the sari again. He stepped behind her once more and his arms encircled her from behind as he swished the fabric around, tickling her ankles with the hem. "And then you pleat it here and pin it to the front of your jeans."

He handed the pleats to Carrie and knelt on the ground to rummage through the box, pulling out a few safety pins. As soon as he moved away from her, Carrie took a few deep breaths, trying to calm the excitement in her chest. This time Dee turned and pinned the pleats to her waistband himself. Carrie had to look away to keep from blushing at the sight of Dee, kneeling in front of her, concentrating on her stomach. But when he was done, he looked up and grinned, which both relaxed Carrie and almost made her swoon at the same time.

He slipped behind her once again and wrapped the sari around her, his palms brushing the small of her back, her waist, her side. By the time he appeared in front of her again to drape the rest of the fabric across her chest and over her shoulder, Carrie could hardly breathe.

"Now you pleat it again," Dee said, gazing into her eyes as he worked. "Lift it and drape it over your shoulder so that the *pullao* hangs behind you."

He slid the silky fabric over her shoulder, brushing her neck and sending a shiver down her side. Stepping even closer, he reached under the sari near her clavicle and pinned the fabric to her shirt to hold it in place. Carrie could smell the scent of his breath, still sweet from the icing on her birthday cake.

"How do you know how to do all this?" Carrie asked.

"I grew up with five women in my house," Dee told her, looking down. "None of them ever looked nearly as beautiful as you do right now."

Carrie swallowed hard again and smiled. Between the beautiful colors and the smoothness of the silk and the warmth of his skin so close to her, she felt as if she were about to implode.

"Are you going to kiss me now?" Carrie asked him breathlessly.

Dee looked into her eyes. "Yes," he said.

Carrie's eyes fluttered closed as he undid the clip that was holding her hair up in a bun. She could feel her blond locks fall around her shoulders. Then she felt him place both of his hands on her cheeks and then his mouth covered her own. She felt as if she had been waiting for this kiss her entire life. His lips were perfectly soft, his touch strong and protective, as if he cared about nothing more than holding her close. She wrapped her arms around Dee's back, clinging to him to keep from falling.

It was, without doubt, the most incredible kiss Carrie Fitzgerald had ever experienced.

And she wasn't even wearing her lucky T.

Chapter Thirteen

"You're doing it again," Dee said to Carrie as they walked back to CCS that night.

"Doing what?" Carrie asked, letting go of the bracelet's beads and dropping her hands to her sides.

"You were off somewhere else," Dee said, adjusting the box that held her sari under his arm. "Is everything okay?"

Carrie smiled sadly. Everything should have been okay. Everything should have been perfect. Dee had kissed her. On a rooftop. Under a rosy Indian sky. She should have been walking on air right about then. And part of her was. But another part—the part she had been trying to ignore all day—was abysmally sad.

She missed home. She missed her friends. She missed her mother. But most of all she missed her dad. And the realization that she had messed up her one and only chance to get the lucky T back and bring him close to her again made her so angry at herself she could cry.

"Carrie, what is it?" Dee said, pausing on the sidewalk. "Whatever it is, you can tell me."

Strangers passed by, talking and laughing, on their way home or out with friends. Even though she was here with Dee, all the bustle made Carrie feel lonely and heartsick.

"I'm sorry. Don't get me wrong, I had an amazing birthday and it was all thanks to you," Carrie said. "I just—"

"You're coming down from your birthday high and you're missing home," Dee said.

Carrie blinked, surprised. "How did you know?"

"Happens to me every year," Dee replied, walking again. "My birthday is in November, so I'm always at school. I party with my friends, we go out for a big dinner, and everything is fine, but the moment I'm in bed with the lights out, all I want is to be here."

Carrie looked at Dee incredulously. He really did understand. Suddenly she knew he wouldn't laugh if she told him the whole backstory about the lucky T. Dee cared about her. In that moment she felt an overwhelming certainty that she could tell him anything.

"There's something else," she said, taking a deep breath as they crossed a street. "The T-shirt isn't just lucky. It was a present from my dad. He gave it to me right after he and my mom got divorced. I hardly ever see him anymore, and it may sound kind of stupid, but whenever I wear it, I sort of feel like he's with me. Like he's watching over me from wherever the heck he is just then." Carrie swallowed hard and glanced up at Dee. "I don't know, but . . . not having it now . . . it's like lately I've been missing him even more than usual."

"Wow," Dee said.

"I know. I'm a loser," Carrie replied, quickly swiping a tear that had irritatingly sprung up.

"No. I was just thinking . . . that's a real reason to want to find a T-shirt," he said.

"Really?" Carrie said, surprised.

Dee smiled slowly and Carrie had to quell another urge to pounce on him. He stopped walking, reached out and ran his fingertips along her temple, then tucked a lock of hair behind her ear. For a moment his hand lingered against her cheek and Dee looked deep into her eyes.

"Does your father know that you traveled halfway across the world to search for this piece of him?" Dee asked.

"No," Carrie said softly.

"You should tell him," Dee said simply. "People like to be told how much they matter. I'm sure it would mean a lot to him to know the lengths you've gone."

Carrie looked down as they started walking again, overwhelmed by a flood of conflicting emotions. She wouldn't mind a little illustration of that from her father once in a while. Why didn't *he* show *her* how much *she* mattered?

But you acted like you didn't care that he wasn't coming to visit, she reminded herself. *How's he supposed to know how much it hurts unless you tell him?*

Carrie wrapped her arms around herself and hung on. What if she called her father and told him she really needed to talk? Could they work all this out, or would he be too busy even to take the time to hear her?

"God, I'm so confused," Carrie said with a sad little laugh.

Dee smiled. "Confusion ultimately leads to a deeper understanding."

"You know, sometimes you sound like a fortune cookie," Carrie teased.

"My mother always tells me that," Dee replied, tugging her arm so that she would sidestep a puddle.

They laughed and Dee cleared his throat. "You are a contradiction, Carrie Fitzgerald."

"How do you figure?" she asked.

"On one hand, you have no fear. You came all the way to India to chase something that is special to you," he said. "That's very brave."

Carrie warmed under the intensity of his admiration. "And on the other hand?"

"On the other hand, you fear all these things that don't really exist," he said. "Breaks in the sidewalk, cracked mirrors, knocking wood. Why the superstitions?"

Carrie shrugged. "I don't know. I guess I just—I started believing in good luck when I got my T-shirt and then it was like I couldn't *not* believe in bad luck as well."

Dee shook his head. "You're too smart for that," he said. "You should start living in the real world."

"I don't think that's really possible," Carrie said, trying to envision herself willingly walking under a ladder or not holding her breath while driving by a cemetery. The very idea made her shudder.

"Just try it. I promise you if you let one thing go, the sky will not fall down," he told her.

"Okay, fine. How about this?" Carrie said. "You break one rule—one real rule—and I'll give up one of my superstitions. I mean, you're telling me to live a little, but you aren't exactly living life to the fullest yourself."

"I think you can live within the rules and still live life," Dee said.

"Not if you've never felt what it's like to do something bad. That total rush," Carrie said, spreading her fingers. "I'm not saying you should knock over a liquor store or anything, just . . . do something you wouldn't normally do under your own strict guidelines. See how it feels."

"Okay . . . so what rule should I break?" Dee asked, his brow furrowed.

"I don't know," Carrie said. "Why don't you . . . do something different at CCS without asking Mr. Banarjee first or something?"

"I can't do that!" Dee said. "He's my boss."

"Well, it's not like he's in the mafia and will whack you," Carrie said. "Next up is breaking a rule."

233

"And if I do that. If I defy my boss . . ."

"I'll do something crazy," Carrie said.

"Like open an umbrella inside?" Dee asked, his eyes bright.

"Like open an umbrella inside," Carrie said with a laugh.

"It's a deal," Dee said, opening up his arm to her. Surprised but touched by the gesture, Carrie slid over and leaned into his side as they walked. Dee wrapped his arm around her and squeezed her shoulder. As the CCS building loomed into view, Carrie started to feel a confidence welling up inside her.

Maybe her life could be okay without her lucky T. After all, right then she was walking along the streets of an exotic city with an amazing birthday present tucked under her arm. She was cuddled up next to a thoughtful, intelligent, intriguing, beautiful guy. And her T-shirt was nowhere in sight.

At that moment anything seemed possible.

The next day was beautiful and sunny and warm, and Carrie woke up with a new outlook. Just deciding to talk to her father made her feel more at ease than she had in weeks. Plus there had been all that blissful daydreaming about Dee she had done the moment she woke up. Everything was going to be fine. Great, even. Carrie could feel it.

To celebrate her giddiness, Carrie decided to take

Dash, Akhtar, Manisha, Trina, and Asha out for a walk. After convincing one of the teachers, Miss Ruma, to sit with the younger kids, her little band of hikers set out, headed for a nice, lush, wide-walked neighborhood Carrie had found on one of her many T-shirt hunts. It was the perfect place to sightsee and get a little exercise away from the crowds and the noise.

"Wow! Look at that one!" Akhtar said, rushing up to the gates of an impressive brick mansion. All the kids grabbed on to the iron bars and pressed their faces up to the openings. "I bet a prince lives there!"

"And the princess is kept in that room at the top," Asha said, pointing to a high window. "Just like in all the stories."

"Maybe it's a princess's house and she keeps the *prince* up there," Manisha said huffily.

Carrie laughed and patted Manisha's head. "I like the way you think."

Manisha beamed and they continued on their walk. Trina and Asha stuck to Carrie's sides like a pair of handbags, while Dash and Akhtar walked a few paces ahead, talking and laughing in that mischievous way boys of their age often did. Manisha brought up the rear, pausing every so often to study another of the amazing houses.

"A basketball man lives here," Asha announced suddenly, pausing at the end of one of the wide driveways.

"What do you mean, a basketball man?" Carrie asked.

"He plays for the Olympic team," Dash told her. "Thinks he's all that."

"He is all that," Akhtar said. "He has the honor of representing our country."

"Wealthy git is what he is," Dash replied, spitting on the ground.

The house was huge and made of white stucco with a red, Spanish-tiled roof like the houses in Carmel back home. Beautiful flowers burst from the window boxes, and the drive was lined with hundreds and hundreds of bright yellow marigolds. The flower beds ran all the way out, past the gate and along the sidewalk in front of Carrie.

"How do you guys know he lives here?" Carrie asked.

"Everyone knows," Manisha said with a shrug. She leaned back against one of the pillars that held the gate. "He's famous."

Asha bent down, plucked one of the marigolds from the flower bed, and held it under her nose.

"Asha! Don't do that!" Trina scolded.

"Why? I like them," Asha said, bending to pick another.

"Asha, Trina's right. They don't belong to us," Carrie said.

"So what? Let her have them. He has enough of them," Dash said, leaning down and plucking a few more. He handed them to Asha, whose entire face lit up at the size of her new bouquet.

"Can I put them by my bed, Miss Carrie?" Asha asked.

"Okay, sure," Carrie said, glancing up at the house and half expecting to see an angry face staring out at them. "Let's get going."

"Wait! I want some too," Manisha said, bending to pluck a few flowers for herself. Dash knelt down to help her and in about five seconds had cleared a space about one foot square.

"Dash! What are you doing?" Carrie hissed, dropping to her knees.

"If Asha and Manisha have flowers, then they're all going to want flowers," Dash said. "Trust me. They're girls."

Dash and Manisha started to fill her bag up with flowers. Trina tucked a bloom behind her ear and Akhtar started to make a chain by tying the stems together.

"I like that one!" Asha said, pointing to a flower Manisha was holding, yellow and fringed with orange petals.

"I'll trade you for that one," Manisha said, taking a light yellow bloom from Asha's bouquet.

Carrie knew she should stop them, but they were having so much fun. She looked up at the house, her heart pounding as the kids laughed and plucked and traded. The place looked deserted enough. And Carrie was sure that the basketball man, whoever he was, wouldn't mind losing a few flowers if he saw the joy this little gardening break was inspiring.

"You guys, let's only take them from the edges so it's

not so noticeable," Carrie said, getting into the act. "We'll decorate the girls' ward with them. The place could use some brightening up anyway."

Too bad Dee's not here, Carrie thought as Manisha passed her a handful of flowers and she deposited them into her bag. This was exactly the kind of rush she'd been talking about, exactly the kind of rule breaking he needed to do. Harmless enough, but thrilling all the same.

Carrie set the last glass of flowers on the windowsill and stepped back to admire her work. Marigolds bloomed from every available surface in the room, adorning not only the three large windows, but the tables between the beds and the dressers at either end of the room. The color and life changed the entire feeling of the ward, making it more welcoming and definitely more cheery. Maybe there really was something to the whole feng shui thing. Carrie would have to look into that before the new school year started back home.

She heard Dee's footsteps in the hall and turned just in time to see him walk in.

"The girls told me you had something to show— whoa," he said, stopping in the middle of the room.

"We pulled a little Martha Stewart," Carrie said, grinning as she executed a curtsy.

"Where did all these flowers come from?" Dee asked.

"Just a little creative gardening," Carrie said with a conspiratorial smirk.

Dee took a few steps toward her, bringing a distinctly unpleasant vibe with him. He looked tense, as if he were waiting for Leatherface to jump out of a corner and hack them all to pieces with a chain saw.

"Carrie, what does that mean, creative gardening?" he asked.

"Well, the kids and I were out for a walk today and we . . . borrowed a few flowers from one of those immense mansions a few blocks up."

"Oh, Carrie. Tell me you didn't," Dee said, covering his face with his hands.

A hard rock of disappointment formed in Carrie's stomach. She knew that taking the flowers was technically wrong, but in the grand scheme of things it had made the kids happy. She had hoped Dee might see it her way. Clearly he did not.

"Look, it's not that big of a deal," Carrie said. "It's not like he's going to miss them. His landscaper will probably have them replaced before he ever even notices they're gone."

"That's not the point, Carrie!" Dee exclaimed. "Do you realize what you did today? You taught those kids it's okay to steal."

Carrie's face flushed. There was no denying that they had taken something that didn't belong to them. But it wasn't as if they had all run out into the streets with crowbars and committed grand theft auto. She looked at Dee, at the disappointment and condescension in his eyes, and a flame of indignation ignited in her chest. Who was he to judge her?

"It's just a few flowers, *Dee,*" Carrie said. "Why are you freaking out like this?"

Dee took a deep breath and glared at her. "Is this what you meant last night by breaking the rules? Did you all get that rush you were talking about by doing something bad?"

Carrie looked at the floor. When he said it like that, it sounded perfectly awful.

"You did, didn't you?" he said. "I bet you all had a grand time! How are we supposed to teach them now that it's wrong?"

Oh, crap. What did I do? Carrie thought, his words sinking in.

"I'm sure they know that stealing, *real* stealing, is bad," she said softly.

"How? Kids are impressionable, you know. They watch you do something like this and they think . . . no, they *know* that it's acceptable," Dee said. "And what do you mean *real* stealing? Is there some size requirement I don't know about? Like stealing is okay as long as whatever you take is smaller than a TV?"

"Well, there are degrees of stealing in the States. The values of the items stolen is the difference between a misdemeanor and a felony," Carrie countered, thanks to hours of watching Court TV.

"Exactly, but either way it's still crime," Dee asked, folding his arms over his chest.

At that moment Carrie had no idea what else to say. A lump formed in her throat. Had she really just scarred Manisha and Dash and the others for life? She had a sudden vision of them as teenagers, running around in black leather jackets with cigarettes hanging out of their mouths, throwing gang signs, and wreaking havoc on the streets of Calcutta. All because of her.

"I'm sorry," Carrie said finally. "I just . . . I thought it would cheer the place up."

"What am I going to tell Mr. Banarjee?" Dee asked, tipping his head back.

At the sound of the director's name a sliver of dread ran through Carrie's heart. If this was the way Dee was reacting, then it was quite possible that Mr. Banarjee would throw her out on the street. He definitely wasn't the most laid-back guy on earth. "Why do you have to tell him anything?" she asked.

"He's going to find out. He always finds out," Dee said with a foul expression.

The stark contrast between the expression on his face now and the admiration he had heaped upon her the night before sent Carrie into a tailspin. She wanted last night back. She wanted that Dee back. She needed him. Plus the last thing she wanted was to be forced to leave and say good-bye to the kids and the friends she had made here. Carrie swallowed her pride and started grasping at straws.

"I'm sorry, all right?" she said, lifting the last glass of flowers off the windowsill. "We'll get rid of them."

"That's not the point," Dee said. "The damage is already done."

"Well, what do you want me to do?" she asked. "I'll . . . I'll talk to the kids. I'll explain that stealing is wrong. I'll—"

"You don't get it, Carrie," Dee said, pacing now. "It's not just this. It's everything. You act like playing basketball and teaching them about fashion is going to help them, but it's not. It's not going to help them get anywhere in the world. And the one time you were asked to do something semi-responsible, you took them out to play again. It's like you think this is circus camp, not real life."

There was nothing inside Carrie but a roiling mess of confused emotions. Was this how Dee really felt about her? That she hadn't contributed one useful thing since she had arrived here?

"Well, if that's what you think of me, then maybe I should save Mr. Banarjee the chore of firing me and just go," Carrie said, her voice breaking.

Oh my God, I can't believe this is happening, she told herself.

For a split second she thought she saw uncertainty in Dee's eyes. She thought he was going to grab her and apologize and tell her they would figure something out. But a moment later he blinked and it was gone. His gaze was completely blank when he said:

"Yes. Maybe you should."

"Why do you have to leave?" Manisha asked for the twenty-fifth time, pulling on Carrie's arm as she stood in the foyer, looking out at the rain. Dash and Akhtar hung off to the side, arms crossed tightly over their chests. Dash kicked at the floor while Akhtar stood still. "Is it our fault?" Manisha asked. "Because we took the flowers?"

Carrie looked up through the window, guilt searing her heart. The clouds were thick as mud. No one would be watching the gorgeous sunset tonight.

"Manisha, none of this is your fault," Carrie told her. "I just . . . I have to go home."

Carrie's voice broke on the word *home* and she was at a loss as to whether it was because she was homesick or because she didn't want to leave yet. Just looking at the dejected faces on these kids—her friends—was making her chest ache. She glanced out at the road, looking for the telltale auto-rickshaw. Celia had promised to come get her at six o'clock sharp. Where was she? Carrie had to get out of here. She couldn't take much more of this long good-bye stuff.

"Don't leave, Carrie," Dash said. "Dee is not your boss."

"No, but Mr. Banarjee is," Carrie said. "And I don't think he really wants me around right now."

"But what if we do?" Akhtar said quietly. "What if we want you around?"

Carrie's eyes welled up with tears, but luckily she was saved by the toy-like engine of an auto-rickshaw pulling up outside. It idled at the curb and Carrie could see Celia inside, huddled away from the open doors, avoiding the rain. Carrie had never been so relieved to see anyone in her life.

"Well, that's my ride," Carrie said. "'Bye, kids."

She reached down to give Manisha a hug. Akhtar simply gave her a quick bow, then turned and ran up the stairs. Carrie couldn't believe how attached these kids had become to her and how much she was attached to them.

"He can't handle anything," Dash said, lifting a shoulder. Then, playing the tough guy, he reached out and slapped Carrie's hand. "See you."

As Dash walked up the stairs, Dee passed him on his way down. Carrie couldn't read his expression to save her life. He might have been sorry for the argument, but he might have just as easily been sorry to find her still there.

Heart heavy, Carrie reached for her umbrella. Out of habit she was going to step outside, then open it, but she paused. Fear and excitement gripped her chest all at once. She could do it. She had to prove to Dee that she wasn't some little idiot consumed by ridiculous fears. No matter how much of a jerk he had been. Carrie was going to be the bigger person.

She looked at Dee over her shoulder and popped open the umbrella, effectively blocking him from view, but not before she saw the stunned look on his face. Then, exhilarated by her outright defiance of everything she believed in for so long, she grabbed up her bags and strode out the door.

It would have been a perfectly elegant exit if Manisha didn't follow her out into the rain.

"Don't go," she said, her eyes brimming with tears.

"I have to," Carrie replied as the rain pounded on the umbrella. "But I'll write to you. I promise."

"You won't. You'll forget," Manisha said sorrowfully, looking at the ground.

"Hey. I don't forget my friends," Carrie said, putting her stuff down and crouching in front of Manisha as rain ran down the little girl's cheeks. "You're the best friend I've got in this place."

Manisha's whole face lit up and she threw her skinny arms around Carrie's neck again, hugging her for real. Finally Carrie had to pull away. She gathered her stuff and got into the auto-rickshaw, blinking back her tears.

"Hey, Carrie," Celia said sympathetically.

"Hey," she replied.

The engine started up and Carrie was jerked backward as it careened forward.

"'Bye, Carrie!" Manisha shouted after her. "'Bye!"

The raindrops smacked at the windshield, and Carrie's tears started to fall. Celia reached over and squeezed her shoulder comfortingly, but it wasn't enough to close up the floodgates. Carrie cried all the way back to the hostel.

Chapter Fourteen

Carrie was exhausted. Her whole body felt weak. Her eyes were heavy and dry. As she looked blankly out the window of the lurching bus, she couldn't imagine sitting through the entire flight back home. It felt as if she would never get there. San Francisco existed in an entirely separate reality.

There hadn't been much sleep for Carrie the night before. Her eyes had refused to close as her mind raced from place to place. She kept seeing Dee's hard and disappointed eyes. Manisha's sorrowful face. One minute she was wishing she had never stepped foot in CCS, the next she was wishing she was back there. She went from feeling indignant about the way Dee had reacted to the flowers to painfully guilty about the fact that she had encouraged the kids to take them. No matter how many times she resolved not to think about it anymore and to get some sleep, her eyes always ended up popping open again. Meanwhile Doreen had snored the night away in the next bed, effectively frustrating Carrie to the point of throwing her pillow at the girl. Repeatedly. She didn't wake up once.

In the midst of all the random stream of consciousness, one thought kept coming back to Carrie over and over again like a mantra. She was going home without her T-shirt and nothing was ever going to be the same again. Not only that, but it felt as if she was leaving a part of her father behind.

Great, now the floodgates are open, Carrie thought.

In her mind's eye she began to imagine herself calling her father when she got back home. She saw herself telling him how much it hurt when he blew her off and that she wanted to see him more often. Then the mental film reel flipped to a classic scene—her dad getting off the plane, dropping his bags, and opening his arms so that Carrie could run right into them. Then he'd hug her and tell her she was the most important person in his life and he would never again let her feel otherwise.

Then her thoughts trailed off into Dee-ville. He was, after all, the one who had put the idea of coming clean with her father into her head. If the whole thing worked out, she would owe it to Dee.

Not that he would even care. He probably hated her now.

Carrie glanced out the window and gasped. Her

hands pressed up against the dusty pane of glass. Her entire mouth went dry. She couldn't be seeing what she thought she was seeing. It had to be a mirage—a hallucination brought on by insomnia and Doreen's buzz saw snoring. But she couldn't take the chance.

"Stop the bus!" she shouted, jumping straight up and slamming her head into the overhead rack. Her skull exploded with pain, but she barely noticed. "Stop! Please!"

She stepped over the knees of the woman sitting next to her, whacking the poor lady in the face with her backpack. The bus stopped the second Carrie got into the aisle, throwing her forward a few feet. Angry passengers all around her grumbled and shot her dirty looks.

Checking out the window to make sure the hallucination was still there, Carrie reached up and yanked her bags out from the shelf above. Grasping everything in both hands, she tottered down the aisle as quickly as possible, thanked the bus driver, and tripped into the street. As she picked herself up and dusted herself off, she stared at the little woman standing on the corner, holding a red moped by its handlebars.

The woman with the birthmark and the nose ring. The woman who had almost run her down with her lucky T.

She knows where my T-shirt is, Carrie thought wildly. *She's the only person who knows!*

"Hey! Moped lady!" Carrie shouted, hoofing it over

to the woman just as the walk light started flashing and the crowd on the corner moved forward as one. "Hey, you! With the bike!"

The woman didn't seem to hear her. She pushed her moped forward, disappearing into the throng, but Carrie wasn't going to let her go this time. She adjusted the straps on her bags and dove into the melee.

Please just don't let her get on that bike, Carrie thought desperately. *If she does, it's all over.*

At the far corner the crowd broke up, some heading toward the shops up ahead, others veering off in various directions. Finally Carrie caught sight of the moped woman again. She was preparing to fire up the engine.

"Step away from the moped! Please!" Carrie shouted, near tears.

But the woman just kept going about her business and sped off. Carrie didn't have to think twice. She took a deep breath and started to run.

With her bags slapping against her thighs and back, Carrie ran as she had never run before. As her feet slammed against the pavement, she dodged a vendor selling sweetmeats from his cart, jumped over a pile of cow dung, and skidded past a group of children playing marbles near a stoop. Her breath became labored and her brow and armpits started to sweat, but she refused to slow down or stop. She was not going to lose her T-shirt. Not this time.

Up ahead, the moped turned into an alleyway,

Carrie's heart plummeted at the thought of the woman disappearing again, and then it happened. A wheelbarrow full of coconuts appeared out of nowhere and Carrie's momentum was too great. She tried to pull up, but she couldn't. She slammed into the side of the cart and fell to the ground. Her bags went flying. Her shin exploded with pain.

The man with the wheelbarrow yelped something in a foreign language and knelt on the ground next to her.

"I did not see you," he said in clipped English. "I am so sorry. I did not see you until you were on the ground. You are cut very badly."

"No! I'm fine. I'm fine!" Carrie said, tears squeezing their way out even as she protested. There was blood everywhere, but Carrie barely reacted. All she could think about was that she was going to lose her lucky T. *Again.*

"We need some help!" the man shouted. He held his hands to the top of his turban and turned around and around. "Anybody? This girl needs help!"

A small crowd quickly formed around Carrie, and she felt someone grab her under the arm to help her up.

"We'll get you to a doctor. Don't worry," a woman's voice said in her ear. "Can you put any weight on it?"

"I don't know." Carrie sniffled. She touched her toe to the ground and winced, but when she tried again, the pain was a little duller.

"Good," the woman said. "We'll just get you inside."

"Thanks," Carrie said, limping along. She looked up at her nursemaid for the first time. Her mouth dropped open and she almost fainted dead away. "Moped Lady," she said under her breath.

The woman stopped and her whole face creased in confusion. Then she clearly recognized Carrie. "You're that *gehra* from the other night. The one I almost killed!" she said.

Carrie looked up at the building they were shuffling into. A sign above the door read *Calcutta Women's Mission*. She was here. The last shelter on her list.

Fifteen minutes later Carrie was clean and bandaged, sitting on the edge of a chair in the Calcutta Women's Mission office, and Moped Lady, whose name turned out to be Payal, was looking at her with an amazed sort of gleam in her dark eyes.

"So you've come all this way, and you were about to give up, when you saw me?" Payal said, lifting her chin from her hand.

"Yup."

"And you jumped off the bus and chased me with all your stuff and ripped up your leg . . . and all this for a T-shirt?"

"Yup."

"Wow," Payal said, shaking her head and blowing out a breath. "You Americans are even crazier than I thought."

Carrie would have laughed, but she was too wrought

with suspense. "So, do you know where my T-shirt is?"

Payal raised her eyebrows. "Actually, I know exactly where it is."

"You do?" Carrie gasped. "Where?"

"I just gave it to someone this morning," Payal said. "Her name's Deena. She's ten years old and she's living here with her mother."

"She's here?" Carrie said, her throat going dry. "Here in this building? Now?"

"Yes. But I have to tell you, I don't know if I like the idea of you taking that shirt back, however far you've come," Payal said. "Deena and her mother have no place else to go. . . no income to speak of. She needs clothes." Payal cast a glance at Carrie's suitcase and backpack, which now stood along the wall of the office. "And from the look of things, you don't."

Carrie swallowed hard. She knew what she was asking sounded ridiculous, and she didn't expect Payal or anyone else to understand, but she needed that shirt. She needed its luck. If the last twenty-four hours were any indication, there was no way she could survive without it.

"I'll give her everything in my suitcase, Payal," Carrie said, leaning forward and looking the woman in the eye so that she wouldn't mistake how serious she was. "All of it."

Payal was clearly impressed. She sat back in her chair and looked Carrie over. "All right," she said. "But you're going to have to ask her yourself."

Carrie followed Payal up a rickety set of metal stairs and over to a door marked #2. She could barely contain her excitement as Payal rapped on the door. Inside that room was Carrie's T-shirt. It was right behind that panel of wood.

The door creaked open and Carrie looked down. There, staring up at her with big brown eyes, was a little girl with two black braids and one seriously nasty bruise on her right cheek. She was wearing the lucky T. Carrie's birthday wish had come true.

"Hi, Payal!" the girl said brightly.

"Hi, Deena. This is my friend Carrie. May we come in?" Payal asked.

"Yes, you may," Deena said politely.

She left the door open and walked back into the room. Carrie stepped inside, the floor creaking beneath her, and looked around. The room was small, about ten feet by ten feet, with one window in the center of the back wall. Two mattresses were laid out on the floor, each with a sheet and a small pillow. Stacked against the wall were a couple of meager piles of clothes and a hot plate was plugged into the one outlet. A pan on top of it held a few mounds of rice, cooked and now congealing at the surface.

"Where's your mum?" Payal asked.

"She went out," Deena said, sitting down on one of the mattresses and picking up a ratty-looking teddy bear.

"How did she get that bruise?" Carrie whispered.

"Her uncle was beating them both," Payal replied, turning her back to Deena and lowering her voice. "The father's dead and the uncle took them in. It took her mother three years to get up the courage to leave. They ended up here."

Carrie felt as if she was going to be sick. Suddenly she began to contemplate how she must look to Payal and what Dee must have thought of her once he found out she was in India to find a T-shirt. She probably came off as an overprivileged, spoiled, sheltered girl who knew nothing about the world around her. Carrie had taken all the blessings of her life for granted for so long—long enough that she had come to believe her only *real* blessing was the lucky T. And while there had been lots of moments this summer that had made her second-guess her superstition, she knew now that she was truly leading a charmed life. T-shirt or no, she had a mom who loved and respected her. She had a father, however absent he was, who cared about her well-being. She had good friends, a beautiful home, a great school, and as much food as she needed. She had so many clothes that she was able to give some away because she no longer needed them.

Two months ago Carrie had been unable to see any of this. Two weeks ago Dee's assessment of her had been right on. But standing there, in the middle of that tiny room with Deena and Payal, it was all too clear. Carrie Fitzgerald was not that person anymore.

"Deena? Carrie has something she wants to ask you," Payal said.

Deena looked up at Carrie as she shakily walked over and sat down next to her on the cot. She was aware that Deena could use all the clothes in her suitcase—that a lot of people would look at the proposed transaction as more than a fair trade. But Carrie knew better. She knew what Deena really needed—hope.

"What did you want to ask me?" Deena asked, her eyes wide.

Carrie swallowed back a lump in her throat and smiled. "I wanted to ask you . . . if you knew . . . that the shirt you're wearing is going to bring you all kinds of luck."

"It's Carrie! Carrie's back!"

Asha's voice sounded out the alarm as Carrie walked up the steps at CCS, her chin held high. Thanks to another quick but effective dousing from the rain gods, she was soaked to the bone. Dash opened the door for her and she swept through, feeling very Katharine Hepburn. Then all the kids rushed in from the lounge area and crowded around her.

"Hey, everyone," Carrie said while dropping her bags. Her shoulders let out a long overdue sigh of relief.

"What are you doing here?" Akhtar asked.

"Are you back to stay?" Manisha demanded.

Dash simply picked up her bags and started upstairs with them, clearly not wanting to risk it.

Just then Dee walked in to see what all the commotion was about. Seeing him brought up a zillion emotions for Carrie—many of them stemmed from the fact that he always looked smoking hot and none of which she felt capable of dealing with at the moment. She was here for a reason and one reason only.

"Hey," Dee said gruffly. Yep, he was still pretty angry.

"Hello," Carrie replied coolly. "Excuse me."

She passed right by him, noticed how he smelled like he'd come right out of a shower, thought about Dee all wet and soapy, and walked right to the back of the house. The door to Mr. Banarjee's office was closed. Carrie took in a deep breath and knocked on the door.

"Come," Mr. Banarjee said.

Here goes nothing, Carrie thought. She opened the door and stepped inside.

"Miss Fitzgerald," the director said, looking up from some papers on his desk. "I'm surprised to see you."

"Not as surprised as I am to be here," Carrie said.

She wiped her hands on her wet jean skirt as she walked farther into the room. It was her first time in Mr. Banarjee's office. A few shelves of books lined the walls, where the only decorations were framed paintings of Mahatma Gandhi and Mother Teresa—two of Calcutta's biggest heroes. His desk was neat as a pin and the shade was drawn over the single window.

"I know Dee told you what happened," Carrie said. "And I know . . . I was wrong. But I'm here to tell you that I think I have a way to make it up to you and the kids, if you'll let me."

Mr. Banarjee sat in silence for a moment and Carrie was really hoping he wouldn't toss her out on her butt. What was Celia going to say when she called and told her she was not, in fact, on a plane and that she needed another extraction from CCS?

Finally Mr. Banarjee removed his small reading glasses and folded them in both hands. He blew out a breath and looked at her.

"What did you have in mind?"

The next day was warm and sunny with white clouds zipping high across the sky. A perfect day for a little gardening.

Carrie sat between Akhtar and Trina, digging little troughs in the lush dirt for the marigold seeds Carrie had bought with the last of her spending money on her way back from her visit with Deena. On the other side of the entrance to the driveway Dash, Manisha, and Asha were patting seeds into the ground. Carrie smiled as she watched them work. It felt good to be teaching them a lesson, especially since she had learned so much from being in their country.

"I still do not understand," Dash said as he moved some dirt around with his spade. "One day we take the flowers, the next day we plant the flowers?"

"I already explained this to you," Carrie said, smirking.

"We made a mistake and this is how we're making up for it. We never should have taken the flowers in the first place."

"But you helped us do it," Trina pointed out.

"Yes, and it was wrong," Carrie replied, amused at how long it was taking for all of this to sink in. "The flowers were never ours to take. They belonged to someone else and you should always respect the property of others."

"Listen to her, kids, she speaks the truth," a new voice proclaimed.

Carrie and the others looked up to find Vijay Shah, the kind older man who had answered the door to them that morning, hovering above them. Mr. Shah was short and stout with graying hair just above his ears and an otherwise bald head. Dressed in khaki pants and a polo shirt, he looked as if he'd just stepped off a golf course. He held out a tray with a pitcher full of whitish juice and a bunch of plastic cups.

Carrie smiled up at him. Mr. Shah had been extremely understanding and kind when she had explained the situation to him that morning.

"I brought you some sugarcane juice," he said.

The kids all jumped up as if he had just offered them chocolate. Carrie slapped her hands against her jeans and got up to help.

"Thank you," she said, lifting the pitcher as all the kids grabbed cups. "You didn't have to do this."

"And likewise, all this is not necessary," Mr. Shah said, looking around at the flower beds.

"No, it is," she told him as she poured out the juice for the kids. "We did something wrong and we want to repay you. Right, kids?"

"Yeah," Dash said, slurping up his drink.

"Sheesh! What *is* that stuff?" Carrie asked as the kids all chugged it and licked their lips. *Whatever it is, it can't be better than Yoo-Hoo, can it?*

"Have you never had sugarcane juice?" Mr. Shah asked.

"No," Carrie replied.

"Oh, then you must try it. It is the sweetest nectar on earth," he told her.

Carrie looked down into the empty pitcher and shrugged.

"No nectar for me," she joked.

"Come inside," Mr. Shah told her. "We will get more."

"Okay. Thanks," Carrie said. "You guys keep working. I'll be right back."

The kids returned to their flower beds with renewed energy. Either the sugarcane juice was magical or it had enough sugar in it to send a small horse into insulin shock. Whatever the case might be, it was all good to Carrie.

"So, tell me more about this CCS you came from," Mr. Shah said as they walked up the long, wide drive.

"It sounds awful, but I don't know much about how it all works—like where they get their funds or anything,"

Carrie said. "What I do know is that the place is run perfectly. The kids take classes with this amazing woman and there's a lot of studying and drawing and sports. It's a great place to work."

"I assume they take donations?" Mr. Shah said.

"I guess," Carrie said. "Why?"

"I would like to make one," Mr. Shah told her as they reached the front door of the house. "You impressed me when you came to my door this morning. Not many people would admit to doing wrong. I would like to support a place that teaches such values."

"Wow. Even though we trashed the place first, then offered to clean it up?" Carrie asked.

"Everyone makes mistakes, Miss Fitzgerald," he said with a small smile. "Not everyone tries to correct them."

Carrie grinned as he opened the door for her. She was so glad that everything was working out. Well, almost everything.

"Whoa," she said as she stepped inside. A cool blast of air hit her like a bolt of lightning. "Do you have *air conditioning?*"

"A guilty pleasure, I'm afraid," he said with a laugh. "You know, it is nice having people around the house again. My children have all moved out."

"That's right," Carrie said, suddenly remembering. "Is one of your sons a basketball player?"

Mr. Shah led Carrie through a plushly decorated living room with colorful pillows and couches strewn everywhere. Deep rugs lined the marble floor and a gilded frame hung over a massive fireplace, holding a painting of one of the Hindu gods. It was a beautiful home, and once again she was struck by the stark differences between this place and the orphanage just blocks away.

"Yes. My youngest, Kunal, is on the India Olympic team," Mr. Shah said, visibly brightening. "We are very proud of him."

They walked into the kitchen together, a huge, bright room with marble countertops and a double oven that her mother would have salivated over.

"Do you like basketball?" Mr. Shah asked as he opened the refrigerator.

"I'm on my team back home and I've been teaching the kids at the shelter," Carrie told him. "They love it."

"I should tell Kunal to stop by when he is in town next," Mr. Shah said. "I am sure he would be happy to play with the kids."

"Really?" Carrie said. "They would *love* that. Is he going to be home soon?"

"Yes. In fact, the whole team will be in Calcutta for some press events the week after next," he said, pouring out a glass of juice for her from another pitcher.

Carrie took the glass when he held it toward her. Some part of her brain knew she should be thanking him, but it was too busy wildly formulating a plan. The entire India Olympic basketball team would be in town in just two weeks? That would put them here just before she had to leave to go home and give her just enough time to pull off the coolest event in the history of cool events.

"Mr. Shah, you know how you said you wanted to support the shelter?" Carrie said. "What if I had an idea of how you could help them in an even bigger way? Maybe more than anybody else has ever done before."

Mr. Shah raised his eyebrows, intrigued, and smiled. "I would say, tell me all about it."

Chapter Fifteen

"Come on, Dash! Pass it! Pass! You can get around him! He's not that big!" Carrie yelled, earning a round of laughter from the spectators behind her. Out on the gleaming court of the St. Xavier College gymnasium, Dash expertly passed the ball by Vijay's son Kunal, who was at least four times his size, right into the waiting hands of Trina, who turned and took the shot. One of Kunal's teammates made a lunge for the ball, but he was too late. It bounced off the backboard and through the hoop.

"Woo-hoo!" Carrie cheered, laughing over the antics of the Olympic team as they all hung their heads. Obviously they were letting the CCS kids win, but they were doing a great job of faking an effort.

Trina and Manisha slapped hands, then rushed down the court to get on defense. The ball was passed to Em Siddiqui, the tallest guy on the Olympic team. As he jogged up court to take his shot, Dash jumped to knock the ball away and ended up tripping into Em's side. Once he was there, Dash seemed to think this was a good defensive strategy and just held on, pressing the side of his face into Em's hip and letting his feet drag.

"Dash! What're you doing!? This isn't tackle football!" Carrie cried.

Em laughed and struggled toward the basket. Then Akhtar and Shiva joined Dash, all of them hanging on to Em around the waist. The audience applauded and cheered as Em continued to crack up laughing, lifting the ball toward the basket. Finally, with all the weight on him, he tripped and the ball bounced away. Shiva instantly let go, grabbed up the ball, and raced for the basket on the other end. He was so tiny that none of his shots had gone anywhere near the hoop all night. But his face was so determined—his lips pressed together, his eyes wide—that Carrie was sure he was going to make this shot.

When Shiva was a few feet from the hoop, Kunal suddenly scooped the little boy up from behind and held him above his head. If Shiva was surprised, he didn't show it. He simply dropped the ball through the hoop and raised his arms in triumph. Just then the buzzer went off, sounding the end of the game. Carrie instinctively glanced at the scoreboard as everyone in the jam-packed stands jumped to their feet, applauding the win of the CCS kids, 44–30, over the India Olympic team.

"Yeah!" Carrie shouted, clapping as hard as she could as the kids and their heroes high-fived and hugged in the center of the court. She glanced to the corner and saw Mr. Banarjee happily shaking hands with Mr. Shah. Thanks to the older man's help, the charity game between CCS and the pride of Indian basketball had been highly publicized in all the right circles. Mr. Shah had persuaded all his friends to buy tickets for their families and word had spread like wildfire. The turnout had been even larger than they had expected and Carrie couldn't help beaming with pride. It was hard to believe she and Mr. Shah had come together to organize the biggest fund-raiser in CCS history.

If I had never gone back to apologize, none of this would have happened, she thought, glancing behind her at Dee, who was sitting halfway up the stands with the other staff members, Doreen, and Celia. He smiled slightly and she smiled back. It was the most civil contact between them in the two weeks since she had strode back into CCS. They had both been avoiding contact with each other. Carrie had tried to get up the nerve to reach out to Dee, but every time she chickened out. There was only one day left, though. If she didn't mend fences with him soon, she might never have the chance.

The kids ran over to Carrie and started shouting.

"We did it, Miss Carrie! We kicked their butts!" Akhtar announced.

"Yes, you did! You guys were amazing," she told them, ruffling Shiva's hair.

"We know," Dash said, puffing his chest out slightly.

"Well, I'm really proud of all of you," Carrie said, looking into each of their smiling faces. She couldn't believe she was going to have to say good-bye to them the very next day, this time for real. But at least she would leave knowing for sure she had done something good here.

She caught a glimpse of Mr. Banarjee walking toward her and stood up straight. Over the last two weeks she and the CCS director had worked together a lot and she had come to realize that he was actually pretty cool, even if he was a little strict. The one thing that was clear was that he cared about these kids more than anything in the world.

"Congratulations, Miss Fitzgerald," he said with a little bow. "We have raised more money tonight than CCS normally sees in a year."

"Whoa," Trina said.

"I second that whoa," Carrie replied. "Really?"

"Yes. I thank you from the bottom of my heart for all your hard work," Mr. Banarjee said. "And so do the children, right, kids?"

"Yeah!" the basketball team cheered, causing Carrie's heart to swell.

There was a sudden peal of feedback from a microphone and then Mr. Shah's voice filled the gym.

"On behalf of my son Kunal and the entire Olympic team, we would like to thank the children of CCS for putting on such a competitive game this evening," he said.

Again the room rang with applause and the kids all stood up a little bit straighter.

"Because of the amazing attendance for tonight's event, Mr. Lalit Banarjee and I have decided to make this game a yearly tradition to benefit CCS," Mr. Shah continued, smiling at Carrie. "So everyone make sure to come back next year. We promise another great match."

Carrie grinned as Mr. Shah and Kunal came over to shake her hand. They were trailed by a few reporters with notepads and tape recorders and a bunch of photographers as well.

"May we take your photograph with your team?" a woman in a purple sari asked, holding up a digital camera. "It's for the *Times* of India."

"Oh, okay," Carrie said, flustered. "Kids! Let's line up for a team picture!"

She and Mr. Banarjee got all the kids in line and Carrie stood at the center in the back, one hand on Dash's shoulder, the other on Trina's. As she grinned for the camera and flashes exploded all around, Carrie really did feel like part of the team. And she had just recorded the biggest win of her life.

Carrie was packing her things that evening in her small bedroom. She was jittery with nerves. In less than two days she would be home and would have to deal with things she had put off thinking about for weeks. Like reuniting with Piper. The whole thing with Jason felt as if it had happened a million years ago. And the less Jason mattered, the more Carrie realized she had been way too hard on her best friend. Now all she could do was hope Piper would be open to seeing her, even though Carrie had never written her back. She had started a few letters, but crumpled each one of them up after writing a few paragraphs. Nothing she wrote seemed to be able to convey how sorry she was for being so cold.

What if things between Piper and me have changed forever? Carrie wondered, her stomach twisting up into a huge knot.

She shook her head and cleared her throat, folding clothes a little more vigorously. There was no use obsessing about it until she was standing in front of Piper, asking if they could put everything behind them.

Manisha knocked on the door, effectively snapping Carrie into the present. She hung back tentatively with Asha and Trina behind her, as if Carrie had some sort of contagious illness and they weren't sure whether it was safe to enter.

"I'm not dying," Carrie said with a laugh, remembering the stupid antics with Doreen. "I'm just going back to America. Come in."

The girls stepped into the room, followed by Dash and Akhtar. All of them looked solemn but somehow excited at the same time. Carrie sensed something was up and then noticed that Manisha had both hands behind her back. This was strange. The girl talked with her hands more than Carrie's aunt Rosalene, the most Italian of the Italian side of her family.

"What's going on?" Carrie asked, narrowing her eyes.

"We got you a going-away present," Dash told her.

"Hope you like it!" Asha put in.

"How sweet! What is it?" Carrie asked, looking at the little line of kids. "Are you going to sing for me or something?"

"No, it's this," Trina said.

She pulled on Manisha's arm, revealing the delicate necklace that hung from the little girl's fingers. It was made of tiny brown and gold beads with one silver medallion hanging in the center.

"Oh, wow," Carrie said, sitting down on the edge of her bed. Manisha placed the necklace reverently in her hands. "It's so pretty."

"We made it!" Asha said proudly.

"You did?" Carrie asked.

"Miss Ruma helped," Dash said. "And Dee bought the beads for us."

Carrie raised her eyebrows in fascination. *He was a part of this? Interesting . . .*

"But I picked out the medallion," Manisha told her.

Carrie lifted the silver disk and studied it for the first time. Etched into the surface was a primitive picture of a human baby with an elephant's head. The creature was vaguely familiar to Carrie, but she couldn't place where she had seen it before.

"Who's this?" she asked.

"That is Ganesha. He is the god who removes all obstacles," Akhtar told Carrie. "We call on him to bless all our important events."

"Like if someone's being born," Trina said.

"Or if someone's getting married," Dash put in.

"Or if someone's going on a trip," Asha said. "Like you."

"He is good luck for us," Manisha told Carrie, reaching out and touching the medallion with the tip of her finger. Then she touched the same finger to Carrie's forehead. "He will be good luck for you."

"Even though he's not a T-shirt," Akhtar said.

Carrie was so touched she barely knew what to say. So she told the simple truth.

"You know what? I'm glad I lost that T-shirt."

"You *are?*" Asha said, her mouth dropping open. "But it's your luck!"

"It was," Carrie said. "But if I hadn't lost it, I never would have met any of you."

The kids all smiled at one another and Carrie held the necklace out to Manisha. "Will you help me put it on?" she asked.

Manisha undid the tiny clasp and Carrie turned her back to the kids, lifting her hair up so Manisha could fasten the necklace around her neck. When she stood up to look in the mirror, all the kids watched her proudly. Carrie smiled at her reflection and laid her hand over the medallion, taking a long, deep breath. She looked at Dash, Akhtar, Manisha, Trina, and Asha in the mirror and grinned. Carrie had been blessed with a lot of luck that summer, both good and bad, and the result of it all was— she was happy. She turned around, crouched down, and wrapped her friends up in one big group hug.

"You really like it?" Akhtar asked.

Carrie squeezed her eyes closed to keep from crying. "I've never loved any gift more."

That night after lights-out, Carrie found Dee standing on the balcony, leaning against the wrought-iron rail. He was wearing a pair of long cargo shorts, a dark blue T-shirt, and the Birkenstocks that she'd seen him walk in all summer. She closed the door behind her and he turned around. His surprise was written all over his unbelievably gorgeous face.

"Hey," Carrie said.

"Hey," he replied.

She took a few steps across the balcony, pushing her hands into the pockets of her lemon-colored capri pants. Now that she was here, she had no idea where to begin.

"How do you like the necklace?" Dee asked, breaking the silence.

"It's beautiful," Carrie said, happy just to be talking. "Was it your idea?"

"No, actually," Dee said. "The kids came up with it all on their own. They really adore you, Carrie."

Carrie walked over to Dee and stood right beside him. She leaned over the balcony too and gazed out into the night sky.

"What about you?" Carrie asked. "It doesn't seem like you adore me anymore."

Just then Carrie and Dee both looked at each other, and their eyes were locked in a magical trance.

"That's not true," Dee said, his face turning red in the cheeks. "I—well, you know, I lo—"

Suddenly a cat made a loud shrieking sound and Dee stopped talking.

Oh God, was he about to say he loves me? Carrie thought. She looked up at the stars and invoked the spirit world. *C'mon, throw me a bone!*

"What were you going to say?"

"Well, I wanted to say that I . . . am sorry, Carrie," Dee said.

Noooooo! "I love you" is way better than "I'm sorry."

But no matter how much Carrie hoped he'd say it, Dee was already off in another direction.

"You were right. Kids need to have fun. If today proved anything, it proved that. And you realized how important that was. I guess I just didn't see it."

Carrie swallowed hard. "Listen, I had it pretty good

growing up. I mean, doing my homework in my own air-conditioned room with my mom's help and everything? Turns out that wasn't quite the tough life I thought it was."

Dee smiled and took her hand. "So, you forgive me?"

"If you forgive me," Carrie said, giving his hand a squeeze.

"Good," Dee said. "Because I couldn't bear the idea of you leaving tomorrow without saying good-bye."

Carrie was seconds away from kidnapping Dee and stuffing him in her duffel bag. "Me neither."

"I can't believe that your time in India is already over."

Carrie looked up at him and grinned. "Oh, it's not over yet."

Half an hour later Carrie skipped onto the dance floor in Dee's marketplace, wearing the sari he gave her, and paused right in the center of the mayhem. The band played a fast, bass-heavy song and the young female singer looked as if she was having the time of her life, her long hair flying everywhere as she danced and swayed and sang. Dee finally caught up to Carrie and stood in front of her, bemused but grinning.

"What are we doing here?" he shouted over the music.

"This!" Carrie said.

She curved one arm over her head, the other out in front of her chest, snapped her fingers, and wiggled her hips. Dee laughed and covered his mouth with both hands, shocked.

"Where did you learn *that?*" he asked.

"I have very talented friends," she said, dancing around him in a circle. Thanks to a few dance lessons from Manisha, Trina, and Asha, Carrie felt totally comfortable with her moves, shuffling along expertly to the beat and holding her head high. "So are you going to dance with me or what?"

"I can't believe you did this," Dee said, moving to the beat and spinning to keep up with her. "It must have taken you hours!"

"Hey, I wasn't *that* bad," Carrie said as everyone around her started to twirl. She jumped right in, spinning and spinning and never getting dizzy. Thanks to a little tip from Asha about whipping her head around to keep one stationary object in sight, Carrie could twirl for hours.

Just like before, Carrie lost Dee in all the blurring lights and colors. She laughed as she spun, feeling like a little kid who had just learned the pleasures of twirling for the first time. Then suddenly Dee grabbed her arm and she stopped, breathless and giddy.

"What?" Carrie asked, looking up into his eyes.

"You're beautiful," he said.

Carrie's heart whirled along with the rest of the dancing crowd. "What?" she shouted, pretending she couldn't hear him.

"You're beautiful!" he said a bit louder.

Carrie narrowed her eyes and shook her head slightly. "Yeah, speak up, Dee, so the people in the cheap seats can hear you."

"You're beautiful!" he shouted at the top of his lungs, throwing his hands in the air.

A few people around them grinned and rolled their eyes. Carrie stepped closer to Dee; every cell in her body was shuddering with anticipation.

"So, were you going to kiss me again?" she said. "Because my time in India's pretty much over and if you don't do it in the next thirty seconds, I may just be forced to attack you."

Dee grinned, took a step back, and crossed his arms over his chest. He raised his eyebrows, challenging her.

Carrie laughed. "All right, then. This is all your fault."

She reached up, slung her arms around his neck, and kissed him, feeling euphoric as her lips touched his. Dee picked her up off the ground and held her close, twirling her around under the stars. When he finally put her down again, Carrie was completely awestruck by the emotion she saw in Dee's eyes

"You know what, Carrie Fitzgerald?" Dee said, touching his forehead to hers. "I can't believe how lucky I am to have fallen in love with you."

Carrie had never felt so relaxed and at ease in her life. "But you don't believe in luck," she murmured.

Dee ran his fingers along her cheekbone, kissed her on the nose, and whispered into her ear, "I do now."

Chapter Sixteen

Carrie kicked back in her aisle seat and stretched her legs as far as they could go. Celia was gazing out the window, looking down at the clouds below them. Doreen was nestled in the middle seat, flipping through a copy of *InStyle* magazine, which Carrie thought was a wonderful change of pace from her usual reading material. Could it be that Doreen was actually going to invest in the art of looking good and being nice? Only time would tell.

Doreen nudged Carrie's arm and pointed to a photo of Donatella Versace, who was wearing a snug-fitting black rayon sheath dress that had a plunging neckline. "What do you think?"

Carrie squinted and made a strange face. "Yeah, that's a little . . . extreme."

"You're right," Doreen agreed. "Not like I could walk into study hall wearing that."

While Doreen kept paging through the pretty pictures of celebrities and their wardrobes, Carrie began wondering what Dee was doing at that very moment. Carrie unzipped the front pouch of her backpack and pulled out the note he had given her that morning with strict instructions for her to read it on the plane. Now was as good a time as any.

Dear Carrie,

I remember you telling me that you hate flying, so I just thought I'd remind you how much you mean to me and how much you mean to the kids. When you start to get anxious, reread this note over and over again and know that we're thinking of you.

Thank you so much for an incredible summer. Can't wait to see you over Thanksgiving break. It'll be my first trip to the States, and I know you'll take good care of me.

Miss you already,
Dee

Carrie sighed. She missed Dee so much that she was actually having physical pain. Doreen leaned in and started reading over Carrie's shoulder. "Aw, a letter from your love machine."

Carrie rolled her eyes. "Stop."

"You *love* him. You're going to have a million of his babies," Doreen teased.

"Are you finished?" Carrie asked.

"Hmmm . . . one more," Doreen replied. "Carrie and Dee, sitting in a tree—"

"All right, enough!" Carrie said, laughing.

"Fine. Ruin my fun." Doreen snickered. "So do you think this is going to work out? There are several continents between you guys."

"Who knows? Maybe. Weirder things have happened, right?" Carrie said with a wink.

"Yes, like you and I sitting next to each other without getting into a catfight," Doreen said, faking a fearful shudder.

Carrie laughed and then began to give Dee's note another read, just so she could have that I'm-so-crazy-for-this-guy feeling all over again.

"Hey, wait a second," Doreen said after catching another glimpse over Carrie's shoulder. "What does that say after the PS?"

Carrie looked down, read it quickly, and her eyes bulged. Then she folded the paper up as swiftly as she could and tried to distract Doreen.

"Hey, check that out. Are we flying over Guam?" Carrie asked, pointing out the window.

"Nice try, Carrie," Doreen said distrustfully, then grabbed the note out of her hand. She took a closer look at the postscript and let out a weary sigh. "Oh my God. 'Tell Doreen about the special medical research they're doing in Brazil'?"

"It's our little inside joke," Carrie said, trying not to laugh.

"Very funny," Doreen replied.

"Oh, Doreen. You know we love you."

"Yeah, yeah. Sure you do," Doreen said, returning her gaze to the magazine. "So what's the first thing you're going to do when you get home?"

Carrie touched her fingers to her Ganesha medallion and began to think of all the loose ends she was going to have to tie up. There was meeting with Piper and getting ready for her junior year of high school. She'd have to do a bunch of shopping with her mom and attend a couple of the summer parties that her friends would be throwing. But there was one thing that Carrie knew she needed to do literally the second she stepped off the plane.

"I'm going to call my dad," she said. "He and I need to have a nice long talk."

"This is Akhtar and Dash on the basketball court," Carrie said, handing her father another picture to add to the rapidly growing pile on the table in front of him. "And this is Dee with the girls."

"Handsome guy," he said, studying the shot. "Not good enough for you, but then, no one ever will be. You should know that up front."

Carrie grinned and sat back in her favorite booth at the Starbucks near her house. A week had passed since she had returned from India and already her father was there, as promised. They had been chilling at the coffee shop for almost two hours, talking about her trip and Dee and the kids and the fund-raiser. Her father had sat there listening the entire time, his brown eyes rapt with attention.

"I'm so proud of you, Carrie," her dad said, flipping through a few of the pictures again. "This looks like it was an amazing trip."

"It was," Carrie said, taking a sip of her latte. "I still can't believe I did it."

"I can. I always knew you were a thrill seeker," her father said with a smile.

"So, Dad, is this okay?" she asked tentatively. "I mean, I hope you didn't get in any trouble for switching your schedule so last minute to come here."

"No, everything's fine," her father said reassuringly.

Carrie noticed there were a few more lines around his eyes than usual and his hair looked lighter, which reminded her just how long it had been since they had seen each other. But even so, her dad still radiated this amazingly positive aura. It was one of the reasons Carrie liked being around him. Just being in his presence made her feel content and loved.

"Carrie, you have no idea what went through me when you told me how much you missed me," he said, taking the conversation in a more serious direction. "I always thought . . . I always thought you were really angry at me for leaving and I suppose I thought you wanted me to stay away."

"You did?" Carrie asked, baffled. "I was only upset because I didn't get to see you enough."

"I know that now," her father replied. "You really need to understand that me being away a lot was just me chickening out. You hadn't done anything wrong. It was just that I was having trouble dealing with the situation. I look back and wish I handled things differently."

Carrie leaned over the table and held his hand. "Well, maybe we can just start fresh."

"I was thinking exactly the same thing," her dad said enthusiastically. "In fact, I talked to my manager the other day and she's working it out so that I'll get one flight through San Francisco per week."

"You're kidding!" Carrie said excitedly. "Once a week?"

Her father grinned widely. "Turns out I actually have enough seniority to pull some strings. Imagine that."

"Wow. Dad, that's amazing," Carrie said. She couldn't believe it. Talk about wanting to handle things differently. If she had talked to her dad about her feelings a long time ago, he would have found a solution, just like he had today.

"Hey! Maybe we'll even take a trip together this year," her dad said.

"That'd be cool," Carrie replied. "Where?"

"I don't know. Anywhere particular you want to go?" her father asked as he swirled the coffee in his cup.

Carrie pretended to ponder the question. "Um . . . I've always wanted to check out London."

Just then her new BlackBerry beeped and she grabbed it off the tabletop. *Incoming message from Dee,* the display read. Automatically she smiled widely.

It said: *How's the reconciliation going? I miss you!*

"Is that lover boy?" her father asked, raising one eyebrow.

"Dad! Ick," Carrie said, wincing. *Dads aren't supposed to say any phrase with the word* lover *in it.*

She typed back a response quickly. *Better than expected! Call U 2nite! Miss U 2!*

A horn honked on the street outside and Carrie and her dad looked out to find her mother waving from the window of her car. Her mom had offered to pick her up from Starbucks and drive her to Piper's, but Carrie knew she wasn't going to come inside and see her dad. Still, it was okay—for now. Carrie couldn't solve everything in one summer. In fact, she had a feeling she should leave her parents' relationship up to them. They would figure out how to be around each other again eventually. And if they didn't, Carrie knew that she'd be all right because even though her parents couldn't be happy with each other, they both wanted their daughter to be happy.

"Well, looks like our time is up," her father said, standing and adjusting his tie. "Good luck with Piper, honey. I hope it all works out."

"Thanks, Dad," Carrie said, and gave him a tight hug. The familiar scent of Polo Sport made her smile. "I'll see you soon, right?"

"Absolutely," he said, not letting go of their embrace. "Seeing each other is never going to be a problem again."

"Lucky me," Carrie said, still breathing in the scent of her father's cologne.

Carrie stared at Piper's house as her mother pulled her car up to the curb. Her heart was break-dancing inside her chest. She had only talked to Piper for five seconds since she got back, and that was to set up this meeting. When they had spoken, Piper had sounded distant and almost wary. There was no telling what would happen.

"So . . . are you going to get out of the car and knock on the door, or are we just going to stare for a while and go home?" her mother asked.

"I'll be ready in a second," Carrie said, not moving a muscle. "Really."

There was a crash outside, as if a trash can had just fallen over, and suddenly a black cat raced by the car followed by a mangy-looking dog. Carrie's heart skipped a beat. Her mother put the car into first and turned her blinker on.

"Mom! What're you doing?" Carrie blurted.

"What?" her mother asked, startled. "That was a sign, right? That we shouldn't be here? I figured we were going home."

Carrie waited for her mother's eyes to crinkle or for her to laugh at her own joke. But then she realized that her mom was 100 percent dead serious.

"God, Mom!" Carrie said, covering her mouth with her hand. "You must think I'm really twisted!"

Her mom put the car back into park and looked at Carrie in confusion. "So you're telling me that the black cat thing had no effect on you whatsoever? You don't have to . . . I don't know, turn three times in a westerly direction, then eat a cinnamon stick or something?"

"Mom! Now you're just making stuff up," Carrie said with a laugh. "Besides, I'm over black cats. I'm working on all my superstitions."

The lines in her mother's face deepened. "What did they do to you over there?"

"I don't know," Carrie said with a shrug. "I guess I just realized life is too short to waste it on stuff like that."

"Wow, Carrie. I'm impressed," her mother said.

"Thanks," Carrie said, feeling a little rush of confidence under her mother's proud gaze. "Okay. I'm goin' in."

Then she picked up her Ganesha medallion, kissed it, and got out of the car.

"Wait a minute, what was that?" her mother asked.

"For good luck," Carrie replied.

"I thought you were over superstitions," her mother replied, laughing.

"I said I was working on it," Carrie said, rolling her eyes as she slammed the door. "One thing at a time."

Shaking her head, Carrie's mother pulled away from the curb. Carrie took a deep breath, steeled herself, and walked up to Piper's front door.

It's just Piper, she told herself, attempting to calm

her racing pulse as she rang the bell. *What's the worst that could happen? She flips out on me and we wrestle for a little while before her brother calls his friends over and charges them ten bucks to watch us roll around in the dirt, smacking each other.*

The door opened before the second *bong* had faded away. Carrie froze the instant she saw Piper's face. Her lips were pressed together, her eyes narrowed, and her eyebrows raised. She had her head cocked to one side and one hand still rested on the doorknob as if she wanted to be ready to slam the door in Carrie's face. In short, she looked really pissed off.

"You're fifteen minutes late," Piper said flatly.

Carrie's heart sank down to her toes. "Uh . . ."

"That's fifteen minutes I've had to wait to do *this.*"

Then Piper threw her arms around Carrie and hugged her so hard she thought her neck was going to break. Carrie heaved a sigh of relief.

"I'm so sorry, Piper!" she said.

"I'm sorry too!" Piper replied. "And I want you to know I haven't talked to Jason once all summer. Well, except the other day when I was at the pool and I needed him to get me a Band-Aid, but that's it. I promise."

"I don't even care," Carrie said with a laugh. "I missed you!"

"I missed you too!"

Carrie pulled back and whacked Piper's shoulder. "What the heck was *that?* Giving me *attitude?*"

"I had to do something to get you back for not writing me," Piper said with a mischievous grin.

"Do you have any idea the size of the coronary you gave me?" Carrie said, holding a hand to her chest. Her poor ticker was still pounding as if it had been given an electric shock.

"Probably about the same as the one I got when I heard you were in *India!*" Piper said, stepping outside and closing the door. "So . . . tell me everything. What did you do over there?"

Carrie sat down on the front steps and clasped her hands. As she started to come back down to earth, she couldn't believe she had been so nervous about this. After all the years she and Piper had been friends, she should have known everything was going to be fine. It was just as her mother said—Piper was a sweet, amazing person. And they had been friends for too long to let anything as dumb as a guy come between them. They didn't need to have some sort of long, drawn-out Dr. Phil session to work things out. All they needed to do was pick up where they left off.

"Well, in a nutshell, I hung out with a bunch of really cool kids, played basketball, did arts and crafts, solved a little plumbing crisis, did a little creative gardening, ate a lot of unbelievable food, saw an amazing sunset or two, and met the India Olympic basketball team," Carrie said. "Oh, and I fell in love with the most perfect guy in the history of guys."

"Whoa," Piper said. "And I was all excited to tell you about the new cafeteria tables at theater geek camp. Got any pictures?"

"I just happen to have a few right here," Carrie said, pulling out the folder of prints she had shared with her dad. "This is Dee," she said, pulling out her favorite shot of him laughing at the breakfast table.

"Oh . . . my . . . God," Piper said, her mouth dropping open. "He's like Brad Pitt, only waaaaay hotter. How'd you guys meet?"

Carrie laughed. "Actually, I just kind of bumped into him."

"Wow, Carrie. This place looks amazing," Piper said, starting to flip through the rest of the pictures. "Wait a minute, what's this?"

Piper handed her a picture and Carrie smiled.

"Oh, that's me and Doreen," she said.

"I know that, genius," Piper said sarcastically. "But why do you have your arms around each other? Are you both drunk?"

"What? No!" Carrie said, completely amused. "We actually got some stuff straightened out. I mean, at first there was these bloody duels and pistols-at-dawn kind of stuff. But what can I say? We had a breakthrough."

"So Dor-mean and you are pals now?" Piper asked curiously.

"Yeah, and if you're cool with it, I thought all three of us could hang out together."

Piper took the picture back from Carrie's grasp and took another look. Then she giggled. "Carrie, you amaze me."

Carrie smiled, absently reaching up to touch her medallion. She thought over all the things she had seen and done that summer. She thought about the kids, about Deena and Payal, about Mr. Banarjee, and about Dee. Leaning her head on Piper's shoulder to watch as the images of her last few weeks flipped by, she did feel amazed herself. She also felt relieved to have her friend back, happy to be home, and perfectly content with everything she had and everything she was.

Maybe this moment wouldn't last forever. Maybe everything wouldn't always be perfect. But just then she felt as if the world were clothed in lucky Ts.

"You know, I may have to start buying into this superstition thing of yours," Piper said, stopping on a picture of Carrie and Dee from her last morning there. "You do have all the luck."

"Yeah," Carrie said, putting her arm around Piper's shoulders. "I guess I really do."

About the Author

Kate Brian is the author of the hot new series Private, as well as the novels *Sweet 16*, *Megan Meade's Guide to the McGowan Boys*, *The Princess & the Pauper*, and *The V Club* (available in paperback as *The Virginity Club*). She has also written many young adult novels under a different name. She lives outside New York City. Her lucky T is nestled safely in her dresser drawer. She thinks.

From bestselling author
KATE BRIAN

♥ ♥ ♥ ♥ ♥

Juicy reads for the sweet and the sassy!

Lucky T
"Fans of Meg Cabot's *The Princess Diaries* will enjoy it." —*SLJ*

Megan Meade's Guide to the McGowan Boys
Featured in *Teen* magazine!

The Virginity Club
"*Sex and the City: High School Edition.*" —*KLIATT*

The Princess & the Pauper
"Truly exceptional chick-lit." —*Kirkus Reviews*

FROM SIMON PULSE
♥ Published by Simon & Schuster ♥